PRAISE FOR THE RADIUM AGE SERIES

"New editions of a host of under-discussed classics of the genre."
—Tor.com

"Neglected classics of early 20th-century sci-fi in spiffily designed
paperback editions."
—*The Financial Times*

"An entertaining, engrossing glimpse into the profound and innovative
literature of the early twentieth century."
—*Foreword*

"Shows that 'proto-sf' was being published much more widely,
alongside other kinds of fiction, before it emerged as a genre."
—*BSFA Review*

"An excellent start at showcasing the strange wonders offered by the
Radium Age."
—*Shelf Awareness*

"Lovingly curated . . . The series' freedom from genre purism lets us
see how a specific set of anxieties—channeled through dystopias,
Lovecraftian horror, arch social satire, and adventure tales—spurred
literary experimentation and the bending of conventions."
—*Los Angeles Review of Books*

"A huge effort to help define a new era of science fiction."
—*Transfer Orbit*

"Admirable . . . and highly recommended."
—*Washington Post*

"Long live the Radium Age."
—*Los Angeles Times*

MAN'S WORLD

The Radium Age Book Series
Joshua Glenn

MAN'S WORLD

Charlotte Haldane

Introduction by Philippa Levine

THE MIT PRESS
CAMBRIDGE, MASSACHUSETTS
LONDON, ENGLAND

© 2024 Massachusetts Institute of Technology

This edition of *Man's World* follows the text of the 1927 edition published by George H. Doran Company, which is in the public domain. All rights reserved. No part of this book may be used to train artificial intelligence systems or reproduced in any form by any electronic or mechanical means (including photocopying, recording, or information storage and retrieval) without permission in writing from the publisher.

This book was set in Arnhem Pro and PF DIN Text Pro by New Best-set Typesetters Ltd. Printed and bound in the United States of America.

Library of Congress Cataloging-in-Publication Data

Names: Haldane, Charlotte, 1894-1969, author. | Levine, Philippa, writer of introduction.
Title: Man's world / Charlotte Haldane ; introduction by Philippa Levine.
Description: Cambridge, Massachusetts ; London, England : The MIT Press, [2024] | Series: Radium Age | Includes bibliographical references.
Identifiers: LCCN 2023013584 (print) | LCCN 2023013585 (ebook) | ISBN 9780262547635 (paperback) | ISBN 9780262378116 (epub) | ISBN 9780262378109 (pdf)
Subjects: LCGFT: Dystopian fiction. | Novels.
Classification: LCC PR6015.A247 M36 2024 (print) | LCC PR6015.A247 (ebook) | DDC 823/.912—dc23/eng/20230621
LC record available at https://lccn.loc.gov/2023013584
LC ebook record available at https://lccn.loc.gov/2023013585

10 9 8 7 6 5 4 3 2 1

CONTENTS

Do we really know science fiction? There were the scientific romance years that stretched from the mid-nineteenth century to circa 1900. And there was the genre's so-called golden age, from circa 1935 through the early 1960s. But between those periods, and overshadowed by them, was an era that has bequeathed us such tropes as the robot (berserk or benevolent), the tyrannical superman, the dystopia, the unfathomable extraterrestrial, the sinister telepath, and the eco-catastrophe. A dozen years ago, writing for the sf blog io9.com at the invitation of Annalee Newitz and Charlie Jane Anders, I became fascinated with the period during which the sf genre as we know it emerged. Inspired by the exactly contemporaneous career of Marie Curie, who shared a Nobel Prize for her discovery of radium in 1903, only to die of radiation-induced leukemia in 1934, I eventually dubbed this three-decade interregnum the "Radium Age."

Curie's development of the theory of radioactivity, which led to the extraordinary, terrifying, awe-inspiring insight that the atom is, at least in part, a state of energy constantly in movement, is an apt metaphor for the twentieth century's first three decades. These years were marked by rising sociocultural strife across various fronts: the founding of the women's suffrage movement, the National Association for the Advancement of Colored People, socialist currents within the labor movement, anticolonial and revolutionary upheaval around the world . . . as well as the associated strengthening of reactionary movements that supported, for example, racial segregation, immigration restriction, eugenics, and sexist policies.

Science—as a system of knowledge, a mode of experimenting, and a method of reasoning—accelerated the pace of change during these years in ways simultaneously liberating and terrifying. As sf author and historian Brian Stableford points out in his 1989 essay "The Plausibility of the Impossible," the universe we discovered by means of the scientific method in the early twentieth century defies common sense: "We are haunted by a sense of the impossibility of ultimately making sense of things." By playing host to certain far-out notions—time travel, faster-than-light travel, and ESP, for example—that we have every reason to judge impossible, science fiction serves as an "instrument of negotiation," Stableford suggests, with which we strive to accomplish "the difficult diplomacy of existence in a scientifically knowable but essentially unimaginable world." This is no less true today than during the Radium Age.

The social, cultural, political, and technological upheavals of the 1900–1935 period are reflected in the proto-sf writings of authors such as Olaf Stapledon, William Hope Hodgson, Muriel Jaeger, Karel Čapek, G. K. Chesterton, Cicely Hamilton, W. E. B. Du Bois, Yevgeny Zamyatin, E. V. Odle, Arthur Conan Doyle, Mikhail

Bulgakov, Pauline Hopkins, Stanisław Ignacy Witkiewicz, Aldous Huxley, Gustave Le Rouge, A. Merritt, Rudyard Kipling, Rose Macaulay, J. D. Beresford, J. J. Connington, S. Fowler Wright, Jack London, Thea von Harbou, and Edgar Rice Burroughs, not to mention the late-period but still incredibly prolific H. G. Wells himself. More cynical than its Victorian precursor yet less hard-boiled than the sf that followed, in the writings of these visionaries we find acerbic social commentary, shock tactics, and also a sense of frustrated idealism—and reactionary cynicism, too—regarding humankind's trajectory.

The MIT Press's Radium Age series represents a much-needed evolution of my own efforts to champion the best proto-sf novels and stories from 1900 to 1935 among scholars already engaged in the fields of utopian and speculative fiction studies, as well as general readers interested in science, technology, history, and thrills and chills. By reissuing literary productions from a time period that hasn't received sufficient attention for its contribution to the emergence of science fiction as a recognizable form—one that exists and has meaning in relation to its own traditions and innovations, as well as within a broader ecosystem of literary genres, each of which, as John Rieder notes in *Science Fiction and the Mass Cultural Genre System* (2017), is itself a product of overlapping "communities of practice"—we hope not only to draw attention to key overlooked works but perhaps also to influence the way scholars and sf fans alike think about this crucial yet neglected and misunderstood moment in the emergence of the sf genre.

John W. Campbell and other Cold War–era sf editors and propagandists dubbed a select group of writers and story types from the pulp era to be the golden age of science fiction. In doing so, they helped fix in the popular imagination a too-narrow understanding of what the sf genre can offer. (In his introduction to the 1974 collection *Before the Golden Age*, for example, Isaac Asimov notes that although it may have possessed a certain exuberance, in general sf from before the mid-1930s moment when Campbell assumed editorship of *Astounding Stories* "seems, to anyone who has experienced the Campbell Revolution, to be clumsy, primitive, naive.") By returning to an international tradition of scientific speculation via fiction from after the Poe–Verne–Wells era and before sf's Golden Age, the Radium Age series will demonstrate—contra Asimov et al.—the breadth, richness, and diversity of the literary works that were responding to a vertiginous historical period, and how they helped innovate a nascent genre (which wouldn't be named until the mid-1920s, by Hugo Gernsback, founder of *Amazing Stories* and namesake of the Hugo Awards) as a mode of speculative imagining.

The MIT Press's Noah J. Springer and I are grateful to the sf writers and scholars who have agreed to serve as this series' advisory board. Aided by their guidance, we'll endeavor to surface a rich variety of texts, along with introductions by a diverse group of sf scholars, sf writers, and others that will situate these remarkable, entertaining, forgotten works within their own social, political, and scientific contexts, while drawing out contemporary parallels.

We hope that reading Radium Age writings, published in times as volatile as our own, will serve to remind us that our own era's seemingly natural, eternal, and inevitable social, economic, and cultural forms and norms are—like Madame Curie's atom—forever in flux.

INTRODUCTION

Philippa Levine

In the decade following World War I, commentaries on and concerns around the devastation it had wrought appeared frequently in newspapers and political commentaries as well as in novels and films. The technologies developed during the war made it possible to think about a science-driven future in more meaningful ways than had previously been possible. Imagining the future was one of the favorite pastimes of science writers and novelists alike. Charlotte Haldane was both of those things. In November 1926, she published her first novel, *Man's World*, an exploration of a future world of tightly controlled gender roles and reproduction.

Earlier that year she had married J. B. S. Haldane, a renowned biologist at the University of Cambridge. Then in her early 30s, the former Charlotte Franken had been married to Jack Burghes for eight years, during which time she was the family's principal breadwinner, first as a press agent for a music publisher and subsequently as a journalist with particular interests in science. Her son Ronald was born some six months into a marriage which had rapidly deteriorated. Jack refused to grant her a divorce so she and Haldane had resorted to a common ruse of the time, sharing a hotel room after having tipped off a detective to witness this "proof" of adultery. Adultery was at the time required for a divorce and Charlotte was well aware that it had been only three years since women could even file for divorce on the same grounds as men. Charlotte was also the right age to enjoy the newly won voting rights of women. Before 1928, only women over thirty had that right, and she had turned thirty in 1924. She was, in many respects, what the press at the time dubbed a "new woman."

Charlotte and JBS, as he was generally known, had met when she approached the eminent scientist for advice as she began work on what would become *Man's World*. She had read his provocative essay *Daedalus, or Science and the Future*, the first book in a new series launched by the London publisher Kegan Paul at the end of 1923. This slender volume predicted changes in how reproduction would be handled in the future and envisaged a world in thrall to science. This hugely successful work established Haldane as a skilled popularizer of science at a time when the scientific future was a topic of broad interest, not least among novelists experimenting with the genre of science fiction.

Futuristic as the control of human reproduction sounded at the time, the interwar years were nonetheless *par excellence* the age of eugenics, a science directly interested in managing and regulating birth and reproduction. The term *eugenics*, coined by British scientist Francis Galton in 1883 from the Greek for "good" and "origin," quite literally meant "well born." Galton dreamed of improving humans by encouraging the fittest to procreate and by ensuring the unfit could not. Eugenicists around the globe—from China to Russia, from the Americas to South Asia, and across Europe, east and west—championed a slew of practices designed in some cases to better birth outcomes and in many cases to prevent births. Unsurprisingly, science fiction writers of the day took up these themes with gusto and, throughout the 1920s and 1930s, science fiction stories in which states and governments intervened to control reproduction proved immensely popular. Some of the best-known are Yevgeny Zamyatin's *We* (1924), Owen Gregory's *Meccania* (1918), Rose Macaulay's *What Not* (1919), and short stories by Efim Zozulya ("The Dictator: The Story of Ak and Humanity" (1919)) and Julian Huxley ("The Tissue-Culture King" (1926)).

In reality, eugenics often did shape reproductive and other social policies in a variety of places, though seldom in the ways these novels predicted. Eugenic policies in the interwar years ranged from tax credits and other incentives designed to help families with the cost of raising children to coercive measures including institutionalization and forced sterilization to ensure that others—those with heritable illnesses or certain kinds of disability, mental or physical—were prevented from ever parenting. Although Britain was the birthplace of eugenics, other nations including the Scandinavian countries, North America, and Germany outstripped it in implementing these strong-arm practices. Britain's 1913 Mental Deficiency Act did allow for the compulsory institutionalization of those deemed "feeble-minded," but the country stopped short of approving involuntary sterilization. Not so elsewhere, as the thousands of forced sterilizations in the United States and across Scandinavia, and the hundreds of thousands of them in Nazi Germany, attest. Nonetheless, though coerced sterilization failed to find a formal footing in interwar Britain, eugenics was not a marginal but a mainstream idea; J. B. S. Haldane and many other prominent scientists of his generation were active in eugenic organizations and by 1911 a professorial post in the field had been established at University College London. This was the milieu that nurtured Charlotte's ideas about sex determination before birth and it was JBS, already well known in eugenic circles, to whom she turned for advice.

Man's World came out a year before her widely reviewed nonfiction book *Motherhood and Its Enemies*. Where *Man's World* separated those who were encouraged to bear and raise children and sterilized the remainder to prevent pregnancy, *Motherhood* damned unmarried and childless women as useless and argued that those with disease or disability should be prevented from having children, a directly eugenic principle. There was something of a contradiction both between the messages of the two books—despite the closeness of their publication dates—and between what both books preached and the manner in which Haldane conducted her own personal life. Charlotte's career was seldom interrupted by motherhood, and though she claimed in her autobiography that she and JBS hoped to start a family together, her son from her first marriage was the only child she ever had.

Man's World chronicles the lives of brother and sister, Christopher and Nicolette, as they grow up in a fictionalized postwar state where reproduction is tightly controlled and social roles highly circumscribed. This is a "man's world" because women are either mothers or "neuters," and those who embrace motherhood are required to engage in prenatal exercises designed to ensure the sex of the infant. The overarching plan is to produce more men than women. Men are divided into three basic categories: scientists, administrators, and the proletarian masses. Men are ordered by their intellect while women are reduced to their biology. Christopher and Nicolette both yearn to break out of the roles allotted to them. Christopher, something of an antihero figure in the story, is resistant to what's expected of him as a man, and the gender fluidity he demonstrates is explained in the book quite literally as an error caused by his mother's failure to pursue the regimen developed to ensure the birth of baby boys. Nicolette, meanwhile, wants to keep her options open rather than committing to one of the prescribed female roles. With the help of some rebel friends, the two siblings find a way to sterilize her temporarily, a process known in this dystopian world as "immunization." It is when she succumbs to conformist expectations, falls in love with a scientist, and chooses motherhood that the plot turns tragic. Christopher, now alienated not only from the world in which he lives but also from his beloved sister, literally flies too close to the sun, in a strange echo of JBS's *Daedalus*.

Reading *Man's World* from a contemporary perspective can be troubling. The disparagement of Jews pops up over and over. Nicolette's ambivalent response to the Jewish painter Arcous Weil includes "fleeting sensations of disgust." We hear of the "Jewish habit of self-depreciation" and Charlotte alludes to what she calls a "Jewish quality of mind." The entire architecture of the world the book describes is the creation of Mensch, a Jew described as physically grotesque yet of tremendous intellectual power and vision.

What makes these seemingly anti-Semitic remarks puzzling is that Charlotte was from a middle-class German-Jewish family who, she claimed, never fully assimilated into the Anglo world. In her autobiography, published in 1949, she notes that "I knew about anti-semitism long before I learned the facts of life. The righteous moral indignation it aroused in my father transmitted itself to me, and left a lasting impression on my youthful mind."[1] Yet her adult life suggests that she consciously distanced herself from Jewish circles; both her marriages were to gentile men and she moved in social circles where Jews would have been thin on the ground. Never fully accepted by Haldane's friends—indeed, sometimes shunned by them—she may well have experienced these slights as anti-Semitic. The Jews in *Man's World* are portrayed as brilliant but ruthless, exceptional in their talents, but always outsiders. It's hard to know what to make of this and it certainly makes for uncomfortable reading today. This handling of anti-Semitism may well have been her attempt to minimize her own Jewishness and merge into the world of the Anglo intelligentsia. It might equally represent a recognition of the difficult tightrope that Anglo-Jewry walked in interwar Britain.

In a similar vein, the novel is also imbued with a race consciousness that draws a stark line between what Haldane calls the "white race and adjoining races." The "Slav" is described as "retrogressive" and we are left in no doubt that the duties of motherhood at the heart of the book lie with reproducing the "white race." In a terrifyingly prescient passage, Haldane speaks of a poison derived from, and deadly to, black people. Haldane was writing at a time when such vocabulary was commonplace and the greater population growth in some non-Western countries was cause for alarm. Books that foretold the "swamping" of whites circulated widely. Australian novelist William Lane's 1887 *White or Yellow?* imagined the social breakdown that would ensue from mass Chinese migration to Australia. In the United States, Lothrop Stoddard's *The Rising Tide of Color: The Threat Against White World-Supremacy* (1920) warned of the collapse of white authority. Madison Grant, author of *The Passing of the Great Race* (1916), provided an approving preface to Stoddard's book echoing this alarm at the higher reproductive rates of nonwhite populations. By the time *Man's World* appeared, immigration laws in many white-dominated nations had become increasingly exclusionary. The Johnson–Reed Act of 1924 radically altered immigration requirements in the United States, excluding Asians completely and severely restricting entrants from southern and eastern Europe. The notorious "White Australia" policy was among the very first laws passed in newly independent Australia in 1901, and in Britain early twentieth-century immigration laws sought to limit Jews and "undesirables." Managing race was a central concern in many developed countries in the early and mid-twentieth century.

In a conversation between Nicolette and her aunt Emmeline, Haldane vocalizes some of the most dominant beliefs of the eugenics movement of the period. Emmeline insists that without safeguards as to who might be permitted to bear children, the future of the race would be imperiled. Without regulation, "children would be born haphazard everywhere, would be bred by the pure and the impure." "The dirty bestial breeding of the past" would doom the race. Eugenicists were prominent advocates of controlling population, either to reduce the unwanted or to increase the "right" kinds of people. In the aftermath of the First World War, which had seen unprecedented mortality rates among young men, population quantity and quality were heavily debated issues. Scientists and science fiction writers explored a range of corrections to the perceived damage done by the loss of so many young men. Asexual reproduction (parthenogenesis), artificial insemination, and ectogenesis (developing the fetus outside the uterus) were all themes explored by writers such as Charlotte Perkins Gilman, Yevgeny Zamyatin, Katharine Burdekin and, most famously, Aldous Huxley.

Charlotte's work, like that of many who lived through the Great War and witnessed its devastation, reveals a preoccupation with the fragility of civilization and what might be needed to shore it up. It was a concern she shared with her husband. In *Daedalus*, JBS had used the literary device of a future undergraduate paper to make his points, and among the opinions the fictional undergraduate shares is that, without ectogenesis, "the greater fertility of the less desirable members of the population in almost all countries" would have hastened the collapse of civilization.[2] This theme was among the central preoccupations of science fiction writing in the 1920s and 1930s. In common with other works of its time, *Man's World* weighs the benefits of promoting the greater good over the desires of individuals; Haldane returns to the theme over and over again, especially in scenes in which rebellious nonconformists express their distaste for what Christopher calls the "herd instinct." It is when Nicolette returns to the herd—to marriage and motherhood—that Christopher knows he is doomed. We do not know whether Charlotte saw herself more as Nicolette or more as Christopher. She yearned—albeit fruitlessly—for more children in her second marriage (as did JBS), yet she was in so many ways an unconventional woman.

Charlotte's unflattering portraits of her Jewish protagonists, her disparaging remarks about women who opted out of motherhood, and her reading of Christopher's gender deviance as a problem induced by his mother's irresponsibility all point to an ambivalence about the key issues driving her writings. Interestingly, the reception of *Man's World* has been equally inconsistent. Some have read it as utopian and others as dystopian. Some see satire at work, others deny its presence. The novel has been read as a feminist tract protesting the narrow scope for women in this man's world while others, finding the female characters unsympathetic, regard it as an antifeminist statement in which women collude in their own subjugation. These wildly different interpretations—both at the time of publication and more recently—are hardly surprising in light of Charlotte's own uncertainties, for, unless we read the novel as satire, its contradictions are unsettling. Does Charlotte champion eugenics or is she warning us about it? Can women be fulfilled without motherhood? Either way, we can be sure that she was sensitive to the big issues of her day and as adept at thinking through the turn to scientific management as any of the better-known male science fiction writers with whom the author of *Man's World* would always compete. Reviewing Huxley's *Brave New World* for the preeminent science journal, *Nature*, in 1932, Haldane offered a double-edged assessment, calling the novel Huxley's second-best work before eviscerating both its understanding of biology and its clumsy failure to comprehend modern women.

Man's World may have been ambivalent about the expectations and the actions of women, and the division of them into the fecund and the barren, but Haldane leaves us in no doubt that she could articulate a variety of female voices whose keen understanding of reproductive politics far surpasses the capacity of most of Huxley's characters to critique the strange world in which they live. This is not an easy novel nor an obvious one. Haldane's attitudes to race, to the role of women, and even to science are complex, and she offers no easy answers. Instead, she takes us on a variety of journeys with remarkably different endings, letting readers choose which of her sometimes conflicting but always robust modernist messages matter the most.

Notes

1. Charlotte Haldane, *Truth Will Out* (London: Weidenfeld & Nicholson, 1949), 2.

2. J. B. S. Haldane, *Daedalus, or Science and the Future* (London: Kegan Paul, 1923), 66–67.

Do thou teach me not only to foresee, but to enjoy, nay, even to feed on future praise. Comfort me by a solemn assurance that, when the little parlour, in which I sit at this instant, shall be reduced to a worse-furnished box, I shall be read, with honour, by those who never knew nor saw me, and whom I shall neither know nor see.

—Fielding, *Tom Jones*

ACKNOWLEDGMENT

The intelligence that had once been known as Ernest Renan and that of his disciple Anatole France sat glimmering away somewhere in vastness.

'So one does remember something both backwards and forwards,' said sacerdotally he who had once been corpulent and sentimental.

'Only occasionally, dear Master.' The tone of the late owner of relics and a thin white beard was apologetic.

RENAN. 'The productions of the female body are human beings; those of the female mind . . . gargoyles.'

FRANCE. 'Yes.' The reminiscence of a white chin wisp wagged with faint malice. 'To be beautiful and good, if I recollect correctly, was, according to you, their mission for ever.'

RENAN. 'Well, you, if it comes to that, are alleged to have declared that you would like to dramatize my *Dialogues philosophiques* . . . a novel, to quote the secretary—or was it the cook?—in which the characters would be merely animated diagrams.'

FRANCE. 'You, dear Master, forestalled me; for you dramatized a wish.'

RENAN. 'Yet observe, this funny little female defies us both with this uncouth flattery.'

FRANCE. 'It is all very earthy. But perhaps we overlooked one point after all?'

RENAN. 'How so?'

FRANCE. '"In the ideal State you can appeal only to God!"'

RENAN. 'The Revolt of the Angels, surely?'

FRANCE. 'Not quite. That was merely Jahveh.'

RENAN. 'You deign to compare?'

FRANCE. 'But certainly. I note with some amusement that they will be hard put to it to attitudinize before this . . . gargoyle. I mean, dear Master is all very well—but, dear Mistress!'

RENAN. 'H'm. We will not pursue the point. Henriette would perhaps . . . But there will be no question of that. This pretentious little volume will not be read.'

FRANCE. 'So I gather. Still, even they might, in memory of us who so clearly inspired it, glance at this scheme of an imaginary, undaunted, though misshapen world.'

RENAN. 'Even we, though classics, can scarcely expect such homage. That our creations should occasionally be thumbed with reverence—it may be, but you cannot expect them to notice a humble imitator even of such as we.'

FRANCE. 'Yet no emanation of the female is entirely unworthy of notice. I approve the scheme of sex relationships——'

RENAN. 'Penguin Island, of course.'

FRANCE. 'Certainly. And "collaboration with God"— your dialogues; and "individual *versus* community" . . .'

RENAN. 'All of us, my dear friend, all of us. I vaguely remember having seen it before.'

FRANCE. Observe the strained avoidance of such definitions as "good" and "evil." The thing has no style, and moreover an air of insincerity.'

RENAN. 'You speak truly. It lacks, don't you see, the fundamental insincerity, the Gallic lightness, which is the point of departure for style.'

FRANCE. 'All we have here is "scientific state"—your idea—"communal interference"—my idea—"systematic breeding"—your idea—"the courtisane-artist."—'

RENAN. 'Entirely your idea; entirely.'

FRANCE. 'Pardon; that was a mere symbol.'

RENAN. 'So that there is really not a single gleam of originality in the whole effusion.'

FRANCE. 'Except perhaps the insistence on the experimental method?'

RENAN. 'My poor friend, Plato will tell you, or, better still, Moses . . .'

FRANCE. 'No, thanks. I was sure at bottom I had heard it all too often before.'

RENAN. 'And you will again. On earth at this moment, for instance . . .'

FRANCE. 'Still hankering, dear Master, still hankering? Let us repose ourselves, surely. Let us look, if look we must, towards some less familiar planet. Perhaps there—though I confess I doubt it—we may find novelty.'

1 THE VISION OF MENSCH

> I cannot believe that political problems differ from those of
> every other aspect of social life in being incapable of solution by
> scientific methods.
> —Dr. W. H. Rivers

I

When Mensch died, or, as was now said, made room for his successors, at the age of one hundred and thirteen, he had looked for eight years on the world he had envisioned for the first time fifty-seven years previously. He had always been grotesquely short in stature, and during the last twenty years of his existence his great, bulging head had appeared far too heavy for his gnarled, shrunken body. As St. John Richmond, Jaques and Adrian, his sons, Walter Lutyens, and a few others watched Conrad Pushkin administer the final hypodermic that released the remnants of life from the body of Mensch, their gaze was drawn and held by that remarkable head.

Pushkin stepped back from the bedside. 'Finished,' he remarked briefly. Pushkin's flat face proclaimed his Slavonic origin; two large tears now gathering in his pale eyes and rolling slowly down his face confirmed it.

'That will be the best job of my career, that brain,' exclaimed Lutyens, his enthusiasm brimming over. His voice still held a remnant of the nasal twang of those far States where Mensch had picked him up so long ago. 'Ah, the brain of Mensch! That should teach us something.'

'He will be ready for you when you want him,' said Jaques.

What was left of Mensch lay there on the bed serenely, done with. Lutyens's pupils, of whom there were several present, crowded nearer as he beckoned to them. 'You see there,' he began, 'the remains of the leading man of this century. Now you will observe . . .'

St. John Richmond, who had said nothing at all, glanced once more at the head, then he touched Pushkin's shoulder and drew him away. They left the room together, Adrian at their heels.

II

St. John and Conrad, these two who had stood nearer to Mensch than any others, faced one another in St. John's room. Each held in his hand a glass filled with liquid. Conrad drained his at a gulp. St. John sipped meditatively. St. John, always an arresting figure, now, at the height of his powers, possessed a magnetic quality to vision. He was tall and thin, but slower in his movements than most thin men. The pitch of his voice was low. His eyes, deep-set, were remarkable for nothing save their glinting intensity of expression. Above them rose a Shakespearian brow, surmounted by untidy reddish-brown hair, flowing in a long sweep down to his neck. His short moustache and pointed beard were of a darker brown. The nose was long and thin, ending in a generous curve of the nostrils. The lips, between reddish beard and moustache looking paler than they were, seemed wide and full when he opened them. In repose they appeared to be rather grimly closed. Hands and feet were long and narrow, nervous and active. He looked and felt at his best when standing or walking. As Nicolette once said to Christopher, 'One never could even imagine St. John sprawling in a chair.'

He now rested his glass on the elbow-high picture-rail that ran round his apartment, and gazed down at Conrad, who, bowed and hunched, his strong, monkeyish hands clasped tightly together, sat silently.

'So. He is gone at last,' Conrad muttered. 'In truth, he had done bravely.'

'Amazing how he endured so long,' said St. John. Each man appeared to be soliloquizing. From long knowledge of one another, their conversation usually ran on such parallel lines. 'When you think of his youth and his middle age, his retention, so long, of his best mental qualities was really remarkable.'

'A practical romanticist. Do you think we are sufficiently careful to maintain among our people to-day those imaginative qualities that were his hall-mark?'

'They are no longer needed to the same degree. Remember, that particularly Jewish quality of the mind, romanticism in eruption, can only flourish in conditions which seek to destroy it. It is a mental gesture, akin to the magniloquent gestures of the actor. It requires a background, a scene. Think how his collection of us, at the beginning, his pride in our obscure origins, appeared in its own time, and appears now. That was, of course, endearingly absurd, amusingly feminine. Yet then it had a grandeur. He had his vision, and as the instruments of its realization he chose from those children the world then condemned to the human scrap-heap. Now there is no more scrap-heap; no more stigma, no more holy matrimony, no more scope for sentimentality in action, except'—St. John smiled on his companion—'in certain remote corners peopled by the retrogressive Slav. You know as well as I do that we not only absorb, nowadays, but fashion our finest material from such among us as retain something of the Menschian qualities.

'He foresaw us. He accurately foresaw the scientist, not as the perverter nor the destroyer of mankind, but as the new director, the inevitable successor to the priest and the politician. He foresaw, but with less accuracy in detail, that under scientific direction mankind would travel a different road. He foresaw the possibility of arousing the scientist's consciousness of, and will to, power. He sought out and educated and set on their way those whose mission it was to do this. But even he, with all his vision, could not foresee that the last war and Perrier would in any event have brought these results about, even had he never been born. Even he did not see that the control of sex, of determination and production, was the essential and only possible foundation on which the edifice of which he dreamed could be erected. Who indeed, until the last war cleared away the mists by ridding the world of most of those who were enfolded in them, could have predicted what now exists?'

'Perrier, then, seems to you the greater of his time?'

St. John, on hearing these words, realized more thoroughly than hitherto that his companion was labouring with peculiar emotional stress. He would have abruptly terminated the conversation, even with Christopher, had the boy dared to relapse into the old-fashioned habit of suggesting vague and unscientific comparison. But had his sympathies been less tolerant, had he been unable occasionally to humour such lapses in his colleagues, they and the people had long loved him less. He himself had not administered the last hypodermic to his and Conrad's spiritual father; it was Conrad's hand which had performed this otherwise common-place operation, and it was Conrad who now suffered because he had been the chosen instrument finally to still the voice and close the eyes of Mensch.

Gently he replied: 'You do not, of course, require an answer. You know that to us both Mensch meant much the same. He has long been acclaimed the greatest politician of his race since Jesus. The empire of the one succeeds the other. But Perrier, to you and to me and to Lutyens and to Braunberg and the others, was a colleague—an admired predecessor, and we should know above all men the value of his contribution to science. Remember, even at this moment, Conrad, that the experiment is what counts; the result matters little. Had there been no Mensch, had there been no Perrier, those two experiments would still have taken place.'

Conrad was humbled and relieved. 'The sense of perspective has returned to me, St. John,' he answered frankly. 'Only, even as I passed him on, I wondered where his successor would be found, and that wonder caused a depression in me. As you say, he needs no one successor; he needs only able instruments, and those he has surely found. He conceived his vision, its epoch gave it birth; it will live, and in its appointed time it will make room for another, no doubt. Now, for all of us, there is much to do.'

III

A science may affect human life in two different ways. On the one hand, without altering men's passions or their general outlook, it may increase their power of gratifying their desires. On the other hand, it may operate through an effect upon the imaginative conception of the world, the theology or philosophy which is accepted in practice by energetic men.

—Bertrand Russell, *Icarus, Or the Future of Science*

The Mensch oration was delivered by Antoine Herville in the principal lecture hall of Nucleus, the settlement that had grown out of and around the original Mensch foundation. Nucleus was the very core and innermost heart of the new world state, whence the principles of scientific rule sprang and were scattered like winged seeds among the new leaders of the remaining people. Herville's oratorical gifts invariably attracted an audience worthy of them, but the five thousand who now awaited his appearance, flattered, in their quality, even his reputation. Among them were the remnants of those who had heard, understood, and accepted the call of Mensch when his was still a new and an isolated voice; those who had in a measure foreseen as he had done the coming and the consequences of the last war; and who, at its end, had rallied to the lead flung them by his heirs and successors, had striven with them for the establishment of the new order, and were even now embarking on the succeeding experiments that should justify its existence. They were of diverse ages, of varying branches of the white race, but of unanimous convictions. All, by the new standards, had been passed into the ruling class; by the old, they would have been admitted to possess such exceptional intellectual merit as was then, for want of an exact definition, vaguely described as genius.

But among them were also two groups of personalities on whom, far more than on any of their predecessors, rested the responsibility of the future development of the world state. There were the young men known as the leaders of the Patrol and the Gay Company; those who had professionally devoted their minds to vigilance and their bodies to experiment on behalf of the commonwealth. All present on this occasion, as befitted its unusual distinction, had given proof of complete submission and loyalty to the cause of the scientific state. The Patrol comprised its administrative and executive officers; the Gay Company of Stalwarts, a smaller and more exclusive body, were those who had placed themselves, physically and mentally, at the disposal of experimental research. They were the flower and the élite of the new orders; those whose gift of themselves had transformed the struggle with disease from a blind, bungling skirmish into a battle royal, fought on man's side with weapons of exquisite precision and the spirit of a religious devotion.

This audience, drawn by air from communities in every continent, contained a minority of women. Those present, each one an epitome of the most desirable qualities of her sex, belonged chiefly to the order of vocational motherhood. These mothers, radiant in the consciousness of their sublime mission to the race, were a group apart and uplifted. They shared with the members of the Gay Company a complete serenity, proclaiming acceptance of the biological law and submission to its dictates.

When Antoine Herville arose to address his audience, conversation was sucked into silence as water is sucked into earth. He was an orator of medium height, of well-rounded head, of visionary, half-shut eyes, and of severe, though occasionally ample gestures. Son of a former renowned French tragedienne and of a flippant Irish poet, he might have been the offspring of an immaculate conception, so little did his character or appearance bear any paternal imprint. He had been the last boy to be adopted by Mensch. The little Jew, enthralled by his precocious gift of self-expression, had made him, instead of the delightful conversationalist he might have remained, the leading orator of his time. To talk was his mission.

'My friends,' he said, and he spoke, as was invariably his way at first, slowly, a little wearily, as if he had not yet warmed his dramatic instincts at the flame of their ardent attention, 'the life of Mensch was ended a little while since by the hand of Conrad Pushkin. What he had to give us was given; nothing of him was lost that we may regret. What he could do for humanity was little; what he could, and did, give, was much. He foresaw,' said Antoine, and spread his arms in a sudden sweeping gesture, bringing them slowly back and cupping his hands against his breast, 'Us. He did not look immeasurably far as the philosophers looked; he did not gaze upwards and search among the stars for whom he hoped or feared might be behind them as the christs did; his imagination painted no fantastic vision on the walls of his mind. He searched neither backward nor forward. The withered hand of the past beckoned him unheeded; an empty hand from which many have endeavoured to grasp something it held not. Hope and fear, twin pillars upholding man's mirage of a future, he disdained. The present always sufficed to this man who made himself thus the master of time.

'There is not one among us who doubts that this world of ours would have come to be had Mensch never existed. We know that it was created by the scientific mastery of man's instincts to fight and to propagate his species. The chemists and the geneticists—the last war and the control of sex—these, modified by contributary developments, wrecked the past habits of our race with the Christian domination. We see now how little Mensch did—Mensch saw then what must be done by us.

'This man, this Jew, was fortunate. In that past the antagonism inevitably met by one of his race forced him early to consider his position. Many times, when relating how his ancestors had come by their name, he regretted that he had not been the Isaac Abraham on whom a Prussian captain in the townlet of Schwindemühl had bestowed it. For he admitted early that the name was both ridiculous and significant.

'We know what a curious little creature he looked, with his gnome head, dwarf body, round shoulders, spindly legs, and great Jew nose.'

Antoine, switching his personality into comedy, made them behold the Jew; humped his back a trifle, threw out his hands, palms upward, fingers and thumbs even tinged with Semitic expressiveness, lolled his head, raised his eyebrows, narrowed his lids, and smiled deprecatingly, insinuatingly.

'Now that original Isaac Abraham—what a caricature of a human form he must have presented to the Herren Offiziere, as, accompanied by his Sarah, her wig awry and trembling with emotion, he appeared before them.' Arms clasped over bosom, fingers clutching an imaginary shawl, he gave them Sarah. '"Ach du lieber Mensch! Ach du lieber Mensch!" the poor crone whined at the Herren Hauptmann who was to name her. Even a mind endowed with a less crude humour than that of the Prussian bully might have seen the joke of christening the little human cartoon before him by the name of Man.

'During early manhood then, this one, "by name of Mensch," was a literary translator. Words of all known languages, common words, thoroughbred words, bastard words, composite words, words like jewels and words like ordures, were his tools and his trade. Sometimes he would spend days seeking, in some particular tongue, the *mot juste*. He was, of course, always of the minority Jews, of the clan of artists, philosophers, and theologians, who, in striking contrast to their majority brethren, possess no money sense. See him travelling then from country to country, a huckster of words; a transcriber, acquiring in time a modest fame among publishers and bookmen and the few polyglot literary men of his day. His formula for comfort was simple—music, tobacco, and debate at the end of the day's or night's labours. It was in his own existence, as he led it for most of his life, that he found the key to one of the principles we have put into action—ceaseless simplification of man's needs; the whittling down to the indispensable minimum of his obligations.

'We realize we could not have done one thousandth part of what we have done, in ten times the years, had we not clearly foreseen what a deal we could leave undone. This state has wilfully neglected or directly abandoned two-thirds of the alleged obligations, moral and social, on which other states were founded. It has therefore been able to satisfy the claims of the final and unavoidable residue. As old Mensch translated words in his youth, giving each its full and just measure, so we, his successors, have translated values, constantly eliminating as many as possible. The former standard of living was so high, so finely patterned, so overburdened with superfluities that the Brains of to-day would be tortured to madness if they attempted to keep pace with it. In our considered reaction against the absurdities of the past, we have sought and found an indispensable minimum standard from which to start our rebuilding operations.

'It was Huxley who flung at his contemporaries that sublime challenge in fifteen words which was the parent of Mensch's philosophy: "I have no faith, very little hope, and as much charity as I can afford." Faith, child of ignorance; hope, twin of fear; charity, pallid ghost stalking in the wake of greed; could a civilization built on faith, hope, and charity be expected by any scientific thinker to last?

'The disciples of Plato have as much to answer for as those of Jesus; they were responsible for the form of behaviour founded on another trio of canting clichés: the good, the beautiful, and the true. They had served for centuries as the basis of schools of humbug, unscientific philosophies. A mere vocal question mark will suffice to cancel them. But let us just once more, before we finally abandon it and pass on to the discussion of relative realities, repeat this litany of nonsense, by which the minds of millions of men, for thousands of years, had been lulled into stupor'—with outstretched finger he beat time, as in mocking voice he repeated the incantation, 'Faith, hope, and charity; the true, the beautiful, and the good'; then dismissed it with a contemptuous rap of the thumb.

'One day Mensch received the commission to translate a number of English, German, Dutch and French scientific works for a Russian university. These were chiefly standard books concerned with the biological sciences. And suddenly he found the eyes of his imagination looking into the laboratories where experiment and observation were unremittingly pursued. Experiment and observation here at last were two definite concepts to be introduced into a mind emptied of all the lumber of cant. He saw them as Renan before him had seen them as two illimitable lines, railroads, on which a vast train, loaded with eager adventurers and intrepid explorers, moved forward.

Sometimes with dazzling speed—sometimes at a snail's crawl; but it moved always. Its progress might be delayed, but it was never stopped. On the lines of experiment and observation a few men were always going forward, well in advance of the bulk of humanity, towards the realms of knowledge. Many came back empty-handed; some brought no more than news of a light which belonged to the future; others found a clue, slight in itself, but pointing to many tracks; and to a rare individual it fell from time to time to make a supreme discovery.

'But at whatever pace the majority of these men advanced, and however far they went, their progress was only in one direction. Despite all they had learnt, and their prodigious facilities for assimilating knowledge, they remained in general ordinary men, brilliant specialists within a small compass, but in character no more developed than the majority. Their judgment, save when it was applied to a concrete scientific problem, was as warped as that of their contemporaries; they fell as easily as any others into the traps laid by the politicians and the theologians; often they helped to make those traps. They too were victims of prejudice, mean-minded and narrow-gutted. Self-deception ruled their minds; self-dissection they could not or would not apply.

'The financiers behind the leading political juntas had therefore plenty of scientific material at their behest. The leaders of the nations found no chemist or physicist unresponsive to their orders, and the result of this docility became for the first time strikingly obvious in the war of 1914–1918, the first chemical war on a fairly large scale.

'That war gave a few people an inkling of what might follow. The lay mind made no attempt to understand the scientific mind, but it became suspicious and frightened of the possible passing of power into the hands of the scientists. For the first time the uneducated thousands were warned, chiefly in the Press, that an entirely new menace might be threatening them.

'In its appointed hour the vision of Mensch broke into flower. For a number of years he had thought the scientific man to be the perfection of human evolution. This type of man had gone ahead and found, not vague theories to dwindle into emptiness at the first attempt at practical application, but the two great principles of experiment and observation. A prophetic artist was needed to realize that these two great principles could be applied to the solution of all human problems; that religion with its faith and fear was an appanage of mental savagery; that philosophy with its ethical wranglings was an even more futile attempt to escape from man's self-imposed burdens; but that all their shams could be broken up, their stranglehold on the mind destroyed, by the vigilant application of these two guiding rules.

'Mensch was that prophetic artist. Once that vision had taken form in his mind, he set out to examine it in detail. It seemed to him logically certain that no deviation from the ancient routine of battle and recuperation, of senseless slaughter and useless recovery, was to be expected, so long as the old laws of thought prevailed; it seemed equally clear that the control of humanity had passed from the theologians to the politicians, and must in due course pass from them to the scientists. Yet it was plain that the scientific point of view did not exist apart from specialization. In the groups and sub-groups of the specialists there were but a handful of first-rate minds; there were thousands of mediocrities and hundreds who were definitely dangerous, either gullible or corruptible to the end of their time.

'He concentrated now exclusively on the translation of scientific works, in order that he might move constantly among their users. Here and there he found a man such as we now term fully developed up to the present pitch; one who was guided in his self-conscious dealing by the principles of experiment and observation. It was a memorable day for him when he met the physiologist M'Grath, who used his own body for the purposes of experiment.

'The passionate capacities his thoughts did not absorb were concentrated into love of little children. Here he followed and was content to follow a charming precedent. The little children suffered him to come unto them, and he sought their company. Wherever he might happen to be his temporary home consisted of one room in a mean city street, wherein all day long and far into the evening the urchins frolicked and fought. Often he would lay down his pen and go to them, teaching them new games, telling them of alien children in far lands, playing a tune on his fiddle that they might dance, or impersonating grotesque and comical beasts to draw their laughter. His dramatic instincts found their complete gratification in the mothering and fathering of the unwanted. He never begot a child himself. Not only promiscuous breeding, but unintelligent motherhood, outraged his sense and disgusted his senses. The necessity of establishing motherhood on a vocational basis was one of his earliest decisions.

'He began to collect infants when he realized that he would one day require disciples. He chose them with discrimination, noting the necessity that the material for his educational experiment should be physically hardy and mentally endowed. He never took a child of less than three years of age or more than five, with rare exceptions. His ambition was to select one boy from each European nation, to transport them to an estate far from all human settlements, and there to prepare them for their mission.

He first chose St. John Richmond and thereafter Conrad Pushkin. In order to provide for these two he whittled down his, and their, needs to the finest point; he worked from eight o'clock each night until four each morning, allowed himself four hours for sleep, and devoted the remainder of the day entirely to their development. At the end of five years he had adopted three boys, having added Carl Winburg to the establishment. He foresaw that his resources would not permit him to do these three justice if he added to their number, but happily just then the legacy of the Dingwall millions befell him. Some years before, the remarkable inventor of the Dingwall car had met Mensch in a Viennese café, where they had talked a night through. Dawn separated them, and the little Jew's reluctance to ally himself with a man of money kept them apart. But Dingwall on his death-bed had forced his millions on the friend of that night. "He shall have his chance to fight with all they imply," thought Dingwall with amusement as he struggled with death, for struggle was his natural medium of self-expression, and he could no more die than live passively. "Let him see what he makes of them." I regret that Dingwall is unable to witness'—Antoine smiled gently and swept his arm slowly towards his auditors—'the result.

'Dingwall knew nothing of the child collection, or he might have been robbed of his satisfaction. The motive behind that legacy was friendly malice. It would have been cheated. Mensch, like other Jews in the wilderness, embraced the manna with praise and benedictions. Within the shortest possible time he was established with his disciples, to whose number each year added, in his isolated citadel, and his educational experiment was in full swing. The Menschlein, as he lovingly called them, had no gods and no parents; they grew up ignorant of all enslaving herd codes of the outer world; Mensch, sweeping away from them the accumulated spiritual rubbish-heaps of centuries of false thought, taught them the true meaning of words. As they grew older he led them back to the ancient Greek fountain-head of science. "The honeyed spirit of those old Greek sages still brooded over them."

'From its inception, Nucleus was a self-governing community, in which reigned a complete anarchy which later had to a large degree to be abandoned, but which will certainly become universal again as soon as the race has been educated up to it.

'Only the most imaginative of you here can possibly guess with what sense of power those boys presently went into the world to teach. The younger ones among you, who have as a matter of course received a similar education to theirs, can barely conceive what it meant at that time, in those political and social conditions, to be a man without fear; a man balancing a healthy body on firmly planted feet, and possessing a brain which could cut with knife-like precision through the common perplexities and doubts of common men. Hemmed in by mental inhibitions impenetrable as barbed-wire entanglements, over-loaded with chimerical responsibilities—thus men lived long after the dawn of the twentieth century. Although in the seventeenth Descartes had declared, "Cogito, ergo sum," many of them could read and write, but to think, as we understand thought, was impossible to most of them. "In the beginning was the word"—small wonder that those who believed that did not inquire whether it might have been a catchword.

'It was inevitable that each of these powerful young men quickly gained adherents and followers, but they were careful to admit to their intimacy only those capable of thought on experimental and searching lines. They took care to be considered by those who might have become their enemies had they taken them seriously, mere theorists. They kept in constant touch with one another and with Mensch himself, and presently they spread like a human cable, linking up every important centre of experiment and research in the world. In a far shorter time than even he had foreseen, their teacher had formed a phalanx of men sufficiently numerous and sufficiently powerful to step into the high places when the moment should call them.

'So we come to the last war; the war of unbounded destruction predicted by a few seers even in the early nineteen-twenties; the *reductio ad absurdum* of the tug-of-war by competitive nationalists, who hitched each his wagon to a star of malevolence, and piled it to the brim with the engines of destruction and annihilation furnished by their prostituted "scientists."

'Mensch, watching at a distance, would have been content to wait. The eruption he had so long ago foreseen did not attract him to close inspection; to attempt to expedite or to stay its progress was not his concern. Most human life, of the quality then being cancelled, did not call to him for rescue. Human life—the cantmongers for centuries had been satisfied to extol its sanctity and to encourage its wasting and rotting by the slow disintegration of disease and death. The swifter process was the cleaner. Let the flames leap and lick, and the gases stifle and strangle.

'But where Mensch could wait, his men could not. Their opportunity was at hand. The holocaust needed guidance and encouragement if it were to sweep in the desired direction. They would need men hereafter; or rather, the raw human material from which might begin to be fashioned the ultimately desired human being. The undermen, untainted by the subversions of the tottering civilization the offspring they would produce were fit to form the bedrock of the new erection. But the tainted, the intelligent savages whose instincts had been trained and sharpened towards this end, whose competitive rabies had reached its climax, must go. They went.

'Thus the battle resolved itself into a straight fight between madmen armed with science, and sane men, compelled to strike them down with the same weapon. While nation had armed against nation, within each had waited the prepared members of another company. Whilst the remnants of armies struck blindly and blunderingly at one another, the soldiers of science looked beyond them, and struck fully and finally at those behind them.

'Mensch was already superseded by the striplings he had reared. The teacher's mission was over; that of the pupils would now begin. We know that it is the experiment which matters and that its result is seldom final; how much his experiment mattered it is for us, his heirs and successors, to prove.'

2 HOW HUMPHREY WAS MADE

When you're married I wish you joy,
First a girl, and then a boy.
—"Poor Jenny Lies A-weeping"

I

Christopher and Nicolette sat at their Aunt Emmeline's feet. She liked to have them there. Her procreative instincts had been sublimated. Now, in early middle age, their entire gratification came from the contemplation of eager, upturned child faces. Child minds to mould, to direct, to develop—she loved them.

She knew, as she watched these two, that their curiosity reached out to her this evening hungrily. She revelled in the anticipation of satisfying it. She loved Christopher especially, as all virgins did. And she knew that to-day, on his seventh birthday, the tale she was about to unfold as her gift to him would draw him still closer to her.

From the moment he had entered, Christopher's blue eyes, which sometimes were dulled by dreams but now shone brightly and exploringly, had tracked her every gesture. While all the preliminary ritual had taken place he had watched, silent and observing. Nicolette, waiting more passively, taking her cue, as she invariably did, from her brother, kept closely by his side; Nicolette being only a small girl. She was still chubby; her short brown curls and the curves of her fat cheeks retained their infantile imprint.

They all three wore a short one-piece garment, of a synthetic silky material, and nothing else but sandals, to protect the soles of their feet. The boy's frock of blue was cunningly patterned in reds and yellows; the baby girl's was white, primrose-bordered; the grey of their aunt's dress matched the tone of her abundant hair.

The room, though airy and comfortably furnished, was cell-like in its simplicity, chiefly because it contained no pictures, whilst the broad ledge reserved for implements and small pieces of sculpture had only one occupant, a stone owl; and eyes which might have gazed at it out of the past would have had to look hard in order to perceive that it was an owl.

Christopher spoke first, having settled himself satisfactorily on the floor, with Nicolette close beside him.

'We are quite ready, Emmeline. Have you all you want?'

'I think so, now.'

'Oh, I am glad. Now listen, Nicolette; you must remember everything. Do you remember? Who was Humphrey?'

'The baby they made a boy,' said Nicolette gravely, 'like they make you and me.'

'Do you remember, Christopher? Emmeline asked. 'Tell me, before I continue, what I explained last time.'

'Before Humphrey came,' began Christopher reflectively, 'the world was very different from what it is now. In those days hardly any important things, like birth and death, were talked about to children. Sometimes they wanted to know, like we do, but all they were told about the beginning and end of their bodies was that they would know later. All that was unpleasant. It hurt mothers to have their children born. People were untaught, so they suffered fear.'

'What is "fear"?' interrupted Nicolette.

'What happens to people who won't ask questions,' he answered. 'People who won't be interested in their own bodies. There are none like that now, but nearly all were like it then. In some places there were too many children, in others not enough, and nearly everywhere a lot were hungry and unhappy and suffered.'

'What is "suffered"?' Nicolette asked again.

'They could not do anything for themselves. They just let things happen to them. Like those seedlings you planted, they all needed a lot of light and air and food, and they could not get them because they were all crowded up together. No one stopped planting or weeded out the weak ones, so they just went on growing—badly, until they were killed somehow. That's all, Emmeline.'

'No, you have forgotten something, Christopher.'

'Yes. Wait.' Thought narrowed the blue eyes. 'There were not enough boys. There were too many girls. Until Professor Perrier made Humphrey. Now, Emmeline, tell us how he did it.'

'It began before Humphrey came,' she took up his tale. 'They had already managed to arrange how many children should be born each year in each country. The war-makers would not have even that at first, but after a while the women paid no attention to them. Several geneticists—that's a long word, but Nicolette need not remember it—had been trying to find out why animals and humans were born either males or females. They began to pair insects, birds, and small mammals in their own workshops. Bit by bit they understood how sex worked. They found out how it was that queen bees laid eggs which later developed into just the sort of bees the hive needed. Professor Perrier bred hundreds of animals, until it became clear what had to be done. Then he did it. And many of these things you will do also, Christopher, if you want to, later on.'

'I have done some already,' he answered eagerly. 'Anatomy on mice and frogs. Nicolette has been looking after them for me, but the other day she overfed Stella, the best one of all. Stella may have to be killed now.'

'Give her to me,' pleaded Nicolette, and her brown eyes grew rounder than ever with entreaty. 'I do like Stella. I'll be ever so careful with the others if you will.'

'It's no use asking me. I must do other things now. I cannot run so fast as you, Nicolette, nor make things with my hands so well. I must learn to.'

'I run faster than all the other children. You cannot help it, darling Christopher,' Nicolette hastened to console.

'I do not want to go fast,' he answered quietly. 'I want to go my own way. I shall, too. I want to be like Humphrey, new and wonderful. How wonderful was Humphrey, Emmeline?'

'Look, and you shall see.' She pressed a button at her side, the light faded out, the projector whirred, the first film appeared on the untinted wall before them.

'Of course this is a very old one, taken long ago,' Emmeline explained to the entranced children. 'It is all flat; there are no colours and no sounds, for they did not know how to reproduce them then.'

There appeared a man and a woman in weird clothes. All of them that emerged clearly were their faces and their hands. Their heads were covered with some ugly and curious things—'hats,'—their bodies were funnelled in heavy, uncouth garments; their feet, bottled up in what the children knew were called boots, were invisible.

'They must have been uncomfortable!' exclaimed Christopher. 'However could they have borne those things?'

'In their day—the early twentieth century—no one could have lived without them. Only towards the middle of it those things began to be discarded in parts of the world.'

'But they never lived as long as we do,' he objected.

'No, they did not know how.'

The woman carried a swathed and veiled bundle, a mass of white draperies. Both parents smiled fatuous smiles of pride and pleasure.

'Where is Humphrey?' asked Nicolette impatiently.

'In the arms of his mother.'

'That bundle, Nicolette. Can we see his face, Emmeline?'

A caption appeared on the wall. 'The World Famous Perrier Baby,' read the children. Then came a large picture of the mite, lying naked on a cushioned table. Its mouth gaped hungrily, dimpled fists beat against the greedy infant lips.

'The darling!' cried Nicolette.

'Just like any other.' Christopher's disappointment was revealed in his eyes and in his voice.

'That was the marvel of it,' said Emmeline quietly, smiling a little at him. 'Just like any other, and yet the herald of a revolution.'

'Why did they want this boy so badly?' asked Christopher, as more pictures of the child passed before them, causing Nicolette to take her brother's arm and snuggle closer to him in her delight. Humphrey year by year; Humphrey with a little girl, his senior, guiding his first steps with maternal care.

'She's like you, Emmeline!' cried Nicolette.

'No, like Antonia—like our mother,' contradicted Christopher.

'You may both be correct. She and Humphrey were ancestors of ours. We are their descendants, and therefore perhaps resemble them.'

The children's chatter ceased as a grave, kindly, bearded man peered at them from the screen, smiled, bowed, and walked out of the camera's focus. 'Perrier,' said Emmeline, with reverence in her voice.

'Those funny things—he's wearing them too,' Nicolette objected.

'Everybody was obliged to dress like that,' her brother explained. 'They thought that if they were shut up in all those things nobody could see the diseases of their bodies and their minds. They tried to cover everything up, as ostriches cover their heads.'

'Well,' said Emmeline, and her voice held a shade of mutiny, 'though your father insists on complete frankness, I know, it may sometimes be unwise.'

'But those were ugly and unnatural in their living, and full of fear and hatred.' Christopher repeated his history lesson loyally.

'And they all stayed where they were put,' chimed in Nicolette. 'We go where we like. If they did not like a place they stayed there all the same. I wouldn't—would you, Christopher?'

'Never. And they frightened the children with gods and bogeys. They said they were in the sky or under the ground. But tell us, Emmeline,' Christopher always returned to his points like a fox-terrier to a rat-hole, 'why did Humphrey's people want a boy so much? The girl was nice. Did they not like girls?'

'They wanted a son who when they were dead would have their title—a special kind of name.'

'But they had her.'

'Girls were not always allowed to take titles. And their ancestor had gone to a lot of expense to get it.'

'To get just a name? Was it a splendid name like——' Christopher searched and presently found, 'like the names in that play the Players gave us? "Commander of the Faithful," "Peacock of the World!" Lovely names!'

'No, not a bit like that. It was just "Sir," "Sir Joseph Dobson." But it was valuable to him. It showed that he had been more successful, as they called it, than most of the others. He wanted it to go on and so did his children.'

'What was ex-pense?' asked Nicolette, pronouncing the new word cautiously.

'It meant a lot of things. Working, for instance, without ever playing. Then the two were not the same thing, but quite different. To this man and other people it meant spending long hours in a horrible place called a Factory. He had to see that lots of men and women kept it going for him, and he kept it going for what was called the Government. He and his friends had to make it impossible for any one to get enough of anything unless they worked all the time at what they were told to do, not what they really enjoyed. Those people didn't know how to look at a picture, or at the stars, or how to listen to music. He could only think of money, for without it he could get nothing.'

'Do you mean coins?' The children were subdued, perplexed, and vaguely sorry, as Emmeline's voice rose above them.

'I cannot tell you all I mean, Christopher. You, my darlings, need never know fear nor greed. Your day shall never breed such a people, nor such a life. And of your day the vision of a different man was the beginning. That man of whom you, Christopher, already know something.'

'Was Humphrey really the first of the new babies?' asked Nicolette, whose mind had wandered back to its favourite maternal musings.

'Not quite the first, dear. There were a lot of animal babies, and then Perrier and his mate had a baby this way themselves. And there were one or two others. But in those days there were very few people who would try a new experiment themselves.'

'No Stalwarts?' asked Christopher in surprise.

'No. They were called soldiers, but they were kept to fight other soldiers, not disease or ignorance. There was no Gay Company. But Humphrey's father, Sir Thomas, the son of Sir Joseph, owned a large estate, on which many cattle and pigs were bred.'

'Like we have.'

'Not quite. You see, they belonged entirely to him and to no one else; but he did not look after them. He also owned two libraries at which he never looked, and dozens of ships on which he never sailed, and sugar and coffee plantations which he never visited. He left his herds in the care of a breeder. Now this man knew a little more about bodies than most men of his time. He liked to learn to do new things. So he began copying some of the experiments on a few animals.'

'One day, Sir Thomas and his mate, or wife as she was called, went to see the farm. This man, Simon, who did not know how they wanted a boy, began telling them what he had been doing. Sir Thomas, who never listened to what any one said except people he was afraid of, kept nodding his head and saying: 'Splendid! Splendid!'

Christopher laughed gaily. He could see, inside him as he used to explain, a picture of Sir Thomas's fat red face wagging between the wings of a stiff collar, the sort those people had worn, and the points of it digging into his fat chin at each nod. He mimicked the nodding and said 'Splendid!' several times in as guttural and deep a voice as he could command. This set Nicolette giggling and nodding in imitation, until she, who had been growing drowsy, nodded herself to sleep.

Emmeline wished to take her in her arms.

'Oh don't bother. Leave her,' begged Christopher. 'The cushions are nice and soft.' Emmeline's curves were angular, and he knew that Nicolette had once called her aunt's arms 'crackly.' He placed another cushion beneath the child's head and said tactfully: 'She is ever so heavy now, and would tire you.'

Emmeline leaned back in her chair and sighed. She knew that Christopher was precociously wise. She began to smoke, and looking at the boy's fair face said, 'You are remarkably like Anne, Christopher.'

'Was she a nodder, too?' he asked with a chuckle.

'She was a fine woman. Brave and keen and intelligent. Fair, like you are, and fearless. Women were mostly braver than men, but not many were as Anne was. She listened carefully to Simon. And though she could not understand all he explained she began to think. If she had been fearful this would have passed her by, and there would have been no Humphrey. When she got home, she sent for all the books she could get about Perrier, and set to study them. After two weeks she wrote to him. Several letters passed between them, and then, when she had come to her decision, she told Sir Thomas what she proposed they should do. He was extremely angry at first. He was as ignorant as all of his kind. He believed in what he called "Nature."

'I suppose he was afraid?'

'Of course he was. Of the idea—of all ideas. But he pretended to be afraid for Anne. She just smiled and let him talk. After a long time, when he could not think of anything more to say, and was about to go to sleep, Anne said softly: "We will call him Humphrey." Then, because he really loved her, and longed almost as much as she longed, he turned to her and kissed her good-night. So Anne knew she would have her boy.'

'Oh, go on; go on quickly, dear Emmeline,' whispered Christopher.

'That is all really,' she answered, smiling her dry smile at the eager, upturned face. 'They went to see Perrier, and even Sir Thomas did not turn back. It was very painful to him when Perrier explained these matters of sex. You see, he could not rid himself of what he thought were his "ideas" on this subject, but which were really unclean mental habits. He had been educated to be interested in the inside of a motor-car, but his own inside he dared not think about. Luckily Anne made it easy for him; she knew that once Humphrey had arrived he would regain what he called his "self-respect."'

'It must have been funny! To respect yourself for not knowing anything. And when Humphrey came——'

'You will understand more fully, when you grow up a little, just what the coming of Humphrey meant. By then you will have learnt about the last war. Humphrey was killed in it. At that time the governments of the world began to see that with the Perrier method they could get plenty of boys. The nations would have an unlimited supply of "Man Power." They only overlooked one person: Mensch.'

'Hullo,' said a soft voice suddenly.

'Just look, will you, dear,' asked Emmeline. Christopher rose from his cushions and moved to the wall behind him. He pushed aside a panel and saw, framed in strips of light metal, a picture of his mother, Antonia, seated in her room. She smiled at him, and out of the picture her voice spoke: 'May I come to you, you two gossipers? Why, that babe's asleep again.'

'Yes, do come, Antonia,' answered Emmeline. Christopher watched his mother rise, then closed the panel. He turned to his aunt. 'Some music will wake Nicolette,' he said. Shall we have some?'

'It will have to be rather loud,' she suggested.

'I'll sing my new marching song,'—and immediately he began in a clear confident voice, stamping his feet and snapping his fingers in time:

The children of the days of old
Just had to do what they were told,
   They were not free
   Like you and me,
But silly lambs within the fold.

They all believed in fairies bold,
And ogres grim, so they were told,
   At dark nightfall
   Would eat them all
If ever they strayed from the fold.

They feared the heat, they feared the cold,
They feared their god so cruel and old,
   With fear they squeaked,
   With pain they shrieked,
And huddled close within the fold.

I'll never do as I am told,
For I am brave and strong and bold;
   It's fine to strive,
   To learn and thrive,
But not to be a lamb within the fold.

Nicolette opened one eye, awakened by the familiar tune, and then the other. 'Oh, Christopher!' she murmured sleepily, 'what a lot of noise.'

Christopher danced around her, with flushed cheeks and shining eyes, waving his arms at her, and repeating:

I'll never do as I am told,
For I am brave and strong and bold. . . .

She scrambled to her feet and began to dance with him. Then Antonia entered. Nicolette ran to her. Christopher continued to dance until he fell, stumbling into the cushions. 'Lovely stories, Antonia,' he called up to his mother, lying where he had fallen, his hands clasped behind his head, his legs outstretched, feet crossed.

'Come, children,' she answered smilingly, and held out her hand to him and raised him. 'You will only just have time to get to the swimming bath. All the others are there already. Come along.'

'Dear Emmeline has told me all about Humphrey at last,' said Christopher, gratefully taking Emmeline's firm hand in his. It was always a cool hand.

'And no one could tell so nicely,' answered his mother, with an affectionate glance, marred by a faint tinge of pity, for her sister. 'Will you come with us?'

'Not now,' Emmeline replied, and watched them as they went together; the tall, soft-bosomed, still beautiful mother; the lithe, ardent boy; the rounded, brown-curled small girl, who turned and threw her kisses as she went. Emmeline, who had chosen another path, watched them go and turned slowly to her books.

II

Emmeline fingered the press-cutting books and thought backward. She tried, not for the first time, to sum up what Humphrey's coming had meant to the world—and to her. In the end it always came back to that, for Emmeline, though remarkable in many ways, retained one of the chief failings of the women of an earlier day and an earlier, more primitive education; she thought from the general to the particular.

Humphrey's coming had meant many things to many people besides Anne and Thomas. To Perrier less than to most of them. To him the boy's birth had been an event inasmuch as the parents were the first, outside his own tiny circle, to place themselves unreservedly in his hands. The Humphrey experiment was a complete success; a satisfactory experiment. It was the fruition of his years of labour. He would have dismissed it at that, but he had reckoned without the psychology of the child's absurd father. Sir Thomas regarded himself, he proudly told the geneticist, as a pioneer. Since, in his schooldays, he had been taught that all pioneers were great and good men and fameworthy, he sought his due. He remembered the Pilgrim Fathers; he liked the phrase and had often used it in public speeches, and jestingly told Anne that he was, in a new and an amazing sense, a Pilgrim Father. Anne, having her heart's desire, let him be. His first gesture was to press on the reluctant Perrier a vast sum of money. This would probably have been refused had Mme. Perrier not insisted on its acceptance.

Sir Thomas then invited all his available friends to a dinner party, the nearest possible approach to a banquet he could command, to celebrate the birth of his heir.

'You see in me,' he told them with post-prandial lack of self-consciousness, 'a sceptic confused, who wishes to pay his small tribute to the greatest man in the world today. Unfortunately he is not here, by my side; you know what these great men are, shy as kittens, ridiculous. But think what this means. Here is a man who gratifies one of the oldest desires of mankind, a desire that has hitherto depended entirely on the will of God. In future, any one who wants can have a son and heir. The nations want men as never before in history; they will now have them. You will naturally understand that I am unable to give you details, but the thing is as simple as can be. It is the beginning of a new world.'

So he talked to his friends and they talked to their friends, and within five days the Press had discovered the Perrier baby. Reporters besieged Sir Thomas's house in Grosvenor Square, London. He received them all with cordiality, to them all he gave answer: You will naturally understand that I am unable to give you details.'

Within four hours the newspaper correspondents from London and New York and a hundred more cities had flung themselves on Perrier's doorstep. Perrier had not yet completed the paper he had been invited to read to the Parisian Society for the Promotion of Genetical Research. Biologists had, of course, been in touch with the experiments he had been carrying out during the past twenty years. His methods with regard to birds and mammals had been tested, adopted, and developed in Cambridge, in Moscow, and in Munich five years previously, and more recently in every centre of biological experiment. It was obvious to his fellow scientists that the next step must be their application and adaptation to the genetics of man. The results of the initial experiments practised by himself and his wife he had not felt justified in publishing. Only his friends, Eugene Delagrêve and Morton Gedding, had been informed of their results. It was Delagrêve, the president of the Parisian Genetical Society, whom he had first informed of the Humphrey experiment, and Delagrêve who, on its successful issue, had urged him to read a paper on the subject to his colleagues.

The fury of Perrier, as this loathed and despised notoriety arose before him, a giant wave that threatened to drown his calm and engulf his peace, knew no bounds. He expressed it with exceeding bitterness and accuracy in a letter to Sir Thomas, which also contained a cheque for the amount bestowed on him by the grateful millionaire, less five hundred francs. He then fled to his ancestral farm in Gascony, and endeavoured to complete his paper.

The coming of Humphrey, however, produced several more unforeseen reactions. Professor Perrier's countrymen heaped academic honours upon him. The French Government, quick to perceive the stimulus this biological invention would give to the birth-rate, placed subsidies at his disposal, while eager bridegrooms sought knowledge and enlightenment. All nations of the European continent sent their biologists to investigate. The Soviet Union offered him laboratories and an unlimited supply of human material on which to continue his experiments. This offer he in due course accepted, in order to escape from the importunities of his would-be disciples.

In England and in the United States, however, the Perrier invention caused greater turmoil than elsewhere in the world. The British and the American nations, led by their clergy, their Press, and their publicists, advanced upon this biological phenomenon from their fortresses of mental turpitude. They gave tongue to their moral battle-cries, and hurled themselves upon that unfortunate who, in a moment of sweet self-delusion, had referred to himself as a pioneer. Those details he had been unable to give must, so argued these peoples in their accustomed manner, be of a revolting nature. Conception control was then still practised by the minority. 'Nature' was still the only geneticist mentioned in public and polite circles. A voluntary, personal control of their sexual mechanism by prospective parents could only be inadequately described as disgusting by people of whom a majority still believed in the Book of Genesis and refused to admit the existence of text-books of genetics.

Sir Thomas knew these people; he had once been of them. But he came of a stock whose chief quality was tenacity developed to a high degree. He stood by his wife with that loyalty that made him lovable despite his absurdities, and told his accusers that he stood by his principles. He was, moreover, a skilled strategist; his father had been a financial power behind a former Government, and Sir Thomas's contributions to political funds had never fallen below the standard set in that respect by the late Sir Joseph, that first baronet of whom Emmeline had told with bitterness the story to her niece and nephew.

Scientific opinion was on Sir Thomas's side; it regarded him as a freakish and comical, but nevertheless respectable instrument in its cause. One or two men of learning descended disdainfully into the arena of public debate and mentioned without emphasis that determination of sex in no way implied the end of the race. The question, as far as England was concerned, was finally settled by a letter, written to the leading journal of the day, diffidently inquiring whether in the Perrier invention might not have been found the final solution of the 'Surplus Women' problem, which threatened at that time to become increasingly vexatious. This brief communication of not more than eight lines was signed A. Mensch, and caused a number of questions to be asked in Parliament which drew from the Minister of Health the reply that the Government saw no reason to prohibit the instruction of the medical practitioners of the country in the application of the Perrier method.

Emmeline's cuttings of that period were beginning to fade, despite their careful preservation. And now, looking back on them in the light of the subsequent astounding revolution, nothing seemed enduringly significant beyond the signature to that letter, A. Mensch.

Even in thinking from the general to the particular, she did not lose her gift of logical and coherent thought. She had voluntarily renounced motherhood in order to assist in the re-creation of the world foreseen and initiated by that man of stupendous vision. This was a fine world that she had helped to make, and she would not have done otherwise. She put books and cinematographic apparatus away, gave a momentary, loving thought to Christopher's shining eyes, and went down to her lecture room.

3 WOMEN AND CHILDREN FIRST

Few but roses.

—Meleager, of the poems of Sappho

I

Nicolette sat on a bank that sloped gently to the edge of the lake. Above her a great cedar spread its velvety branches to the blue afternoon sky, dotted with lamb-like clouds. The dipping sun made a pattern of branch shadows on the lawn around her. A little breeze rustled the iris at the furthermost edge of the water.

A shade of melancholy seemed to tinge the atmosphere, the pleasant kind of melancholy loved by French poets and young girls unconsciously becoming aware of a change in themselves, that natural and impressive physiological change which attunes adolescent mind and body to the meanings beneath Nature's pageant.

Nicolette was growing fast. She had lost some of her childhood's prettiness, and had not yet gained the beauty of young womanhood. The adaptation of her mind and body from the old to the new standards was proceeding normally, for her environment was admirably planned. A slight heightening of her emotional capacities was her only apparent mental symptom.

Now she wrote down, easily and yet with concentration, the doubts and perplexities which filled her young mind. Auto-suggestion by such written confession provided both the youthful and the mature of her day with a wholesome outlet for their conflicts, and all were taught to practise it from childhood onward. This was the last form of examination which survived in these days of more subtle educational methods.

'Ever since I was a tiny girl,' wrote Nicolette to herself, 'I have been looking forward to the day when I should have my own babies. The lovely darling creatures are all wonderful, but none could be so precious as my own. Before I came here to begin my I training I used to dream of my first one; what he would look like and feel like, and how I would try always to understand his every need. I would serve him truly and wholly, and he would be the loveliest and the most adorable baby ever born. I know I should not have thought like that; but although we know it is stupid, Christopher and I have always wanted secretly to have the best and be the best.

'Since I came here I can see how stupid I was. But I am not sensible yet. All the babies are perfect, but I cannot help thinking my Toodles is more wonderful than the others. I do not think such a perfect baby has ever existed. And I love him so much that it makes me miserable to think I shall have one of my own that could never, possibly, be like him. I could never have such a baby. He is just like his mother, Leila, the loveliest thing I have ever seen, and she is kind and wise, too. I am a little fool and I know it. I am a fool to imagine these things which instead of helping me make things more difficult. I do not know what is the matter with me, and I despise myself so much sometimes that I do not think I am fit to be here. I am probably not fit for this vocation at all. But I cannot help it. I feel I never, never want a baby of my own if he is not just like that one, and I know he could never, never possibly be.'

At this moment there was a step on the grass above her, and the shadow of a woman fell across Nicolette's page. The girl looked up and saw Leila, who stood a little higher up the bank and smiled down on her. Nicolette made no self-conscious attempt to conceal her writing. It was according to the prevailing standards, a part of herself, and therefore inviolable unless she chose to reveal it.

The woman came slowly towards her. A simple garment of apple green embroidered all over with small coloured starlike flowers moved in graceful folds from waist to ankle as she walked. A loose girdle, of the same colour as her bright brown hair, held the dress in a soft pouch over the hips. Ornaments she had none.

'Nicolette, child,' said Leila, 'I am going in. Are you coming with me?'

'I will, but just sit down for a minute,' the girl answered. 'Is it not lovely here? So quiet, so calm, and yet a little sad.'

'Are you sad, dear?' asked Leila, with a glance at the eyes that were slightly circled and the cheeks that seemed pale.

Nicolette replied indirectly. 'I was thinking of you,' she admitted. 'And of Toodles. I love him so much that I was thinking all sorts of foolish things.'

'But why should you not love him? That is what he and I are here for. If you did not love the child who teaches you, your lessons would be a waste of time, and we should not be training you for your vocation.'

'You are a dear, Leila,' Nicolette said gratefully, 'but this is my fault. I love him much more than all the other babies. I could never love any child in the world like him.'

'I know what you mean,' Leila said, and her smiling eyes were all sympathy. 'But you must remember that he is the first baby you have actually handled yourself. You are instinctively a little mother, and it is quite natural that you could not perform your first lessons without having such feelings. They are excellent, provided you understand them.'

'Oh, I do not. I mean I am sure I am very foolish. I make more fuss over him than you do. I—I wish he were mine and not yours!'

Leila laughed gaily. 'Well, you see, I have already had many children and you have none, so that is rather natural. When you have your own, you will feel just the same about the first, and afterwards you will not find it so much of a novelty and get used to them all.'

'But Leila,' Nicolette leant forward and gazed at the lake, and her voice was weighed down with the burden of her problem, 'do you really think I could love a baby of my own as I do yours?'

'You will love him quite differently. You see, Nicolette, at the period which you are now entering, nearly all girls feel very deeply. You must remember that your body is going through an important change. That of course stimulates your perceptions and puts a slight strain for the time being on your powers of self-control, while it sharpens your emotions. But if you stop thinking of yourself for a moment you will realize that this is usual, and not exceptional in your case. The more deeply this change affects a girl as a rule, the more certainly is she destined for motherhood. Those we call Neuters do not react so strongly. But this which is now happening to you is your preparation for your future. You will find in time that the bearing of children brings a love for them that is quite in harmony with self-control and intelligence. In the old days, when any woman could breed, before it was realized that motherhood was a vocation, and should therefore be carefully prepared for, many women had a sensual and passionate affection for their children that harmed both. Foolish men encouraged those women in that false affection that was about as noble as the feelings of a tiger for her cubs. They talked a lot of drivel about maternal instinct. Many of those mothers were hysterical or neurotic, and their children also lacked self-control. Then there were women forced into motherhood by custom. They feared it and revolted from it secretly. So that when they had borne a child they imagined they had done something abnormal and wonderful, instead of something to which not the least merit was attached. Thus they spoiled their own minds and those of their offspring.

'Love is an excellent thing so long as it harmonizes with the laws which govern our thoughts and feelings. But it should never be allowed to become degrading to the lover and the loved. You may be sure that by the old standards our mothers, many of them, would be accused of indifference. But those were unscientific standards.

'We are the vessels singled out for the propagation of our race. It is our mission to make ourselves perfect vessels. But once the child has left the mother's womb, his individual existence and development are what she must bear in mind. In proportion to his excellence as an individual and a servant of the race is her honour and her joy.'

'Thank you, dear Leila. I do understand all you say. But tell me just one thing more. Do you like bringing your babies to these gardens to teach us?'

'Of course. It is glorious. Remember that it is an honour to be chosen to do so. To make our motherhood useful to our successors expands its purposes. You see, in the old days a mother of the white race was required to be an employee in the home of the father of her children. How they attempted it we cannot imagine, but we know that an individual cannot accomplish more than one important task successfully, could not expect to. Some one always suffered, and the order of the sufferers was first the mothers, then the children, then the man. But by giving ourselves wholly to motherhood we do not surrender our own chances of development. Our service to you is a service to ourselves and to our children.'

'I cannot imagine why it took women so long to find out these things. Why, even if their minds could not grasp that the system was unfair, did they not revolt from the strain imposed on them?'

'Well, that is quite easily explained. You must remember that the burden did not become really acute in Europe and North America until the dawn of the twentieth century. Then things developed very rapidly. And it was only then that large numbers of men began to think scientifically. It was scientific thinking by men that abolished war. About the same time as your father and his colleagues solved such problems by scientific thinking, other men and women began to apply the same methods to ours.'

'And they met with terrific opposition?'

'Of course, at first. Opposition is the soil in which the seeds of all reform are planted.' Leila rose as she spoke. 'That, however, is a long tale, my dear. And we must return now. Come.'

'I do thank you, Leila, for helping me. I feel quite gay and jolly again. Wait, let me take my papers. I will make them into boats for Toodles.'

The girl and the woman smiled happily at one another as they strolled towards their Common Rooms. And by that smile, intimate, friendly and frank as their conversation, Nicolette was helped across the Rubicon dividing her past and her future.

II

The atmosphere of the entire settlement was one of gay calm. It was not designed for the pregnant women; no births took place there. For these other nurseries were reserved, where each mother resided during sixteen months; seven previous to and nine subsequent to the birth of her child. Here came, for another three months at the most, only those whose services were required by the commonwealth in order that their successors, the mothers of the future, might be apprenticed to learn the elements of their craft.

The mother settlements lay in the most exquisite spots on the North American, Australasian, and European continents. Wherever nature, encouraged and directed by the hand of man, could create a setting of unsurpassable beauty, wherever the climate was gentle and clement, they nestled among sloping hills, decked with blue lakes and painted with flower gardens.

These settlements, covering thousands of acres, were the breeding grounds, the nurseries, in the true horticultural sense, of the white race. Here women congregated to bear, not in agony nor in anguish, not in pain, distress, misery, filth, nor poverty, no longer anticipating in dread the hour of their delivery, but gladly, proudly, majestically. Here they came, conscious of their chosen vocation, submitting willingly to the stringent discipline of hygiene, striving to attain physical and mental perfection, poise, and balance, and to transmit it to those born to the high wonder of scientifically directed living. All they had done was to exchange the haphazard, pitiful, and inadequate discipline of sorrow and suffering for the acceptance of proven laws. Each mother knew in advance what would be the sex of the child to be born to her, and could aid its shaping to its destined end by judicious application under expert direction of the necessary mental and physical exercises. Pre-natal ill-health and pangs of labour no longer existed; foolish self-indulgence would have been scorned; fear was cast out.

III

Only those mothers who possessed certain specific qualities were chosen as teachers of the young. For vocational motherhood was a career which had its grades like all others. These women were at the head of their profession, and most of them passed on, when they had produced the number of children expected of them, to administrative duties in the linking up of their own special problems with those of the world in general. They had by then mastered the theory, as well as the practice, of race-production. To meet such mothers, to exchange views with them, to enjoy their conversation and companionship, was part of the unvarying custom of those men whose province touched theirs.

But all maternal settlements played an inspiring part in the social life. It was here that informal counsel was most often taken; here that men sought inspiration; here that an intercourse almost holy in its purity took place between men and women, when the meaning of friendship in all its wealth and beauty was discovered.

The small girls had gone to their dormitories; the infants lay aligned in their guarded nurseries; all was silence in the spacious buildings which housed them. But not far away, the pleasure halls were gay with light and colour; some were given up to music and games, others to quiet, reflective talk.

While her child slept and Nicolette, her little protégée, lay dreaming, the mother Leila walked calmly through gardens and passages until she came to a small, cosy saloon. When she entered it she found only four people there—the president of the settlement, two other young women destined, like herself, for wider responsibility in the future, and a young man, who had collaborated with one of them in producing her last child.

'Has he arrived?' asked Leila eagerly.

'Yes,' answered the older mother, Mary. 'He will be with us directly. This young man,' she said with a smile at him, is Bruce Wayland, who has brought him to us.'

'Oh yes,' Leila nodded and also smiled, 'I know your name. You are of the Gay Company surely?'

'Of the other side,' he answered. 'I flew across with Peter Minden and thought you might like to talk to him. He was naturally delighted to come. The mothers of Nucleus have a reputation.'

'How are his cattle? I have not yet seen any of them, although of course we have our own.'

'Well, naturally, his are models, as they were the originals of all. I am not an expert, as it is not my line. But last year his workers turned out seventy-eight ectogenetic calves; the aseptic cows produced in the past two years are apparently giving excellent milk.'

'I understand his beasts really are free from all harmful bacteria,' put in Elspeth, the younger woman. 'But I should think it will be a long time before he can rear them in sufficient numbers.'

'It takes time, of course,' answered Bruce. 'As far as he is concerned, the interest is only in the experiment of producing them.'

'Given the land and the animals,' said Leila reflectively, 'I imagine you will be able to support an increasing number. But I suppose they will never compete seriously with those bred normally?'

'Oh no. Nor would the rearing of ectogenetic children have an effect on the human birth-rate in our time. Not on a large scale. But, of course, we don't know how fast things will change. It is a year-to-year matter.'

The man they were talking about came in. He was short and thin, an almost shrunken little man. Yet this was Peter Minden, the geneticist whose performance might one day revolutionize the breeding of all animals on whose products man still depended.

'I am delighted to see you, mothers,' he said in a gentle, jerky voice, while he beamed at them bird-fashion, and turned his bright glances from one to the other. 'Our young friend did not need to persuade me to come here. Such visits are my chief pleasure. I think we have some things to discuss, yes?'

'We welcome you,' said Mary on behalf of them all. 'I expect we have much to learn from you.'

'I am at your disposal. But I wish to reassure you at once on the chief point. We have failed until now with the human embryo.'

'We had not yet considered you as a possible rival,' said Leila.

'I am not so sure,' warned Bruce. 'Beware of him!'

'Of course,' cut in Mary with her clear quiet voice, 'we have thought of that. But not nearly enough. There are many people, Minden, who refuse to take you seriously. What do you think of them?'

'Ah, my dear mother, what a mistake to take anything or any one seriously! Nevertheless, I may have a problem to put to humanity later on. And as it particularly concerns your sex and your profession, I seek an opportunity whenever possible to discuss it with you. Inevitably the day will come, and we might as well consider now what it may bring.'

'You will be a bold man,' said Bruce mockingly, 'if you challenge the mothers on their own ground.'

The ectogeneticist joined in the laugh, but returned to his point.

'That will not be my affair,' he declared. 'It is an inevitable result of discovery. Its various implications will affect me as well as every one else; but principally these women. How do you think,' he asked, turning to them, 'the suggestion of human ectogenesis will be generally received?'

'You will be the most unpopular man in the world,' they told him.

'I disclaim all responsibility,' he repeated. 'Let us look back a little. First you had birth control, then you had sex control. The two enabled you to impose your will on us in collective bargaining. Both met, in the beginning, with opposition from those of you who would not realize the advantages they brought you. But when you did, you knew an era was beginning for you such as motherhood had never known since dim antiquity.'

'It's curious, when one thinks of it,' said the president, 'how, after nearly two thousand years, women do occupy the same relative rôles they bore in Greece and Rome. There you had mothers, prostitutes, and slaves, forming the female hierarchy. The Patrician mothers had then, as now, no more to do than to produce and rear children. Slaves ran their households for them, and courtesans spared them the lust of men.'

'We,' added Leila, 'have mechanical slaves, neuters to perform the more highly skilled jobs, and entertainers to deal with the other matter.'

'But,' interrupted Minden, pointing a warning finger at her, 'remember the time it has taken you to get back to that pleasant situation. Remember the heyday of Christianity, when one woman per man, to speak roughly, was expected to perform the triple rôle of wife, mistress, and slave. Remember the day of the factory, when in millions of cases a fourth job was added to the burden. It was woman who built up "family life," and it was that that threatened to destroy her when she revolted—in the nick of time.'

'Surely,' suggested Bruce, 'it was not woman, but the Church who invented that myth. It was the Church that took all the asexuals into the convents, and persecuted the "fallen." It was not until the mothers were completely under the sway of the priests that they were duped into bearing every one else's burdens. Woman outgrew the family just as government outgrew empire and thought outgrew religion. Science had nothing to do with contraception, and its other inventions only aided and abetted the female effort to find its own level.'

'But science soon turned that to its own advantage,' declared Leila.

'That, again, was not science, but male human nature,' he answered with a grin. 'Obviously it suited us to find you so ready to fall in with our views. A little knowledge of practical psychology enabled us to convince you that the interests of both sexes were identical. At least up to the present.'

'Yes,' reflected Minden. 'I can almost foresee a day in which we shall return even further than to Greece and Rome. When we shall go even beyond Egypt, to the dawn of human society. When the goddess World-Mother shall become the supreme reality again.'

'What!' said Leila, and the other women half laughed, half frowned at her words. 'A sort of human termite queen? From whom the entire race shall be bred? Luckily that will not be for a few thousand years yet!'

'In all ages, everywhere, human beings have declared "Save us from the future!" It has been the abiding terror of all imaginative cowards. For the future alone is inexorable. Death can be cheated again and again—the future never. But those who resent it forget that they themselves will not have to endure it. Those whose present it is, learn to adapt themselves.'

Minden's voice as he had spoken had undergone a slight change. The audacity of the vision they were creating between them had its hold on them all. For a few moments they were no longer individuals—only vehicles for the expression of the thought which gripped them collectively.

'Imagine it,' Bruce took up the completion of its form, 'ectogenesis provides the means to select on the most strictly accurate lines. The numbers of mothers chosen diminish year by year. Until at last, those who supply the race are the supreme female types humanity can produce. Pyramidal.'

'But you really do not think'—Elspeth, the youngest of them there, turned appealingly to Minden—'that this thing will begin in our time?'

'There is no need whatever to distress yourself,' he reassured her. Once more he had become his quaint, outwardly flippant self. We are hundreds, even thousands of years away from that goal. No one, in our day, even desires it. But since all living and striving has become amenable to experiment, no possibility, however remote, can be entirely ignored. Certainly I think that my results have brought that day nearer. But it is still sufficiently far away for you to remain easy.'

'What is the quality and quantity of the milk produced by your cows, as compared to that given by normally reared beasts?' asked the presiding mother.

And forthwith Minden plunged into details of considerable, but merely technical interest.

4 FROM THE GENERAL TO THE PARTICULAR

Remarquez de plus que je me place dans l'hypothèse d'un progrès immense de la conscience humaine, d'une réalisation du vrai et du juste dont il n'y a eu aucun exemple jusqu'ici. Je suppose (et je me crois ici dans le vrai) ce progrès accompli, non par tous, mais par une aristocracie servant de tête à l'humanité, et en laquelle la masse aurait mis le dépôt de sa raison.

—Renan, *Dialogues Philosophiques*

I

'Brains' were in council. When the propagandists, through whom a tiny minority of men supplied and controlled the imaginative concepts of millions, had provided the imagery which would make the masses submissive to the works of the Patrol, they had translated the terms of social organization into those of the human body. The Body then stood symbolically for the entire white race.

Of the individual 'brain-cells' a few were now gathered together in a small and adequately protected hall. Their duties corresponded vaguely to those of former Ministers of State. But, being planned on supernational lines, the scope and power of each individual was napoleonic. Each man, aided by scientific method and scientifically trained subordinates, had at his command countless infallible messengers of communication and direction; his resources were equalled only by his opportunities, but neither had been possible had they not been preceded by a definite plan of scientific thinking and acting.

Here was McKie, in whom was vested the guardianship of the Outer Zones—those artificially created desert tracts which marked the boundary lines between the white and adjoining races; on which nothing during long years either moved or stirred save the shadows of the watchers in the blue above them. The tropical sources of oil, cotton, quinine, and other vegetable products whose cultivation had formerly demanded thousands of white and coloured sacrifices, were abandoned in these synthetic days to their earlier disorder.

Here was Winburg, the fat, mild, amiable Brain of chemical warfare, who had invented the dreaded Thanatil, which, on combining with the human plasma protein pseudoglobulin 2c, formed a deadly poison of the cobra venom type. His particular young men alone knew the secret of its manufacture and its antibody. The gentle Winburg, too, had first suggested the exploitation of that enzyme which produces the black pigment in negroes, and which, when attacking the tyrosine ester of Thanatil absorbed by the dusky skin, gradually liberates the poison till the central nervous system is invaded, causing paralysis and death.

Here, too, was Lutyens, the chief liaison officer between the Gay Company and the Patrol, who had founded that branch of the latter named 'Ears.' Those Ears heard all complaints and grievances, and their legal administration was founded strictly on the principles laid down by their psycho-pathological researchers.

Finally, here was St. John Richmond, with his son and auxiliary Adrian; St. John who, as the only one among them looked on as the possible successor to Mensch, co-ordinated their various functions.

'Well, what about these Japanese?' challenged McKie.

St. John, strolling as usual restlessly about, turned sharply and faced him. McKie was still rather young; to ferret for dangers unseen was his hobby, his pleasure to devise plans of defence against attacks which only he anticipated. That kind of sensationalism was the only luxury he permitted himself. It amused his colleagues to indulge him at times like the present, when his words related to a matter of fact.

'Well,' encouraged the adipose Winburg, 'and what then?'

Lutyens and Adrian Richmond remained silent. The same question had presented itself to both minds already; not with the dramatic insistence it adopted in McKie's case, but still as one which might as well now be discussed and answered.

The glint of a mocking smile appeared in St. John's eyes as he glanced around and noted with what ill-concealed eagerness his reply was awaited. The smile deepened a trifle as he contemplated Adrian, his son; the only one of all the sons to whom the father's word was the word of a ruler. Adrian, incarnation of filial loyalty, amused, flattered, and irritated his parent alternately. Still, Adrian, despite his mental dull patches, was an indispensable lieutenant, a repository of secrets which would be kept, a delegate of responsibilities that could not be averted.

The bold and perturbed McKie gave his leader—as they tacitly acknowledged St. John to be—glance for glance. 'Day on,' Richmond encouraged him, speaking softly through almost closed jaws.

'I say,' retorted McKie, 'that we must take a line regarding these people.' He used lip-talk—a precaution used whenever confidential matters were discussed. Existing arrangements for secrecy appeared adequate, but sound-catchers had before this been smuggled by these same people into council chambers. The others took his cue without comment. 'I suppose tours of this kind are unavoidable. But this one will be protracted. What they want to see and examine ostensibly, we know. Ostensibly . . . How much exactly are we going to let them know?'

'Everything, as usual, of course.' St. John's brevity was ironical.

'H'm. You appear to be quite satisfied about it.'

'So am I,' chimed in Lutyens. They all got fun out of McKie. 'Let there be light. Some, unaccustomed to its intensity, may be blinded or stricken by it. But let there be light.'

'What about Marshall's new stuff?' It was the fat Winburg, joining in the game, who asked the question.

'Certainly, by all means,' nodded St. John, and almost grinned. 'I look forward, Adrian,' he added, as he leaned against a convenient ledge and mischievously contemplated his son, 'to an appreciation of our star turn by the tourists.'

Adrian responded enthusiastically. 'You heard yourself what Godling, Kuck, and Lanion reported on it. Marshall has exceeded his own and our expectations. He has proved his case completely. Since we had his last paper his views have been reinforced by the tests of Barrillon.'

'I am no physicist, but just a plain Patrolman,' burst from McKie. 'So perhaps I may be allowed to doubt whether Marshall's invention really does set the seal on our security. But even if so, I can only repeat, the line ought to be drawn somewhere.'

'My friend,' gurgled Winburg with heavy flippancy, 'you are always drawing lines, and they are very straight ones. Let us be frank with our Oriental friends. If, in their case, seeing proves believing, there is no reason to suppose that faith removes vapours more easily than mountains. And even the Oriental arts in eliminating man from a sphere of noxious activity are not inimitable. I think past events have proven conclusively the efficiency of the "miserable Patrolmen."'

McKie subsided.

'Well, you are apparently satisfied. But it would teach us a lesson if one day our weapons were effectively turned against us.'

'Be comforted, dear friend,' concluded Winburg, 'with the maxim, doubtless of Oriental origin: "The brains of the hydra reside in its head, and the number of all heads is finite."'

'I think you will find,' St. John concluded the discussion, 'that our plans for the entertainment of our visitors will satisfy you. I can assure you that your prejudices are shared by us all to this extent at any rate: we shall use our customary caution in every matter and as much in addition as may be found necessary. We do not propose to pledge our own, nor white posterity's security, to theories or principles. All may come and all may see what happens to be visible. But Marshall's new stuff has not yet reached the point of publicity. Its practical applicability has been tested by the four men mentioned by Adrian only. Their report is in careful hands, and at present only ourselves have access to it. It is not proposed that any of these people shall be on the committee of hospitality. They will be occupied elsewhere for the duration of this visit. Past experience encourages me to think that we shall be in a position to meet any menace such as you seem to suggest. I should be delighted to discuss details with you some other time. I have had a somewhat strenuous eighteen hours. But let me remind you, if I may, that our power still depends on two facts: the small number of us who wield it, and the even smaller numbers of those who might prove our enemies—if they could adapt our methods to their own purposes.'

'Oh, I grant you those points,' answered McKie, mollified, but regretful to abandon his scare.

'Well, then, my dear fellow,' concluded St. John, 'let us be consistent. We have laid down the principle of the open door. We cannot now bar it. But even an open door may be guarded. I forget whether the gates of heaven were supposed to be closed or merely ajar. St. Peter, however, I understand to have been a fairly efficient goalkeeper. It is a pity,' he grinned at Adrian as he spoke, 'that my youngest son, whom I believe to be something of a theological expert, is not here to advise us on the point. The fact remains that the core of our "kingdom," according to the venerated precedent, will remain invisible to all save those of unblemished vision. Our visitors may learn all they *can*. And I think we may confidently forecast exactly how much that will be.'

'I will call on you to-morrow,' said McKie as he rose. 'In the meantime I am at the disposal of the entertainment committee.'

'They will be delighted,' rejoined St. John with twinkling eyes. 'At the end of the visit your own mind, no doubt, will be steeped in Oriental guilelessness.'

'Impossible,' declared Lutyens emphatically, 'even you will never deprive him of his little joke.'

'You will not,' McKie pleasantly flung at them as he went. 'For myself, I find this world "far too good to be true," as our ancestors used to say.'

II

'And now,' said St. John, turning to his colleagues and resuming the tone of ordinary conversation, 'will you excuse me also? Adrian is chafing with impatience, as you see, to get me to himself. It is time for my nightly curtain lecture, and he will burst if he cannot relieve himself of it soon.'

'In that case, decidedly not,' grunted Winburg, whom Adrian frequently irritated. 'I consider he has a deplorable influence on you. His gloating approval of all you do and say nauseates me. Why not send him to Isola or Centrosome, and get that young anchorite of yours to take you in hand for a while?' Winburg's placid humour was so well attested that his remarks gave no offence.

'My dear Carl,' said Adrian dryly, 'you need a mentor yourself. Your latest affair is the talk of the administration. Personally, I cannot understand how buxom contraltos ever became enlisted among the Entertainers.'

'Ah, my boy, you will; one day you will. What a voice! A bird she is . . .' and he sighed with lyrical emotion.

'With all the pectoral development but none of the instincts of the pelican,' added Lutyens. 'By the way, St. John, what news of that boy of yours? They tell me he has a marvellous ear. At certain types of sound matching he is absolutely unrivalled already, they say. There is also a young female with musical gifts who would like to mate with him.'

'You shall bring her along for inspection, Walter. But I cannot encourage you. The boy is all sublimation just now. Besides,' he added, 'I really have not the vaguest idea where he is.'

'Ah well,' said Lutyens, 'these young people can perhaps afford to waste a little time. As for myself,'—he glanced encouragingly at Winburg—'if that Samson can reach his feet, I will deliver him to his Delilah. I am all for a little light warbling to-night.'

After they had gone, St. John paced slowly up and down, while Adrian busied himself with some drinks and glasses which he had drawn from a wall-cupboard. 'Do come and sit down,' he implored, 'you must have walked miles to-day.'

'I do feel a little weary,' admitted his father. 'I will go to Antonia soon. But as I know you wish to know, I will tell you that Christopher is not to be interfered with.'

'I cannot quite approach the matter from your point of view,' he continued, as he slid into the first, which happened also to be the smallest and hardest, chair available.

Adrian sipped his drink and said nothing.

'You dislike the boy's attitude, and are allowing yourself to become prejudiced. Now I happen to like him.'

'But so do I, enormously,' protested Adrian, for the first time with some heat. 'So much so that I cannot become reconciled to his absurdities. It is just because I know he is, or could be, so brilliant, that I think we ought to do something about him.'

'It is too soon, my lad. Give him time.'

'But he has had time. I know quite well that puberty is always a nuisance. I did not want to be impatient. But he is increasingly disappointing.'

'That is entirely your own fault. It is rather abominable, the way you are apt to await a reward for your labours. You looked on him as your own private little prodigy, without the least justification. I admire him for his independence.'

'I admit part of that; I did want to make him of some use. There was every reason to suppose I would. But this religious nonsense is preposterous.'

'Not in the least. Perfectly normal, at his age. He'll outgrow it.'

'I doubt it, or I would not insist in the matter. You know how we have to watch these reactions. All religious mania is dangerous. It's one of the most serious forms of undisciplined auto-suggestion, and I am sorry to see it in one of us.'

'Oh, pooh-pooh. What do you expect, at that age? Christopher knows enough to stop taking himself too seriously in time.'

'Well, I do not see why that time should not be soon.'

'Now, Adrian, you must look after yourself. You are becoming a meddler. I should have thought I provided you with all the material you needed for the exercise of that vice of yours. You can be my confessor, my adviser, my wet-nurse, if you like. But for your own sake, I shall be compelled to send you away if you suggest again the slightest interference with Christopher's metabolism.'

'Righto! I bow. I don't mind if all your other sons get Messianic mania, so long as I can stay where I am.'

'Neither do I. When does Nicolette return?'

'Shortly, I think.'

'We will soon have Raymond with us again. He is an excellent fellow, and the mating should be a success.'

'Yes. They are both lovely children. Nicolette is adorable, and he should satisfy her if Christopher has not planted his seeds of discontent in her mind.'

'There you start again! Why should she not love the boy? We all do, and she, dear little mother-girl, naturally wants to encourage him. You will find that as soon as sexual instincts are awakened and fulfilled in her, she will humanize the boy also. Let my children be, Adrian, and learn a little from your own. They, at any rate, are unlikely to cause you anxiety. And now come along and talk to Antonia for a little,' he added with an affectionate smile, 'and be lectured yourself for a change.'

5 THE VOYAGES OF CHRISTOPHER

Belief is not voluntary; it is not an action, but a passion of the mind.

—Shelley, in a letter to his father

I

Christopher's airplane crept smoothly through the clouds until it had got above them. Even then they were still comparatively low, though they were well provided with oxygen in case he should feel inclined to soar. But at the moment they neither looked up nor down. Nicolette knew quite well the meaning of those casual invitations he flung her from time to time. 'Coming up?' more as statement than query, meant, from him to her, 'I need you.' It meant that he must talk to her, indulge in one of those increasing moods when the urge of speech was upon him, but when the matter for discussion was for her ears alone. She noted that he had carefully disconnected all apparatus which could instantly put them in touch with the rest of the world. He had cut them off.

There was a physical delight in flying with Christopher. His control of hands and feet was exquisite and precise. His control, through them, of the machine, appeared automatic. Inseparable as snail and shell seemed Christopher and the *Makara* when once he was ensconced in her.

Nicolette's thoughts had been running on the loveliness of young things and small things. Moving through the air beside Christopher, she remembered a living carpet of scillas which she had tended in the spring, until it had broken into a stretch of unblemished blue, still and clear as the waters of an inland lake. She tried to hold on to the picture and the mood, for she knew quite well that in a moment or two both would vanish.

'Do you ever feel, Christopher,' she asked presently, looking straight ahead, 'as if you were one of those nice, fat, stone jars, filled to the brim with cool wine?'

'No, you nice, fat, little mother-pot,' he smiled on her. 'Your thoughts are as podgy as your body. I do know what you mean though. I can almost feel it now, with you here, and this'—his hand gently patted the control beneath it—'under my hands. But there's something all the time escaping me. There always has been. There's something, not somebody, but something intangible, that's always just beyond my seeking. I shall never know that sort of peace you mean till I've found it.'

After a moment he went on, 'There's somewhere I want to go to alone where it must be waiting for me.'

'That's poetry, Christopher, isn't it?' she said softly. 'What all the artists, or mystics, are said to have felt, anyway. But what else are you going to do?'

'Nothing,' he answered, and his brows came together sharply. 'Why should I? It's all very well for Adrian to say I should know by now. How can I settle to do anything until I am something?'

'But it is so easy for you to do things.' Nicolette was always gentle with him. 'It never seems necessary for you to learn anything.'

'That's my trouble. Action, don't you understand, is merely a drug. People who can't or won't think are always doing things. There's no adventure in action at all. It's all in the mind. I'm going away to think. I'm going to walk. My walking and what I meet on my walks—will those matter?'

'You have your music, your poetry—you have more chances than most of us to make things and to know the joy of creation.'

'Not yet. For one thing, I'm immature. Sixteen years old —an infant. And there are things you cannot be expected quite to understand. You have the happy certainty that you can control yourself and your works. You can say "I too will something make, and joy in the making, though to-morrow it seem like the words of a dream remembered on waking."'

'You're a renegade'—she admonished him with a smile that took the sting from her mockery. 'What you really want is a spiritual gamble. You want to imagine for yourself a nice little old-fashioned heaven and hell, and then lead an attack on a golden throne where a fat Jewish god with a beard will sit ready to hurl you into pits or something like that, if you dare him.'

'I do.' The boy responded fiercely, so that she glanced at him in quick surprise and quickly away again. 'I do. I want something like old-fashioned religion to throw myself into. What fun they must have got out of it. And the Christians, with their mortification of the flesh.'

'Christopher!'

'I don't think it was so beastly as it sounds. Remember our people have translated the ideas of vice and wickedness to terms of ill-health and foolishness and ignorance. If I went and wrote out ninety-five theses and nailed them on a door, the investigators would just glance through them, see that I was a bit off balance, and order me some dope to put me in order. My only chance of fun—these I have to take you up in the air to tell you these things. I have to switch off. Otherwise, it might be awkward.'

Suddenly he dived rather vindictively towards the earth beneath them. They found themselves on the edge of a rocky forlorn coast, tattered and gutted by waves which now rolled in false gentleness towards it. And, beneath the clear blue of the sky, under the full sun, it seemed to await them contentedly enough. For what he still wanted to say Christopher felt he needed the hot, rough contact of those rocks.

'Hullo,' he said abruptly, 'here is the sea. Let's go down and bathe. There's a broad strip of sandy beach where we can land.'

They descended slowly.

II

They sat quietly for a little, with their backs against the same smooth hot rock, letting the sun suck the moisture from them. Hard to tell at a short distance which was the boy, which the girl. Each had peculiar grace; he in his hairless slimness, she in her rounder, sturdier curves.

At first they had frolicked and bathed and quite forgotten in their physical pleasure that they were growing so fast that adolescence with its queer pangs and momentous changes was upon them both. But Nicolette knew her Christopher, needed no further telling to know that her happy mood of the morning was dissipated. He was going to leave her quite soon.

'And whom shall I share with?' she pleaded. 'Oh, I may be peevish and absurd, but what on earth do people, does any one else matter to me? Always we have been together; always. Now—you do not want me to be there any more.'

Christopher, watching her dig her toes into the sand, watching them stab little holes in it and wriggle impatiently out of them, suddenly realized the change in her. The round child face he had adored was thinning to a less soft oval. Her eyes had lost some of their infant candour and were now almost darkened by tears. She had lost her smile and gained expression. All that was happening could so clearly be read that it awed him by its uncompromising advance.

Tormented by his own 'growing pains,' he had never before detected the symptoms in his little sister. Now they appeared plainly to him.

'My love,' he explained gently, 'for both our sakes we must part for a while. All our lives we have mattered far more to one another than is usual. Nowadays family ties are so loose. They can hardly be tightened as much as we have tightened ours. If you depend on me as much as you have just revealed, there is all the more reason for our separation.'

'It is rather a bluff for you to be so sensible suddenly,' she answered reproachfully. 'You want me as I want you, and you cannot deny it! Who understands you as I do? Who can comfort you as I can? Whom will you have if I agree to do as you say?'

'I am not going to deny anything. Of course I have always needed you. But I intend to cut that need out now;' he glanced at her and then added, 'or rather cut it down.' He had been lying on his back beside her, in his favourite attitude, hands clasped beneath his neck, knees crossed, gazing into the sky. He turned now, and leaning on his right elbow, his chin cupped in one hand, looked at her steadfastly. 'I am going to ask something of you now, Nicolette, something of your love—and your understanding.' He spoke very softly and shook a little. 'I have known fear in these last months—real fear; terror of myself.'

She did not attempt to answer, but gazed at him. Fear had little place in the minds of those of her day and race. She had never known it herself, but knew its name as that of a nervous symptom. Yet this kind of fear which Christopher felt was not, apparently, like that. She read in his eyes that it was only part of some new and significant emotion.

'Be patient with me,' he went on, because what I am trying to explain to you I can hardly, as yet, explain to myself. You know, Nicolette, I have never known the sort of love most people feel nowadays. It is a comfortable kind, simply an easy benevolence, sometimes no more than tolerance. Ours is not an emotional race—our Leaders take care of that. But moderate affection is not in me. Even when I was quite small, I was often surprised at my coldness. Then I was proud; I thought I was more reasonable than any one. Two years ago, Adrian suddenly drove me into a fury. I had to run to get away before I lost my self-control. I just managed to, and then I walked miles, struggling with my rage. It kept coming on, almost choking me. At last it left me, worn out, in the middle of a field. I lay down under some trees and soon I went to sleep. I did not analyse my feelings when I woke up, but went back, jolly glad I had escaped before any one noticed anything, and feeling I had made a fool of myself. But after that sort of thing had happened once or twice, I began to suspect. And then you.'

'Me? What of me?' asked Nicolette.

'Because you were the only creature in the world I loved. I loved you as I hated Adrian, passionately. I could not bear you to be keen on any one else, or anything we could not share. It grew on me with me. It was only through you and with you I could be really happy. Only you could satisfy my need to love and to be loved. Our mutual dependence has got too great,' he finished abruptly.

'But, Christopher,' said Nicolette (and as there were tears in her eyes she watched the hot sand dribbling through her fingers instead of looking at him), 'if one's emotions get out of control one can put them in order. Why didn't you tell St. John? He would have helped you.'

'Exactly.' Christopher spoke with repressed passion. 'He would. With a little effort I could become quite calm and steady. And I tell you, life would not be worth a dog's bite to me! Perverse, reactionary, I am. But my emotions are myself. I refuse to purge myself of them as of waste matter. I will keep them!'

'Come what may?'

'What may! And I will tell you what that will be. There is only one possible outlet for me. Only one.'

'You mean——'

'I mean religion.'

There was a pause. Nicolette was trying hard to understand.

Then, 'How did you come to it? Did you wilfully convince yourself? Are you trying to justify yourself?'

'Great stars, no. I dread it. That is how fear came to me. But because my emotions are stronger than reason I won't stifle them for reason. It cannot supply what I want. It is not with me a matter of becoming reasonable as I grow up—putting away childish things. Religions, from the fetish worship of the savage to that of the late unlamented Roman church, supply every reason for not believing. In spite of that I need my god. That is the only thing than can be said in his favour.'

'What is your belief, Christopher?'

'I cannot tell at the moment. I am going to try to define it. All I feel just now is that there seems to be an Antagonist with whom I shall struggle. And that he or it will get me. I shall probably end,' he said with a smile, 'like that valiant nigger of whom a missionary wrote: "Our poor convert has lost his reason, but I rejoice to say that he retains his faith." It's a grim prospect.'

'So you think I cannot share it with you?'

'I do, and I will tell you why. To get to the bottom of my problem I *must* tackle it absolutely alone at first. I do not know my future. But I do yours. You must learn to go your own way, so that when it leads you to mating and mother-hood I shall not stand on it like a sinister shadow to lead you back. And I foresee danger in this condition of mine. Faith is the seed of all rebellions. The religious life is one endless revolt against the social life; the individual's sole effective protest against the community. Only in the name of his god can man truly rebel against the law of man. The only citizen of Rome who dares not to do as the Romans do is he who claims authority from his "father in heaven." If it comes to that with me, you shall not be concerned.'

'And if I refuse to stand aside?'

'Then we shall see. But now, darling, be kind to me! Help me as you have always done. Let me be free.'

'I will. I can do nothing else. But I am sure that in the end you will come back to me, as I shall come back to you, and that then nothing will ever separate us again!'

'May it be so, my dear little mother-pot!'

They rose then and turned their backs on the rustling sea. Instinctively, as they had been taught from childhood to do, they rose on tip-toe, raised their arms, stretched to the finger-tips, and threw back their heads. But Christo-pher's gesture was one of significance.

III

Christopher talked violently in the first person singular, for he could never consider his mind as a welter of hereditary tendencies. His maternal forbears, nevertheless, were dominant. There was the gentle persistence of the Lady Anne whom he resembled physically, the coolly obstinate creature who had borne Humphrey. Behind her was the ruthless wilfulness of the first baronet whom Humphrey did not succeed. The steadfast Richmond blood was at any rate responsible for those self-questionings which for a time acted as a brake on Christopher's impetuosity. But allied to these various influences was one destined to cause him the most exquisite suffering: the streak of femininity perversely bequeathed to him by his mother.

Antonia, true descendant of the emotional Thomas, had responded wholeheartedly to the lyrical wooing of young St. John Richmond. To be mated to a man even in youth plainly destined to great things, the first 'child' of Mensch, handsome and brilliant, satisfied ambition as well as passion. Gladly she threw herself into his arms and his plans; proudly acquiescent, she bore him five robust sons. Only after the birth of Christopher did she realize how much she had wished the sixth child to be a daughter.

But the independence shown from their earliest days by her five boy babies had wearied her maternal vigilance. To have one that might remain, in spite of the custom of the day, a clinging, cuddling babe when other small sons already asserted their claim to individuality, was at first an unconscious but irresistible desire. Physically Antonia was in as healthy a condition as ever during her sixth pregnancy, but mentally, she weakened. She carried on all those exercises prescribed to develop the masculinity of the growing embryo listlessly. She was not disobedient but rather unobedient. She indulged herself in hours of dreamy reverie. She cut short her walks and neglected her gardening tools and spent hours in romantic solitude, with books and music, among luxurious scenery that roused her emotions to a high pitch. She cheated even in the matters of her diet and her exercises. It was a negative rebellion, such as the high-spirited Anne would have scorned, but at a time when sex was still a matter more or less of experiment and the most stringent precautions were necessary in order successfully to coerce nature, it had its effect. It was only much later apparent that Christopher, though in no definite way physiologically abnormal, had more than his due share of emotionalism; with adolescence his lack of balance became clear to himself, though to few others. In accordance with his temperament he strove to hide it. He had, from childhood, an affinity with women that attracted their passionate devotion. Yet he did not respond as a normal boy of his age and day would have done; he was and grew with the years increasingly ascetic; a mystical understanding of the ways of women filled him to the exclusion of passion for them.

His attempt to take refuge in religious mysticism was symptomatic, but not necessarily of a mental flaw. St. John and every one else knew that such behaviour was strictly in accordance with the mental condition of youth during puberty. But those who clung to such a state, who held and openly proclaimed religious views, were all of the intellectually inferior kinds, those who were still anthropologically on a lower plane of development.

Wisely, and in accordance with their principles of simplification, the Leaders let them be; knowing that with the passing of years their disciples would grow ever fewer, that, provided life could be lived to the full, the pitiful desire for after-life would wilt and fade away.

There were no epidemics of childhood now. But puberty was a state all had to pass through; a normal state in most, prolonged or violent in some, while others never outgrew it.

And finally even in this, 'Man's World,' there were men who longed to assume the world was still God's, and gamble their very lives away on the odds—Man *versus* his 'Maker.'

6   A PEOPLE UNBOUND

Certes, nous avons eu tous, à nos propres dépens, la preuve fâcheuse que ceux qui font des expériences peuvent se tromper; mais qu'arrive-t-il, je vous prie, à ceux qui n'en font pas?
—Paul Bert, *Leçons sur la Respiration*

I

Nicolette lay unclothed on a bed in a strange room. But they might have been her usual bed and her usual room. If the mode of her day had destroyed family life, it had at the same time enormously simplified community living. Having 'no home' meant being 'at home' everywhere. This clean, simple cubicle, which she occupied during her visit to Centrosome, was familiar; as familiar as the types of buildings, the plan of the roads, the hangars, whence she could at any time embark for Nucleus, outside.

The door was opened and the jolly brown eyes of her friend Anna, sister to Bruce Wayland, peeped round it.

'Hurry up,' said Nicolette, and Anna hurried. At a bound she landed noisily on the narrow bed, and while the springs recovered themselves they looked at each other smiling, and said nothing.

There was just that instant's hesitation before the plunge into all there was to tell and to be told, born of their consciousness of the changes in one another, and the desire to bridge the small gap which separated them from their former intimacy.

'Do you like being here?' asked Anna then.

'Yes, I do,' answered Nicolette. Without Christopher, Nucleus had been unbearable.

'Tired?'

'Not a bit.'

'Then let's talk. I wish you had been here yesterday. Lois was singing.'

'Lois—the Entertainer with the beautiful voice?'

'Yes, *the* Lois. And where do you think she has gone now? To Nucleus. And to find whom?' Anna paused dramatically. 'Christopher!'

Nicolette sat up. 'To find Christopher?' she repeated, 'my brother?'

'Yes. She has heard from some one, apparently, all about his extraordinary ear and his gift for music. She lives for nothing else, you know, and is always looking for people to help her. She is starting a new kind of music, so she has gone to enlist him.'

'But Christopher is not in Nucleus. That is really why I came here. It was so dull without him. He has gone away to study.'

'I dare say she'll find him.' Nicolette restlessly got up and went to switch on the neighbouring bath. 'Every one thinks he's a wonder boy. Is he?'

'Of course.' Nicolette bent to the bath, but Anna could see her face in the mirror.

'Do come back,' she said impatiently, 'there is plenty of time yet. Are there any difficulties about Christopher?'

'No,' Nicolette answered stoutly and came back. 'But he is not certain yet what he wants to do, and they say that he ought to be.'

'I don't agree. I think he should be left alone to do as he likes. I won't have you worry him.'

Anna, delightful and absurd, could still soothe Nicolette. 'A nice way for you to talk,' she smiled as she returned to the bed, 'after you have shamelessly thrown him over. I always thought you wanted Christopher, Anna, and now you have gone and mixed yourself up with a big fat Patrolman, they tell me.'

'He is not big and fat,' rejoined Anna indignantly; 'he is lithe and graceful. And don't tease. You know Christopher is years too young for me, and probably wouldn't have me, anyway. But, if we must be blood allies, you can have Bruce. He is big enough, and he puts on fat in a night.'

'I don't want a fat man or any other kind of man. But tell me about yours.' Nicolette did not want to think about Lois or Christopher. 'When are you going to be mated?'

'In three months' time. I am so excited. He's lovely and Latin and dark, and I call him Angelo to annoy him.'

'Sounds pleasant. What does he do?'

'Patrol. Frontiersman. The only drawback is, I shall not see him very much afterwards, unless he's transferred.'

'Where is he now?'

'Here. You shall meet him. He will be here for about six months, or, at any rate, until I am ready to go to the Garden.'

'How splendid. Has he mated before?'

'No, isn't it lovely? He should have, of course he's twenty-one; but he went straight to the Patrol and did a long spell over the Eastern frontier. Then he came down on a Company job, because there was not a man available just then, and as he was coming back on leave soon in any case they let him volunteer. They should not have allowed it, and as he was not in perfect condition, after they had used him for experiments on Meissner's plexus he developed some horrid complication. But it's all over now, and Bruce says it was an entirely new bit of work and very useful.'

'Is Bruce here, too?'

'He is. You will find him like a bear, because he's forbidden to do any more stunts at the Miracle House for at least a year. He was in the chair for nine hours, for an experiment he'd planned himself, before two hundred teachers of physiology. They exposed rather too much of his brain, and the Company Director Formant was annoyed about it. He said Bruce was not justified in taking such risks with himself, because he is wanted for important work later. Bruce is sulking. He told them it was an insult to his intelligence to suggest he did not know how far it was safe to go; that his body belonged to him and he could do what he liked with it, anyway. They retorted that masochism was beyond the allowed limit, which made him angrier still, because he had to admit a tendency to it. But of course he will listen to reason. He is keen enough on discipline and example, and they know it. The young men love him, too. Still, the whole thing has been a bit of a nuisance. You must try to distract him a little.'

'I, Anna? How can I do anything?'

'You might try. It would help us. Surely you know how beautiful you are? Men are really easy to manage once you know them.'

'You are a conceited little creature. Just because you are going to be mated to your Angelo.'

'I am not a bit conceited, only it is such fun. What do you suppose it is like to be kissed?'

'I've never thought about it.'

'I have thought of nothing else for three weeks.'

Anna's bright round eyes shone with eagerness. Nicolette, watching her with a little surprise, realized that her own day of mating would soon come. The thought depressed her. Talk of love merely brought her back to Christopher, whom alone she loved. She would certainly have babies presently, but what friendship or passion could mating bring her to equal the joys of being with Christopher? Yet she must prepare herself, as he had said. She had finished her training and the time was drawing near. The present was every moment becoming the future, everything was moving, growing, urging, expanding; stay still as she would, it was carrying her onward like a moving pathway to the unknown with its pressure of conflicting emotions—she *did not* want to grow up.

She herself had to move violently to escape from this sudden indefinable panic; she plunged into the bath.

'Don't bother now,' called Anna, who, obsessed by her own pleasant dreamings, had noticed nothing. 'We're going to swim in a minute.'

'I want to *wash*, little idiot,' shouted Nicolette angrily. She felt both younger and much older than her friend at that moment.

II

Anna led the way to the lift and out of the building through the Great Hall, down the broad steps to lawns framed by buildings tinted yellow, orange, and glowing pink. They walked slowly down a broad avenue of limes which led to the wide open-air swimming-pool, meeting and passing several people and a few children. No one hurried or lagged, but walked at a beautifully even pace with a grace that would have been foreign to the grimy cities and narrow pathways of an earlier age. There were several gardening parties, each led by a supervisor; for the enormous increase of ornamental grounds had led to an equal extension of this branch of art. It was cultivated by asexual horticulturists, who applied themselves almost exclusively to all arts and crafts, and who had attained an exquisite proficiency in carrying out large-scale designs.

Long low pavilions stood here and there on the banks of the pool. They were built of wood, or stone, or cement, or sometimes of a combination of these materials in such a way as to harmonize with their surroundings. In all the temperature was carefully regulated according to their uses: some contained gymnastic and massage appliances; others were designed for various types of baths; a few had rest and study rooms or were stocked with refreshments. In the summer people spent only the shortest possible time indoors, and at all times many hours were given to physical culture.

'Shall we sit here?' asked Anna, and as Nicolette nodded agreement, they sat on the grass at the pool's edge, Anna quickly kicking off her sandals and dangling her feet in it ankle-deep.

'I can never keep away from the water when I am not busy,' she said. 'Angelo will know where to find us. I expect he will come along soon.'

'What is the topography of this place, Anna?' asked Nicolette. 'You might as well explain now.'

'Well, as you know, this is all part of Administrative Dwellings. This group runs from A to H, and our building is G—Maternal Prep. A, B, C, D, and E are offices. If you look straight across from here you will see the roofs of B just above those trees. In case you want to communicate with any one in Nucleus, wireless central is in C, block 5. Entertainments and studies are in H; over there in the left-hand corner. F and G are all dwellings. The *gyms*, baths, and electrics are at the top of each block; I expect yours are the same.'

'Yes, it all seems pretty much the same. I suppose the cooking *labs* and dining halls are on the right of Great Hall, and the stock rooms on the left?'

'Exactly. The theatre, in H, has just been renovated, and we are rather proud of it. All the decorative work is pure pattern and depends for its changing effect on the lighting. You people in Nucleus still cling to the pictorial style, I know, but you must come and see ours.'

'Old Weil may be getting a bit old-fashioned, but Arcous, his son, would even please you, I think.'

'Well, anyway, you must come to the theatre tomorrow afternoon.'

'No, she must not,' a voice suddenly boomed behind them, and a very large man squatted down by Nicolette, and slid from her side into the water, where he stood, the ripples turning his body, from waist to feet, to a caricature of itself.

'I shall take her to the Miracle House tomorrow afternoon; new programme, adults only. You need not apply.'

Anna immediately did, plunging her foot into the water, and sending a mighty shower of drops over his head and shoulders. He lifted her with one arm from the grass, grasped her kicking toes with the other, and set her down beside him.

'Coming too?' he grinned at Nicolette. 'It's jolly.'

She looked at his big head, perched comically to one side, while a twinkle shone wickedly in his eyes. He had not seen her since she was quite a child, and was evidently wondering whether to await her reply, or whether he dared introduce her to the pool in the same manner as Anna.

'If he touches you,' his sister anticipated, 'bite him, Nicolette. You wait till I set my Angelo on to you,' she threatened her brother. 'Where on earth is he? You might have had the decency to wait for a man of your own size.'

'Nicolette has no doubt trained Christopher to treat her gently,' laughed Bruce, as, postponing further mischief, he climbed out and sat down by her side.

'Now I am in, I may as well have a swim,' remarked Anna; 'but if you're not gone when I come back, I might show Nicolette a trick or two.'

'Let me look at you,' he continued, ignoring his sister's threat with the phlegm of a sea-lion. 'I have not seen you for years. Last time I was in Nucleus you had just gone to the Garden to begin your course.'

'Yes, I remember hearing about you. From Christopher. You annoyed Adrian. He said, "Bruce boomed round the place, while Adrian shrilled like a night-jar, and St. John chuckled like a jackass." I forget why.'

'Oh, because I suggested some tests for the Admins to find out whether they were getting over-stabilized. They always are, you know. And they do test them everywhere now, at five-yearly intervals. But Adrian thought it would have a harmful effect from the propaganda point of view. Letting the people in our little secrets.'

'Adrian is over-stabilized.'

'What—already? I only think he's a bit priggish. But we do rather tend to one extreme or the other. Now I——' he laughed a little guiltily and left it at that.

But she could see what he meant. It was in his eyes. The exceptionally broad forehead, the large curved nose, the red, narrow lips, proclaimed him a future leader of men; but the blue eyes still held a boyish sparkle of daring; the eyes of a boy perpetually in pursuit of fun, of novel sensations, of excitement. He was still busily living and experimenting, with and on himself. The material was all there; in contrast to her slim, almost girlish Christopher, Bruce's form was Herculean, though his hands were surprisingly small, with sensitive pointed finger-tips.

Many groups now came to the lake, and it seemed to Nicolette, who was young enough to be a trifle self-conscious among strangers, that they were suddenly surrounded by youths, all engaged in the obviously congenial task of worshipping Bruce. He introduced them by shouting their names at her as they came up, and in the usual Centrosome fashion they ignored her save for a brief nod, and continued a conversation chiefly composed of jokes, topical allusions and nicknames. Turning to the water, she saw Anna trudging in wild haste towards them, and making violent gestures with alternate arms, which seemed to include herself and an approaching man at the back of the small crowd.

Anna bounded up the steps from the water, and Angelo gallantly swooped down in time to lend her a lean brown hand as she leapt the last three. Nicolette took him in at a glance; tall, thin as a rake, and very dark. He was hairy, too; his eyes were merry, and his ears suggested points. A delightfully faun-like creature. Nicolette was glad for Anna.

III

'So you've never been to a Miracle House before?' asked Bruce, as he and Nicolette set out together for the House of the Sick.

'No. I'm very pleased to come,'—but she would have been pleased to go anywhere with Bruce, for she also felt the spell of his jovial intelligence and vitality.

'I shall be interested in your impressions. I don't often get the chance of taking a novice, and, of course, this is rather my own pet show. By the way, I found out something funny to-day. Did you ever know that there was once a worldwide so-called religious organization called "The Salvation Army"?'

'Yes, I've heard of it from Christopher. They were, apparently, on intimate terms with devils, and made a great rival organization to the Catholic Church on confession.'

'The amusing point, I think, is that our propagandists nearly chose the same name before they decided on the Gay Company. I suppose in the old days religion did really absorb all the best publicity names, as well as being the only civil organization founded on a military model, like the Company.'

They now had reached the House of the Sick, which stood in its own large grounds, well away from all other dwelling-places. Not far from it was a circular building, in somewhat the same relationship to it as are some of the ancient baptisteries to their cathedrals.

'You mustn't think,' said Bruce, 'because the Miracle House is next to the House of the Sick that you are going to see anything pathological. The whole point about Miracle Houses is to show people ordinary normal physiology—what their insides look like, and how they work. Of course, at the very beginning, when they got their name, they were chiefly used for public performances on private soldiers in the Company—sick people. But those shows are not so popular now, because we are on a different emotional plane; disease is considered an enemy to be fought by private and officer—and ordinary people uninterested in medicine or surgery are rather bored with it. But when it comes to normal functions of the body or mind it is quite different. Come along.'

The circular building was quite small. About five hundred people could be placed in its rising tiers of seats, facing a revolving stage. By the sides of and behind this were dressing-rooms, sterilizing-rooms, and others containing instruments and apparatus. The interior was beautifully decorated with emblems of the Gay Company of Stalwarts; pictures, historical and allegorical, depicting scenes from its record, and one or two pieces of statuary flanking the stage. From time to time automatic sprays filled the air with delightful and antibacterial perfume.

A cinematograph screen ran behind the entire length of the stage. The house was full, for this afternoon's programme was expected to be particularly thrilling. Bruce was constantly greeting friends, but Nicolette had no interest in them. A bell rang, conversation died away, and a voice addressed the audience.

'We are going to show you this afternoon,' it said, 'some experiments which may make clear to you the functions of the cerebral cortex. The subject will only be locally anaesthetized. If he feels any pain he will tell us so, but it should be unlikely. We are first of all going to open his head and expose the brain. You will see everything very plainly on the screen by means of the epidiascope. At certain points of the experiment it will be necessary for us to inform you of what we are going to do without the subject's knowledge, and the words will not be spoken, but will appear on the screen.'

'Who is the subject?' Nicolette asked.

'Well, names are not announced, you know; it's a Company rule. I can't tell you till they arrive.'

The stage was now set revolving, and there were wheeled into view several people. In a comfortable chair with a head-rest reclined a young, sturdily built man whose most prominent feature was bright red hair. The operator and two assistants adjusted the chair, while the communicator, whose voice had been heard off-stage, prepared to work the epidiascope and the microphone. Between the operating chair and the screen was the complete electrical equipment necessary for the tests. On one side of the stage was a smallish black box fitted with innumerable stops.

'Now then,' said Bruce to Nicolette, as one of the assistants attached an electrode—rather like a pad on a long wire—to the red-haired man's chest, and another prepared the anæsthetic, 'we are going to see a fine show. The subject is Larssen, and the operator Carlier. They are both first-rate men, and generally work together.'

The red-haired man now appeared on the screen, and Nicolette saw that he was not red-haired at all. They pulled off the red rubber cap from his head, which was completely shaven, and then wiped it with ether. The anesthetic was run into the skin, and Carlier began to prick his colleague's head with needles until he received the smiling reply, 'No sensation.' Deftly he then cut through the skin, exposing the skull.

The anæsthetic was again administered, and Nicolette watched with admiration as the deft fingers of Carlier manipulated a small but rapidly buzzing circular saw, which cut swiftly down until he turned back a flap of bone and skin, and a small part of the brain on the left side of the head was revealed.

'Why is there no bleeding?' Nicolette asked Bruce, with her eyes on the screen. Larssen appeared perfectly comfortable, and was joking with the men holding the flap of bone and skin in warm towels in Ringer's solution.

'They ran in adrenalin with the anæsthetic,' answered Bruce. 'Bleeding would obstruct the view.'

The communicator then spoke quietly into a tube in his hand, and his words appeared in rapid writing on the screen.

'We are going to stimulate the centres controlling the movements of the right arm.'

Carlier took a small electrode and moved it gently about on the exposed brain. Suddenly Larssen raised his right arm, the control of which had now passed beyond his will. As the electrode dictated the arm obeyed, until a smaller implement was substituted, by means of which the middle finger was made to perform antics similar to those previously carried out by the whole arm.

'How are you feeling?' they saw Carlier ask, and almost simultaneously read the words on the screen:

'Pretty unpleasant . . . numb or tickly feeling . . . no pain,' came the answer, and 'carry on.'

'We are now going to stop him talking,' flashed the communicator; 'that is to say, we will shut down the action of the centres controlling his speech muscles.' The electrode was moved a little further downwards. At the same time an assistant held up to Larssen his own photograph, with the question: 'What is this?' While the answer could be read in his eyes, his mouth was unable to form it; the electrode was removed—instantly there came his voice through the microphone, clear and strong, course; what a rotten one! My photograph, of course; what a rotten one!'

'Now we will inhibit recognition; we are going to inter-
fere with his thinking arrangements.'

'Watch this carefully,' said Bruce to Nicolette, whose
eyes did not leave the screen as she nodded.

'It's the star turn.'

'What would Christopher think of it, I wonder?'

The question inevitably came to her mind, but there
was no time to ponder it. Again the electrode was moved,
and Larssen was shown a rabbit, to the accompaniment
of a roar of delight from the audience. Every face smiled,
except that of Larssen. His showed only the pathetic
effort, the sadly puzzled look seen on the faces of victims
of aphasia. And the laughter quickly subsided as it sank
into them that the man with the electrode was deliber-
ately preventing this man from thinking, and that this
man in the chair, this Larssen, would *not* think until the
moment came when he would be released. Still, he was
making the effort and the tension broke into another
ripple of laughter as, his strenuous endeavour ended, he
bravely muttered. 'Think . . . cow . . . .'

After this they fitted on to his brain a caplike object,
from which a multitude of fine wires ran to the box with
the keyboard. Carlier went to this apparatus, and sat
down before it.

'Now,' announced the communicator, we are—or rather
members of the audience who wish to are—going to
make him think of something. But don't be long about it.'

A young man at the end of Nicolette's row got up and
went to a speaking tube similar to that held by the communicator. There flashed on the screen, 'Think of a girl';

the audience, careful to indicate nothing to the subject, giggled softly. Carlier glanced swiftly at the screen, smiled, flashed in his turn 'Too easy,' and began manipulating his keyboard.

Larssen, wearing the headpiece, had during this short interval been reclining with closed eyes in his chair. Now he began to manifest signs of growing emotion; first he drummed a little with his fingers, clenched each hand loosely, unclenched, fidgeted; he half-opened his eyes, and eyes and mouth smiled; slowly the lips smiled and very gradually pouted to kissing shape; his arms rose from his sides, were stretched before him, and the sound of a series of little kisses was heard quite distinctly by the audience. Carlier thought it time to switch off; the experiment was unequivocally positive; and as soon as Larssen was released the audience broke into irrepressible laughter and applause.

'That,' said Carlier, was pretty simple. We will try something a little more difficult, though, as the technique of this experiment is only in its early stages, we cannot expect complete success.'

On to the screen came 'Make him think of a green square.'

This time there was a longish pause ere Larssen gave any reaction; then, in answer to Carlier's encouraging 'What are you thinking of?' there came the slow answer: 'What in the world is that out on my right? . . . It looks like a sort of box, and keeps changing colour from green to purple. . . .' Carlier concentrated on the keyboard—then, from Larssen: 'Now it's a steady green . . . not quite . . .

square . . . rectangle . . . about fifty per cent. longer than broad. . . .'

Next—'Think of 483 . . .' The same procedure; Larssen and Carlier both now images of concentration; Larssen's eyes were shut; you could see the sweat running down Carlier's face as his fingers played with the stops of his miraculous keyboard; at last from Larssen: '47 . . . no, wait . . . 48 . . . 48 . . . 3 . . . no, I can't do it.'

'That's all.' Whilst the stage revolved, taking Larssen away to be sewn up, the voice sounded again:

'There will be no more demonstrations this afternoon. But we can give you a good televistic view of the night sky of the southern hemisphere, with Barronda's comet. As you know, there is an eclipse of the moon on there just now, and the comet will look rather well, we expect, by the side of the coppery moon.'

But Bruce, not wishing to overload Nicolette with impressions, led the way out. She followed him meekly; the Miracle House had more than fulfilled her expectations; but now she wanted to think it out; to wonder what on earth Christopher would have said to it all!

IV

Nicolette, without in the least precisely realizing the cause of it, enjoyed a new and delightful contentment when she was with Bruce. His influence on her virginal mind was akin to that of dry, full sunshine on her growing body. She found his personality pervasive, and gave herself without reservation. She responded warmly to the purely physical stimulation of his company. The booming of his deep voice, with its occasionally slurred intonations, the slow and yet expressive gestures of his hands, the narrowing of his eyelids when he sought a definite phrase; his laugh, his frown, the carriage of his body and his intense virility; all these contented her fully. She had not once thought about Bruce, but from the moment when he had loomed into view by the swimming pool, had taken him for granted.

All the time they were together he had flung facts and information at her. He had the schoolmasterish quality of his type in a remarkable degree. Herein he differed profoundly from Christopher, who, impatient of scientific accuracy of thought, looked on facts as dry mental bread and was always eager to enrich them with the butter of fancy. Nicolette had been born a disciple; she was acutely sensitive and responsive to personal influences of all kinds, and her love and admiration grew always in proportion to the power of the mind that bent itself towards her own.

A great deal of Bruce's information was more or less incomprehensible to her; he had the habit of assuming that every one with whom he shared an experience possessed *a priori* his own vast knowledge of science. Nicolette, listening to him, felt more than once like a small child of old legend trotting breathlessly along by the side of a giant in seven-leagued boots; it became as exciting as a race to endeavour to keep up with him, and she was satisfied if she could more or less master the general outline of his argument, while the infinite detail flashed past her.

Bruce also was pleased. Already at twenty-five his unusual ability had forced him into more or less constant contact with men many years his seniors. In his day it was taken for granted that a young man should be able more or less to measure his own powers against those of his contemporaries, and Bruce, with his keen and scientifically trained judgment, had yet to meet the man of his own age to whom he could forfeit his self-respect. Women had so far played no part at all in his mental development. A number of attractive and expert entertainers had, since his seventeenth year, adequately slaked the thirst of his physical passions. He had mated several times, and on one occasion had experienced a short but fairly intense sentimental affection; for none of his children had he so far known a more than decorous friendliness. The son of his dreams had not yet been given him; the son for whose mother he longed to feel deep and permanent love.

Bruce summed up Nicolette to himself as 'a charming little creature.' He was devoted to Anna, robust, practical, physically courageous, and healthily sensual, but for Nicolette he now felt a big-brotherly emotion that delighted him by the protective instincts it aroused. She was not in the least fragile, yet to him she appeared of flower-like delicacy; her skin, her hair, her hands and feet all seemed of finer texture and moulding than those of any girl or woman he had hitherto encountered. The eager plasticity of her mind aroused in him the wonder and joy of a sculptor who feels beneath his fingers the perfect clay from which to fashion his masterpiece, and in his pleasure at these discoveries he tended to consider her both as more childish and more intelligent than she was, overlooking the influence of Christopher's whetting personality. To know Nicolette without Christopher was like seeing the reflection of the rainbow in the pool.

At the end of her stay Bruce had promised himself a long visit to Nucleus as a reward for his serious work of the next few months. Nicolette had only remembered her brother when it had seemed to her that a certain phrase of Bruce's would have particularly pleased him; of her own future and of its various implications she had not thought once. Their conversation had been continuously impersonal; yet at the journey's end, unperceived, a new road had opened before them both.

7 NO NEW GODS FOR OLD

Now faith is the substance of things hoped for, the evidence of things not seen.
—St. Paul

I

Christopher had 'gone away to think.' Men and women who had a problem to solve often found it easier to isolate themselves until they had done so. There was no reason to dread solitude, and those who sought it had no feeling of loss or deprivation. All over the world hermitages were dotted about in beautiful spots; capable of resisting wild weather, and amply provisioned. They served also as refuges for fliers forced to descend. If the wanderer found one already tenanted, it was customary for him or her to pass on, unless specially asked by the occupant to share it.

Christopher had spent the night as usual in such a hut, thinking particularly about music. All the older forms had been exhausted before his time; one had repeated the same thing to the point of weariness. Yet never, until now, had music been so loved and studied. The new orientation had first been suggested, long ago, by a twentieth-century writer, one W.H. Hudson. Christopher, one of his ardent devotees, had for months been groping, timidly at first, and the with growing courage and success, for a set of symbols to express it. He had begun to make a catalogue of 'nature's' sounds, and to attempt to find a scale whereby they could be truly mimicked.

The longer he remained apart from his fellows, the more difficult Christopher found it to define his god in any terms agreeable to his imagination. So long as he was surrounded by men and women, so long as their laws and their manners chafed him, he felt that their very inadequacy was guarantee of a possible alternative and complete solution to his problem elsewhere. While it was the fashion of the day to praise lavishly its benefits and endowments, the richness and variety of its life, the tolerance and acuteness of its judgments, to Christopher all this was futility and chaos. With a Miracle House round every corner, he longed for a god to arise or descend who would, with one unimaginable and stunning revelation, prove how presumptuous were the creatures who dared to force him into competition.

His imagination rejoiced when there came to it the splendid image of the god antagonist, such as the Jahveh of the ancient Hebrews. The destroyer of all would-be usurpers, the hater of even a mythical rival, the *sole* creator and arbiter of the world—how those old Jews had thrilled, in their moments of anguish and degradation, to the evocation of him! The more daring of them had even aspired to wrestle with this unseen and unrelenting will; to defy it; those, such as Job, who truly 'feared God' must surely have experienced the most voluptuous emotion possible to man.

Christopher would find himself, during walks through forests, up mountains and down into valleys, marching with a phantom procession of the gods of past days and dead peoples. He slaked his own god-hunger in the contemplation of the methods his forbears had invented in order to appease theirs.

To him the religious craving appeared simply as the incarnation of man's supreme desire. In the beginning it had been satisfied by the means which lay at hand. Fruits of the earth, sources of fertility, valleys and rivers, mountains and oceans, and later, sun, moon, planets and stars. The number and complexity of the gods grew as men grew towards richer and more intellectual means of self-expression. Together they grew to consciousness and to morality. Nevertheless, the difference between the religious ambitions of man as personified by Christopher and those of man in his early simplicity was conditioned by development alone. Fundamentally their yearning was the same.

This proved nothing, but it cleared the ground. For if the religious urge was indeed basic and essential to humanity, it must be gratified. Christopher's contemporaries denied it; when they met it, they attempted to pervert and sublimate it. In other days, when men had been less meddlesome, they had continued on the road that lay before them, and had worshipped such gods as came to meet them thereon; might all these not have been the various forms, progressively adapted to human development, in which the supreme spirit had chosen to incarnate itself? Might there not still be waiting a god whom human beings might adore without retrogression? If so, in order to find him, it would only be necessary to continue on that path, using the knowledge gained by science as an instrument, but refusing to be turned aside or back. One could not go back—the old religions had served their purpose, and the old gods, having accomplished their tasks, now slept everlastingly; but faith might still live, and the eternally spiritual might still be evoked in new guise.

Christopher had written:

There is every reason for not believing in God and for not seeking Him. His sole justification is the inadequacy of reason.

He had written:

I care not a fig for life if it be not eternal. For this life I care not.

He had read:

The purely human needs a corrective. It is not sufficiently humbling.

And he had written below:

The only adequate corrective is Faith.

He had also written:

You cannot expect the religious temperament to submit to the discipline of reason. It prefers the promise of eternal hell to the finality of death. The longing for immortality is so strong that only blind belief in its eventuality can appease it. And it is wiser to choose death in this belief than to await it without hope.

Where science dare not tread, there faith steps in.

The scientific mind is invariably middle-aged. But the religious mind is always either very young or very old.

Having arrived at this point in his speculations, he decided to return to Nucleus. He thought he had found a first principle, at any rate, with which to arm himself. It would be useless to seek a second, until he had tested this one. All his criticism, hitherto, had been destructive; had he been able to tear down the edifice the Leaders had built, he would have had no substitute ready to put in its place.

It was nearly two years since his separation from Nicolette. He wanted, if not to resume their old intimacy, at least to see her again, to talk with her, to fondle her, to know if with her all was well. He remembered now that Raymond must be there, and that her mating time was approaching; and in spite of his resolves he wanted, at least once before she entered on her career and became absorbed in it, to claim her again and to feel that he had yet no rival in her affection.

His musical studies had progressed well. He was already able to imitate the cries of many birds so accurately that they carried on conversations with him. He could disentangle the rhythm and the tune of the most faintly running water at a distance; the various speeds of the winds brought him each one their message; the flexion of grasses, the whirring of insects and the splashing and padding of small mammals; all minute sounds had come to him during solitary hours, when he had sat motionless, his ears attuned and receptive to all movement in that profound stillness. Already he had noted down many of their intertwined themes and was rearranging them into a vocal symphony that should be worked out one day.

One evening he came to a fir-covered hill down which a waterfall bubbled, a streak of flashing white, into a velvety green pool. He could see a long way below him, gently veiled in mist, the buildings of a community. It was almost sunset, and Christopher, gazing to the west, was again made happy by the glowing blue palette on which the sun splashed his golds, scarlets and crimsons. He paused an instant to absorb the long-drawn, rounded plaint of a wood-pigeon, and after allowing the appropriate interval to pass, he answered it in scrupulous mimicry. He forgot his intention to bathe, and sat down on the soft spongy moss, delighting in its prickliness. Then he forgot the wood-pigeon, too, and began to sing—softly at first—a bird-song that now came to him as naturally as once had come the songs of human beings. It gained in volume soon, blending as it soared the notes of joy and wistfulness. Christopher, listening to his own creation, could hardly believe that he was himself producing it. When the last note had glided like a bubble into the air, apparently reluctant to dissolve, he prepared to memorize the song. As he paused there was the comparative silence that came when only the water, the wind, the trees and the grass spoke. But then began an answering bird. Christopher, jerking up his head to catch a rising note, realized that he had hardly been aware of its predecessors, so gradually had they evolved from the accompaniment of those other sounds. He listened with growing attention and amazement, for this was the song of no bird he had ever known. His own themes were sent dancing back to him in a manner which indicated a human intelligence at work. There was in this music the gladness of the lark, the languor of the nightingale, the throbbing pride of the blackbird, even, occasionally, the staccato laugh of the rook; it was a human throat that produced so rapidly and so perfectly these diverse sounds.

Christopher sat and listened, and when the voice had finally ceased he did not in his turn, a move, but sang gay, chirrupy song, full of amusement and inquiry. Presently he was answered by half a dozen notes on an ascending scale. He waited, but no more followed. Then he began again, looking straight into the western sky, where the colour was splashed about wildly at the climax of its beauty. This time he pleaded, called, entreated the owner of the voice; high and penetrating his notes arose as if to pierce the mystery, then lost themselves among the trees. The answer was a seductive murmur; the notes flowed along one by one, enchained by desire, infinitely caressing, irresistible as the tones of a siren. Christopher, in an access of he knew not what strange, passionate exultation, thought no more of bird music; his was now a human voice also, pouring forth the infinity of human dreams, the hunger and thirst of the senses, an emotion inexpressible in words, but which in this musical medium made its meaning as crystal clear as the waters of the fall.

It was then that, unconsciously changing his position as the moss beneath his right thigh pricked a little too harshly, he saw the owner of the other voice, saw a woman leaning against the smooth wet rock, saw her body glisten as the spray sparkled on it like a garment of faery diamonds. His song then turned as his body had turned; he directed the stream of it straight at her, then, as she did not move, but smiled slowly at him, it surged into a great triumphant song of welcome. Now she sent her voice to answer his, together their notes soared and swooped, joined, recoiled, joined again; it seemed to Christopher that a cloud had come before the sunset, that every other sound was stilled as the woods listened to such music as had never echoed there since the beginning. He feared to lose breath with the violence of his emotion, when, the duet having risen to its almost unendurable climax, she suddenly, with one last rousing call, stretched serpentine arms above her head and dived into the dark pool below her.

Icy water smacked against Christopher's breast as, panting, he dived in after her. There in the centre they met. Just above the pines, in a sky darkly blue, the first ironic stars began to twinkle.

II

'Now you were the sort of person they worshipped once,' said Christopher slowly, gazing at Lois. The assault of her beauty on his vision was becoming less irresistible. Its power was waning. Soon, even his senses would once again be free.

She knew it. Possibly a certain malice tinted her words as she answered, no less slowly, 'And so were you.'

Matters were not progressing as she wished, as she had planned. During the past six weeks they had learned to know one another, and now the barrier between them had become so obvious that it could no longer be ignored.

'Why,' he challenged, assuming the offensive in order to protect himself, 'did you seek me out?'

'Why not, beautiful one?' she repeated in mockery. 'You have only to look at yourself if you want to know.'

'Oh, that!' Christopher was impatient of her praise. 'I should have thought you were satiated by now with mere beauty.'

Lois responded quickly to the taunt.

'Who are you to know or to understand me, ridiculous boy? You have not even a glimmer of knowledge about yourself. And how much do you expect me to teach you, with your absurd air of self-sufficiency?'

'But I do not know why that should annoy you. Why reproach me? All that a woman can have of me, you have had; all a woman could give me, you have given. I tell you that once you would have been hailed as a goddess. I mean it. Don't even my compliments satisfy you?'

'No more than the compliments of Adonis would have satisfied Venus. Look here—at me!' She moved closer to him, wound her arms around his neck, held his head in her palms and forced his eyes to meet hers. Now then! Can't you see you give me a sense of failure? A sense that infuriates me. This has never happened to me before. Whatever I do you remain unattainable. There is something in you I cannot reach; you have consistently withheld what I really wanted. Give it me.'

'I can't,' he said sullenly, turning away, and she released him. 'Do understand. It is nothing to do with you at all.' She had succeeded in driving him towards that which he wished to evade. He was on the defensive. Seeing him so she became compassionate. 'My dear, be careful,' she said. 'You are so young, but I foresee serious troubles for you. Whatever more you want it would be wiser for you to forget. You must stay with me for a little while, if only because of your art. I advise you to stay with me. If that, at least, satisfies you, cling to it.'

'There, anyway, we are in harmony,' he assented, and took her hand and pressed it affectionately. 'I have been unfair,' he went on after a moment. 'I did not tell you before, because I wanted you to have your way of me, but I will tell you now. When you came on me so suddenly, my mind was very busy. I was trying to follow out something, a thought, which matters to me above everything. Perhaps it was unfortunate that I followed you. But you offered me an exquisite novelty. I thought at first you were going to be a stimulant—the kind I had never tried before. But you became a narcotic. Oh, Lois,' he murmured sadly, 'it was no use. I don't want anything—anything you have to give.'

'Do you really mean that I was the first?' Her desire for him was only increased by this curious confession, but she held it in check. She was savouring a new, delightful sensation.

'Absolutely,' Christopher answered candidly, 'and—the last.'

'No other woman at all?' she pursued, unbelieving.

'*No*,' he emphasized almost roughly. 'Do understand—I am trying to explain. No woman—nor any one. No emotion of that kind at all. I told you—I was after something quite different. But that I cannot explain. All I can tell you I'll repeat. Those experiences you have given me, the nearest to the sublime, I suppose, most people would get (for you are a goddess among women), to me they mean nothing pleasurable; on the whole, rather distasteful.'

There was silence for a moment. For she was beginning to understand, and all the malice dropped from her, leaving only pity.

'What do you think is the reason for it?' she demanded quietly then. 'How do you expect to be an artist, missing all that?'

'Art is not the important thing with me,' he answered at once, decisively—'except as an expression of something else. Myself I have not cared how or why I am as I am. I don't see that it matters. Things that to other people (not only this, but lots of things) are so important, don't matter to me. I am looking for something above and beyond it all and that is all I can tell you.'

'It seems to me, dear boy,' she answered, a trifle impatiently, 'you are looking for the Absolute. I should have thought that had by now been proved a futile research.'

'What I am looking for, or what I shall find, is my own affair. Please, do leave me to it.'

'I could say many things—but I won't. I will only ask that you stay with me a little longer. However you think about your music you do take it sufficiently seriously to make me want you. If I consent to the rest—won't you, for your sake and for mine, stay?'

'I want to go back to Nucleus now; I want to see my little sister. She is going to be mated soon. But afterwards, for a short time anyway, I will come back to you.'

'Ah, I remember her. Now what do you feel for her?'

'Something I never have felt nor ever shall feel, for any other woman in the world; you see, she alone is a very part of me, of my own inner life. You need not mind; it is all so different from ordinary feelings, that; something I cannot explain; friendship, love, none of those words are adequate—do you want me to go on . . . ?'

'No. It does not interest me so much that you need torture yourself to explain. But if she is to be mated soon,' Lois smiled at him, and he could make little of her look— 'if that is so, I do not doubt that you will return to me.'

8 RECONSTRUCTION

> The philosophy of art has no other aim than to bring together as far as possible into one view all that there is in the world's memory—to make a history in which the characters shall speak for themselves, become themselves the interpreters of the history. It will regard the artists as helping to create the mind of the ages in which they live—the mind is only what it knows and worships, and the artists are the means by which the different nations and ages come to have characters of their own.
>
> —W.P. Ker, *On the Philosophy of Art*

I

'Where will you sit, Nicolette?'

'Oh, in a corner somewhere; I do dislike having the light pour into my eyes.'

'Well, choose your own corner. Have you heard from Anna?'

'Yes, I spoke to her to-day. She's like a child with a marvellous new toy. She can talk of nothing but love, as if it had been invented for her special benefit.'

'Why, aren't you the same? Surely that is quite natural at your age.'

'Is it? I feel rather bewildered. Raymond is a dear—but a little—well, oppressive.'

'How so?'

'Difficult to explain. He seems so young to me. We have hardly enough to talk about. He is delicious to look at and to touch, but—is that enough, do you think?'

'If you respect him ardently and want a child, I should think it is.'

'Oh, he is brilliant at his job, but it is so technical, and Raymond gets bored with trying to explain physics to me. He is nice to play with, though. I have never met any one who could do everything so competently. There is not a sport at which he doesn't excel. I never knew what swimming and dancing could be like until now. Glorious!'

'That's splendid. It is so important to be able to play together, you know.'

'He's so clever at inventing new games, too. Every one likes him.'

'But you,' Emmeline added in her dry way.

'No, Emmeline, I do like him, really, very much. But do I not like him enough, or is it that I am not yet ready?'

'How do you mean, child?'

'There must be something not quite normal about me, I think, Emmeline. Perhaps it's congenital, for I have been like it now for nearly two years. I love babies, I want to have them, yet as the opportunity comes nearer I shrink more from it. I don't feel ready. I feel as if I would not be ready for years. As long as it was a lovely vision, to be realized in the distant future, my imagination leapt to meet it; I could hardly wait for the day. Now it is approaching, I recoil.'

'Have you told your mother?'

'Emmeline! You know I can't tell Antonia things. I would like to, she is so sympathetic, she so wants to be consulted; but one can't, and there it is.'

'Well, perhaps Raymond is not the man for you.'

'Perhaps not. And yet I like him so much; I like him physically too, to hold me in his arms, to touch and kiss me. He gives me tremendous pleasure. But something is lacking. I may have to wait; if it does not come, to renounce motherhood altogether. If only I could do something else in the meantime, just to see how things turn out.'

'That might be arranged, but it would be a little difficult. You know the regulations in these matters are rather stringent. They have to be. Either you become a mother or you must be immunized. It is the only safeguard that *must* be taken for the future of the race. As soon as you abandoned it, children would be born haphazard everywhere, would be bred by the pure and the impure; it would be impossible to exercise the necessary hygienic control, and those who had no vocation for motherhood would cheat and lie, would refuse or neglect the years of preparation, the pregnancy exercises—it would simply lead to the dirty, bestial breeding of the past again. The race would be doomed.'

'I quite agree. It would not do. And perhaps, if I am sensible, I shall find myself again. I shall be ready.'

'Well, see how matters shape. Do not try to force yourself to this union with Raymond, and do not repress your aversions, nor suggest longings that are not really there. If necessary I will consult the council about a respite for you; only it may not be simple to find an alternative, as it was always taken for granted that you would become a mother. I often thought Antonia might not have been quite so certain.'

'Emmeline, you are a dear! You are so helpful.'

'When is Christopher due?'

Nicolette's face betrayed none of her secret longing.

'Any time, now.'

'If I were you, I would not make any decision until you have talked the matter over with him.'

'I don't know if I can; he has such a lot to think of just now.'

'Nonsense, you must.'

'Must, nonsense.' Nicolette smiled, for Emmeline's briskness was wonderfully stimulating. 'Will you come for a ride in one of the cars?'

'No, you might break my neck.'

'Well, what would it matter? However, Raymond shall take us. Let me call him; I assure you, you will be quite safe.'

'Oh, I'm willing to trust Raymond.'

'Insulting creature. Well, get ready, and meet us at the garage in an hour.'

II

What was the matter with Nicolette? That was the question she constantly asked herself, and that soon her perplexed relations were asking one another. Here was Raymond, beautiful, blond, upright, kind-hearted and well-intentioned, universally popular, a youth with whom any maiden might be proud to mate, and yet Nicolette, whenever she contemplated their future union and the thought of having a child by him, was thrown into a fever of restlessness and discontent. When she was with him the physical contact of his clean manliness soothed her; she welcomed and even sought his caresses, yet afterwards it seemed as if his kisses had only intensified her longing for something he could not give her.

Antonia adored Raymond, as mothers so often adore the youthful mates chosen for their daughters; from her point of view he was the perfect young man, and she sang his praises so constantly that Nicolette employed a hundred schemes in order to avoid her without hurting her feelings. Her brothers, her friends, all apparently conspired to remind her day and night of Raymond's suitability. St. John even, when he occasionally parted the curtains of abstruse speculation that veiled his mind more and more completely as time went on, approved and encouraged. Only Emmeline, hitherto, had given Nicolette the practical comfort of a critical point of view.

Anna's delirious happiness at the progress of her own affair only intensified Nicolette's apparent aversion to love, mating, and child-bearing. She began to take more interest in women who were not devoted to motherhood. The Neuters, from those who performed comparatively menial tasks to such important members of their order as Emmeline, seemed wholly contented. Their interests were wide and entirely communal; they led calm and beautiful lives; their friendships were lifelong and many, and between those of all communities there was constant interchange of visits, and stimulating contact.

Again, it appeared to Nicolette that nothing could be more joyous than the existence of an Entertainer. Beauty was their cult; they were perfectly trained and fashioned to bring beauty to all the world. They were dancers, actors, singers, poets, novelists, essayists, painters, sculptors, architects—in art they found their supreme satisfaction. They smiled perpetually.

Nicolette had once gloried in the knowledge that to be a mother was to fulfil the most difficult function a woman could perform; she had thought she understood what sacrifices that career entailed, and seemed passionately willing to make them; but now she wondered often whether she might not, after all, find her vocation elsewhere.

Raymond could be summed up in two words—his own. Whatever he achieved, whatever he missed, this less than a phrase, illuminating his character by what it left unsaid, invariably came to his lips: 'Oh, well . . .' He had an unusual capacity for not noticing incidents that had a distressing effect on those more sensitive. He was not unobservant, but unaffected. His attention was concentrated into certain channels whence it rarely cared to deviate. A rather machine-like person, who performed automatically, as was expected of him. So little mattered, after all; yourself, your world, the larger but still unimportant solar system—they might have a significance, but that was not his business. A case might be made out for any hypothetical system by a competently trained philosopher. That done, what next? Raymond's occasional thoughts on matters such as these were really a series of punctuation marks, interspersed with monosyllabic words which hardly ever formed complete sentences. 'Oh, well . . .'

Raymond came from Isola, which turned out the world's extremely valuable mediocrities according to plan. Isola had begun only a little later than Nucleus, but its aims had been entirely different from the beginning. It had been founded, not by one genius, such as Mensch, but by a group of people interested solely in maintaining the highest possible temporary average. 'If it takes a century of apparently useless people to produce three or four genii who leave the average pretty much as they found it,' they had said, 'let us take our chances of genii and concentrate on raising the average. Let us formulate a few simple standards just slightly more ambitious than now obtain, but let us endeavour rigorously to abide by them.' They had mostly been teachers and moderate politicians, these pioneers of Isola, discouraged by years spent in struggling with apparently incurable stupidity, but resolved to attempt one final experiment before their enthusiasm flickered out. Their own average age at the time was forty. They mated and had children, none of whom was destined to became an infant prodigy. Exceptional gifts were held to be a defect rather than an advantage, since over-development of one faculty appeared to inhibit the uniform expansion of the whole. All-round consistency was their aim, and they set about scientifically to obtain it.

Isola supplied the mortar which bound into a solid edifice the bricks fashioned by Mensch in Nucleus. It became famous as the source of brilliant second-raters. Imitators sprang up in several places, and when their less severely controlled efforts wavered or failed, the rate of ambition was slowed down. Very gradually, however, the rate for the average human intelligence rose. Between Isola and Nucleus there had always been friendly co-operation, and much inter-breeding.

How indeed was Raymond to know that Nicolette was behaving inappropriately, sometimes even outrageously, towards him? She felt herself that she was being unfair, but she did not understand, nor try to know, why. After their visit to the Miracle House together, Bruce had gone off again on his travels, and she had seen almost nothing of him during the remainder of her trip to Centrosome. Her training for motherhood did not include the clear interpretation of very obscure emotions. She was not at all conscious of a budding love for Bruce struggling with her established love for Christopher. Bruce was very, very nice—and a wee bit awe-inspiring; another big brother. But it was not in the least a sisterly sort of feeling that, in its desire for recognition, made things so extremely difficult for Raymond.

III

After his conversation with Lois, Christopher realized how futile had been this pilgrimage into the wilderness. He smiled rather bitterly as he recalled the earnestness of his search for a god that had resulted in the finding of an Entertainer. Already the reaction that any one less emotional would have anticipated had overtaken him.

For his own ends he had withdrawn abruptly from Nicolette's companionship, leaving her to find any substitute. Knowing nothing of the friendship she had established with Bruce, he imagined her journey to Centrosome to have been a period of boredom, for which he held himself almost entirely responsible. Yet all that was nothing compared with this affair of Raymond. How had it developed? Was all well with her? He had the sense to realize that their relationship could not be in any way comparable to that between himself and Lois. He had never loved Lois nor ceased to love Nicolette, yet he had abandoned that child to the chance of her fate, passively accepting on her behalf conventions of which, when they threatened at all to impinge on his own affairs, he had an acute horror. How could he have supposed that Nicolette would obtain somehow from another—and, moreover, from the first who offered himself to her—all that he had himself given her?

He was almost seized with panic as he imagined what his abandonment must have meant to her, and all she might have had to endure as a result of it; and driven by a storm of intertwined emotions, he hastened back to Nucleus.

He found them both there, late one afternoon, in the Reconstruction Hall, where Venice of the seventeenth century was arising slowly from a heaped litter of material and implements. Reconstruction was the game of the day, and it was played all over the world. The history of its origin was interesting. Josef Weil, the man responsible for most of the architectural beauties of Nucleus, had a passion for making small-scale models of ancient cities. At the age of sixteen he had begun to construct a series showing the development of Rome, from the earliest described time until the seventeenth century. Paris had followed, then Brussels, London, Stockholm, Pekin, Chicago, and San Francisco. Soon his friends, painters, sculptors, writers and archæologists, had become interested in this hobby. The houses were furnished, decked with books and pictures; minute figures of the outstanding men of the periods began to people the streets and the squares of the cities.

Then, one day, some one conceived the notion of Reconstruction on a large scale. They were all familiar with the type of pageant flimsily designed and carried out by stage and film producers in the past. Those had been attempts and failures along commercial lines. The new efforts were directed by the creative instincts of whole cities, on communal lines. Co-operation under learned direction achieved remarkable results. A section of one of Weil's models was copied under his supervision and rebuilt on the actual scale. Costumes were made under equally expert guidance, down to the jewels and pins which held them together. The 'town' was stocked with all necessary utensils, whenever possible genuine. Then the fun began. All the people in turn went to live for days or weeks in this resurrected city. They re-imagined and even re-enacted the religions, the wars, the pastimes, the crafts, and the politics of those vanished days; cooked and ate their food, and used only the implements then known, making shift without the inventions which since had been created to facilitate—or complicate—existence. What had been lost or forgotten was replaced as adequately as possible. What had since been won was ignored.

The section of the ancient city stood on a convenient site close to the modern one, and the inhabitants of one went for their sojourn of as long as they pleased to the other. They all went; old and young, grown-ups and children; administrators, organizers, teachers, research workers, artists, mothers, and entertainers. Those whose imaginations were the more vivid, or who were more learned, helped the others; but soon ambition came to the aid of the natural gift of mimicry. St. John Richmond as a Doge of Old Venice; an air pilot as the gondolier; a member of the Gay Company as a Jesuit—all, needing only to turn from the latest forms of self-expression to earlier ones, learned from the game the closeness of the links which bound human nature in one long chain, and the relationship of environment to thought and action.

In all the larger communities Reconstruction was played on a grand scale. In some places a new city, or portion of one, arose year by year; in others different places and different eras were resurrected every twelvemonth, but gradually a historical sequence began to shape itself. The imagination of the people was aroused; various types were attracted by various phases of bygone culture, but all, in these days when travel was so easy as to make their own world familiar to every one, saw, through the evocation of the past, their own affairs in true perspective.

In Nucleus they still built from the models supplied by Weil, who, now an old man, conserved the enthusiasm of his youth. When Christopher entered the Reconstruction Hall, he found Nicolette and Raymond in the centre of a noisy group, eagerly discussing details of costume and comparing their models. People were coming and going amid a whirl of brocades and ribbons; armour rattled here and there; in a distant corner gut sounded a melodious ping as musicians were put into rehearsal. Antoine Herville was delivering an impromptu sermon, which was cut short when some one dropped a pile of ancient books which scattered venerable dust as they fell. Christopher was soon helping to arrange drapery—for his eye was quicker and his fingers more sensitive than those of a woman—when Raymond came to ask his criticism of a telescope he had reconstructed from an old drawing.

Raymond began explaining his telescope slowly and thoroughly. 'Comic toys they had in those days,' said he, his eyes twinkling as he screwed them up to inspect the instrument more closely. He was really rather likeable. 'No wonder they could not see very far with them. I'll take it up when the daylight goes, and find out just what it will reveal. I shall have to practise if I am to perform my part properly.'

'But no,' said a girl called Ruth, who was to be found near him as often as she could get there, 'that is just what you must not do. You see, the whole point is to wait until you are actually in the city. There must be only the minimum of preparation and rehearsal. How can you see what they saw until you are back in the atmosphere through which they saw?'

'I want to see what my telescope will reveal. Atmosphere can wait.'

'Then you cannot play this game.' She turned to Christopher for corroboration. 'Isn't that the rule?'

'It may be,' he said, 'though every one does not interpret it the same way. They can't all forget themselves so completely.'

'I could not, I am sure,' said Raymond.

'Well, how do you play, then?' she asked.

'Just like all the rest do, I suppose. Surely the interest of the whole thing lies in finding out how they managed with the instruments at their disposal?'

'But what were the instruments? How do you define them?' Christopher saw the trend of Raymond's argument and was ready with his challenge. 'Surely the chief reason why they did not see what we do was not that their telescopes were toys compared to ours?'

'Well, of course they were not trained observers like we are.'

'Oh yes, they were. They were highly trained to fit their observations to their interpretations. Remember we are reconstructing a period. It would be a sheer waste of time to look through a Galilean telescope and note down what it revealed of the stars. What it reveals of those observers is what we are after.'

'You mean ... ?'

'I mean their religion, their politics, and therefore their hopes, their anxieties. Every time they sat down to observe the stars they looked at them through all those things—through prejudice and conviction, as well as through their toys.'

'But that did not make any difference to what they saw. I am after that.'

'It made all the difference between their century and ours.'

'Surely, Christopher, progress depends on the methods and instruments available?'

'Progress?' Christopher paused to savour the full implications of the word, which he detested. 'I don't know what you mean by it, but if you mean what we learn by discovery, I say that is entirely a question of interpretation.'

'But science or learning is a question of measurement. We, for example, can only learn certain things by measuring them with instruments which our ancestors did not have. That is why the instruments they did have and use are so interesting.'

'You will see how happily they got on in spite of them. As far as your "progress" goes, we have probably lost far more than we have gained. We have almost lost the desire, for instance, of seeking the immeasurable. You people, who go on noting and measuring, measuring and noting, how often do you dare try to interpret? When it comes to that, you are more medieval. They at least had a system of interpretation, into which they endeavoured to fit their facts. They sought to exalt the glory of God, and everything they found they proclaimed to be a part of that glory.'

'Medieval nonsense,' said Raymond briefly.

'If you like, but well-sustained nonsense, all the same. It achieved Christendom. It made us. What are you achieving?'

'We are getting to know how things work. That is worth all Christendom put together.'

'The only thing that matters is the Why, not the How. Tell us that.'

'My dear boy, you talk like a poet or a mystic or a priest. Nobody cares about that but you. One might find out or one might not, but in the meantime let us look through our telescopes.'

'Well, Candide, go on looking and I will go on hoping.'

'Well, Pangloss, go on yourself. Perhaps one day you will tell us all about it.'

They smiled at one another; Raymond frankly and prosaically, as he thought; Christopher, passionately and maliciously, as he felt. The pessimist and the optimist, the man of measurement and the man of vision.

Raymond now saw Nicolette, who had come towards them during the conversation and was standing close to Christopher. She was looking at him, and her eyes were filled with pity, wonder, and alarm. If he had paused to interpret their expression, he would have thought the pity love, and the wonder shyness, and the alarm anticipation. But Raymond was no interpreter.

'Oh, well,' said Raymond, grasping his telescope, 'I am going to have a look through this.'

Christopher and Nicolette then looked at one another, and both knew that the episode was definitely at an end. He could not—and could never—play their game. After all, a mating was not a marriage.

'Oh, well——' had said Raymond, and had been charming about the whole thing. He was disappointed, or thought he was, but it was clear to him that Nicolette was surprisingly childish and immature for her age. He wondered afterwards what had been the quality in her that had attracted him (for he had been sincerely attracted by her), and concluded that it was a certain intensity, a look of the eyes, a wistfulness about the mouth, an atmosphere of spiritual stretching out, a keenness that he could not well define in words. However . . .

His period of enforced chastity having thus abruptly terminated, he formed a liaison with Karen Glaum, a well-known broadcaster of stories and poems, and also gave a child to Ruth, at her own request. He remained only a few months longer in Nucleus, and in later years attained a certain limited eminence as a physicist, owing to his discovery of two important minor facts about the behaviour of polyphenols under very high pressure.

9 CATALYSIS

One word, which he seemed to worship, often entered into his conversation: 'Intelligence.' And he pronounced it with such force of feeling that a little bubble of froth could be seen on his lips.

—Jacques de Lacretelle, *Silbermann*

I

When Christopher, all penitent, begged Nicolette's forgiveness for his temporary desertion, she remembered her prediction with silent joy. 'In the end you will come back to me and I to you,' she had said at their parting, and already it was so. Within a week or two of its ending she could look on the Raymond episode as a joke. St. John was absent from Nucleus at this time, and as she had merely had to soothe Antonia's disappointment and listen to a short disapproving homily from Adrian, she could only see its comical aspect. Nevertheless, having taken pleasure in Raymond's caresses at least, she felt now confirmed in her reaction against the physical preliminaries to motherhood. Christopher could give all the love she needed, and her inward discomfort at certain recollections (innocent kisses though they had been) appeared to her as a sign that she did not choose to penetrate the dark avenue of sex.

'The point is,' said Christopher, 'what do you want to do now?'

It was midday and they were sitting on some sandhills, taking a sun-bath. A pine forest behind them poured out scent; there was a silver shimmer over everything. Christopher was sweating slightly; small beads were on his forehead and upper lip. Nicolette lay on her stomach and with sensual delight felt the warmth travel down her spine.

'Just bask,' she murmured. 'Oh, Christopher, I'm so lazy. I haven't the slightest ambition to do anything at all. I don't care about anything just now but sleeping and eating and watching other people do things. You, for instance, and Weil. I've been spending hours with him, watching him make those adorable models of his. His sight is not very sharp any more, and I've been helping him with the more delicate parts. What a baby I am, playing with my little toys!'

'Not at all. That's art.'

'All right. I'm too hot to argue. Anyhow, I should like to go on helping Weil; he needs an assistant. Now he wants to make models illustrating the development of various arts and sciences. It means a lot of research, copying, donkey-work for which he has not enough time.'

'Well, do. We will get him to apply to the council for you if you think he wants you.'

'I am sure he will.'

'So much, then, for your laziness.'

'Yes, it isn't done, is it? Councils here and councils there, and a job for every one. I suppose it's inevitable, though.'

'Apparently. Only such reactionaries as you and I would like to see the old times back, when everybody was not classed according to capacity by practical psychologists. And when one could comfortably take a job beneath one's intelligence if one were merely lazy.'

'I don't think I would, really. But I do wish provision were made for oddities like you and me. Something ought to be done about us.'

'We must do it ourselves, or others will. Particularly about you. We must make a plan and go very carefully. You had the three usual alternatives. If you help Weil for a time you may shelve a decision, but it cannot be postponed indefinitely. Sooner or later you will either be mated or immunized.'

Nicolette looked at him with anger in her eyes. Indignation brought out the perspiration that the hottest rays of the sun had not called forth.

'I shall refuse!'

'Splendid! But you must think it out before any one else does. They will possibly allow you a year before you decide. Do you think making toys with Weil will be adequate substitute for making babies?'

'I don't want one now, but I probably shall some time.'

'Exactly. But under our system you can hardly work up to that in your own time. In a short while you will find yourself wanting some emotional stimulation. You will say, "I have gone so far, I want to go a little further." You won't want to go back, or rather to jump right on, to begin breeding. You will want to taste and test, possibly to sample the existence of an Entertainer. This, at any rate, is what they will anticipate. Then they will talk about example and precedent. They will never let you risk it, because they will be risking a revolutionary change in dissolving the demarcation lines between the orders. After all, the rigidity of the present breeding arrangement is not surprising: the whole scheme, practically, is feminine in inception and administration.'

'Well, something must be done about it. There must be women of all kinds who rebel against it.'

'Of course there are. Emmeline, for instance. But it is an extremely difficult thing to organize satisfactorily in any other way. Remember the dangers for them. Once the women raise the race slogan, the men will rally to them. You wouldn't have a chance.'

'I shall make Emmeline talk to St. John for me. She has promised to already.'

'But you don't imagine that he would make a difference between you and any one else? St. John is not a Jesuit, he does not play into their hands for his own advantage; he wouldn't for yours. He will never put the particular case before the general. Perhaps I should not say "never," but certainly not yours. He likes people to be definite, too, to know what they want (don't I know it?). If you come to him and plead that you cannot make up your mind, he will send you away and tell you to practise some exercises until you can. All that muddle, that lack of self-determination, that miasma of mixed emotions which impede clear judgment, he will tell you, belongs to the past. It should have gone, with better and worse and such nonsensical comparatives. There is no room for it in the scientific world.'

'Then if no one will help me, I will defy them all. I will cheat and lie and procrastinate; I will await my own time and act according to my own judgment, obscure or not.'

'And I, my darling, will help you. You will need me and you shall have me. I will never, never desert you again as I did. They need a lesson, and we will teach it them together. Then they can draw their own deductions, and if they want to, make a real example of us both. I will find an authority whereby I can refute them. Even if reason be wholly on their side, we will discover something on ours beyond the laws of reason. But we must go slowly.'

Thus was the pact concluded.

A few minutes later they both lay sleeping. The sun looked down on them unwinkingly. The forest breathed and each exhalation was a perfumed sigh.

II

Weil's workshops and museum occupied several acres in the Arts and Crafts section. They were surrounded by other architectural ateliers. All the buildings branched out like the spokes of a wheel from the central lecture and demonstration hall, which raised its lovely poised dome far above them. This had been one of his earliest and best achievements, but it lacked its final glory until Arcous Weil had begun to paint on its walls frescoes depicting the arts and the sciences at the service of humanity. Most of the representative figures were portraits, some of them still uncompleted. Political science was personified by St. John, oratory by Herville, architecture by old Weil himself. For the portrait of the World Mother, Arcous had drawn on his imagination. Behind her lay a crowd of figures symbolizing man's slow development: great louty shapes crouched, squatted, and, slowly assuming an erect posture, acquired at the same time a softer outline, until there appeared from among them, as Apollo might have appeared among the gibbering, trembling satyrs of an ancient wood, modern man. He was drawn in profile, standing proudly alone, poised on tiptoe, ready it seemed to run or to fly. A darker, slightly negroid type a little to his right and behind him, had a hand still on his shoulder, but it was being shaken off by the glorious one, whose own two palms were laid fearlessly in the mighty fist of his mother. She was turned in an attitude of expectation towards a group to her right. Each of the figures who composed it looked towards and behind her, yet the artist's brush had given their glances a slight slant, so that they seemed to travel further than the objects of their sight, further and higher. Of these men the foremost figure was instantly recognizable as Mensch. At the feet of the World Mother sprawled young children of all ages. They became more beautiful as they approached Mensch; they clung to his hands and his arms, one of which was crooked to hold a sleeping infant. Behind Mensch was Jesus with his Cross, on either side of whom stood a martyr and inquisitor. Moses, Socrates, Plato, and Aristotle formed a group raised a little above and to one side of these, while Buddha, and close to him Confucius, were the last recognizable figures in the rear of the procession that faded slowly into a dimmer and dimmer twilight. The drawing was ascetically severe, almost childishly diagrammatical; the colour, designed strictly with a view to the concordant lighting, alone gave the work a warm, emotional appeal.

Panels, each symbolical of an art or science, entirely covered the walls of the hall; organic and inorganic chemistry preceded sculpture and painting; physics and mathematics were followed by music and poetry, and so each fell into appropriate position to form the interlinked chain. Into these, also, portraits were wrought, for this was the hall that commemorated the achievement of man for man.

The genius of Arcous Weil expressed itself mainly in composition. In the making of his 'patterns,' as he always called them, he was sternly traditional. Wherever you find a romantic in any of the arts,' he would say, 'you know that a tradition is impossible. Romanticism is a form of adult infantilism—it leads to the clinic, not the school. Even the romantic can occasionally make patterns . . . Cezanne . . . Van Gogh . . . Gauguin. There is no real reason why a romantic artist should not have a sense of decency. These men succeeded because they knew when to stop, what to leave out. But the romantic is easiest to imitate, and the imitator confesses his all. Dreadful consequence! You cannot repeat the pattern of the romantics. Whereas the classicist can, as they did of old, tell the same story over and over again. Why are nearly all the world's pictures that count representations of a conventional theme, such as "Mother and Child" or "Crucifixion"? Because such pictures are mere abstractions, strictly patterned. In them the artist can let himself go on form, colour, composition. As subjects for civilized human beings neither landscape nor portraiture as such can exist. In such works we see the man who wrought them, not the subjects as seen universally. The other day I discovered a portrait of a banker—a money-broker—by a nineteenth-century fellow called Sargent. Please note, a portrait of a money broker.'

Arcous was talking to a group of students, and his eyes flashed from face to face to see if the point had gone home. 'As a matter of fact,' he continued, as their laughter urged him on, 'you might as well paint a banker as a cow. Except that the former are extinct and the latter getting rather rare. But you will paint landscape and figure. You will paint them as design; you will incorporate them in your patterns. And your patterns will not be mere hermaphroditic, sterile scrawls, such as the romantic infantilists of the twentieth century produced, but they will be great, glorious, allegorical wall-coverings, which can be enjoyed as abstractions by those cultured enough to want nothing more, and at the same time as inspiring pictorial stories by the Body. You will call your figures goddesses, or cities, or demons, or sciences, or heroes, or philosophies, or whatever you choose; your rivers Rhines, or St. Lawrences, or Volgas, or Amazons; use as many personal names as you like, so long as your representation is utterly impersonal; your pattern a mere pattern. You will not—luckily for you we are past the stage when that was possible—reproduce mere accurate photographic copies of dwellings or individuals or scenes; nor will you jot down a shorthand smudge and inform the world that it has no business to come prying at your picture and demand to recognize a familiar object; any one working here will create as simply and precisely as a bee creates a honey cell; let your watchword be "Enough." And now get out.'

Arcous Weil was nineteen years of age. Though the design of the decorations was his own creation he had not attempted to carry it out unaided. Some of his followers could paint robes and folds, hands and feet, almost as well as he could; sixteen had contributed to the completion of the scheme. If they wanted to infuriate Arcous they had only to compare him to Raphael. For he had none of the ingenuousness and insipidity of that boy painter. His genius was rather of the same quality as Blake's. There was a mystical passion in his conceptions and in his manner of expressing them. The Weils could trace their ancestry back in a direct line to one of Sephardim who had made ancient Spanish Jewry famous throughout the medieval world; and there were few families of their race now extant who could substantiate such a claim. Old Weil, absorbed in his models and the Talmudic studies which gave him equal inspiration in another way, had not taken much notice of the fact that his boy had been hailed as a prodigy at the age of seven. Arcous had had the freedom of the studios since babyhood; why then should he not profit by it? In later years, however, the son not only set his seal on the father's fame, but attracted to the Weil workshops men and women who could not remain indifferent to the influence of his Semitic brilliance. They in their turn influenced not his art but his character. Their adulation stiffened his pride, their easy laughter his indifference. Of his own race he acknowledged no superior in intelligence save Mensch, which meant that in his opinion he was the second most remarkable man in his world. Nicolette could not ignore Arcous, even if he himself had been willing to let her do so. That catalytic power, which was the essence of Jewish influence everywhere and at all times, could leave her no more untroubled by its mysterious presence than any of the others. From the beginning he was physically antipathetic to her. Little things about him, the shape of his finger-nails, the extreme whiteness of his teeth, the shininess of his dark eyes, the curliness of his hair, gave her curious fleeting sensations of disgust. But his influence went further than this.

It was clear that he admired her, yet his admiration never lost its critical quality. His youthful self-assertiveness not only challenged her own, but his irony made it necessary for her to be constantly on guard. It was a new experience for Nicolette, this discovery of a person in whose presence one simply could not be natural, be oneself. Arcous compelled one to play his game, at his pace and in his time. She did not like him, but what did that matter compared to the fascination he exercised by forcing her into a new rôle? When he looked at her she saw herself through alien eyes, and often revolting at the unfamiliar picture, she would have wished to protest, to cry out to him: 'But I am not like that! Why cannot you see me as I am and leave me alone?'

He treated her always with a mock respect which was so obvious that he himself felt obliged to apologize for it and explain it away.

'You see,' he said one day in the course of a general discussion, 'it is impossible for a Jew to respect a woman, or even a man, of another race. We only respect intelligence, and therefore acknowledge no overlordship, whether of sex or personality. That would have been our supreme asset, if only we could have hidden it. But we can't. So we were persecuted for centuries. Christianity had little to do with our tribulations, for we were equally hated by all Gentiles, and this was the cause of their antagonism. They did not suspect it, but we did, and enjoyed their vain cruelties for this reason. The same with women. What we could not give to our own, the most obedient, the most loyal, the most steadfast in the world, we could give to no others. Chivalry was not in us.'

'But that was all of the past,' answered Nicolette, somehow ashamed for him, though she knew not why. 'Nowadays you are losing your sharply defined contours.'

'Unfortunately, most of us are,' he answered. 'I know I am an exception, but then look what I have done.'

'Do you really think that is the cause of it? Surely such pride is not essential for achievement?'

'To me, absolutely. Has it ever struck you that I always express myself in comparatives? We invented them, or rather foisted them on the whole of western civilization. Better and worse, a little, more, all those expressions are characteristic. Abolish them as applied to achievement, and you lose a mean, a standard. You get mediocrities at once.'

'Ambition!' he went on after a momentary pause, 'I don't think anyone but a Jew truly knows the meaning of that word. In Yiddish, which is now almost as dead an idiom as Hebrew, there is another one, a good foil to it. "Nebbich." How can I translate it? "Poor mutt" is about the nearest I can get to it. It need hardly be spoken among Jews; it flashes from the thoughts of one to the mind of another. Applied to one of our own race it had just a slight tinge of pity; towards all others it was a term of scorn, of derision, of contempt. Now there is nothing in the world a Jew would not rather be than a "nebbich." Luckily for us no one else knew just what epithet would pierce our mulish indifference. Don't you forget it!'

'But why should I wish to remember it?'

'The day might come when you would wish to insult me.'

Abruptly he turned and left her then.

It was when he said such things that Nicolette was most aware of his physical qualities and disliked him most intensely. She did not in the least object to his superlative egotism, which confined his conversation mostly to himself, his race, his art, and allied topics. Arcous's self-esteem was not only fed and increased by nearly all his companions, fellow-workers and pupils, but it served him as a standard whereby he judged his own creations with far more severity than he applied to those of others. It was all in order that people like Vogt and his friends should be mediocrities; they felt neither shame nor anger at the prospect of moderate success; he burned to rank beside the leaders in his art, and this passionate desire had never, since his twelfth year, left him in peace. 'Ambition and arrogance,' he would say, 'are twin brothers. One feeds the other. You cannot possibly attain your ambition unless you have an arrogant confidence in your own judgment. That is what is the matter with you, Christopher, as a man and an artist. You lack improper pride.'

Christopher had been drawn by Nicolette into the radius of Arcous's catalytic influence. He at once responded even more intensely than she had; Arcous's penetrating intelligence, his domineering will, quickened all the thought processes that were at work in Christopher's brain. The young Jew seemed to feel as strong an anger and disgust as his own with many of the customs and institutions of their time. He spoke even more disparagingly about them; nor had he the least respect for persons, hitting them off with a light irony like the flick of a whip. But he did not propose to do anything about it.

'To me nothing matters but my art, and I don't care how great a mess my fellowmen make of the world so long as they leave me my colours and a wall or two to spread them on in my patterns. I have not the least quarrel with your father, who, surprisingly, is not a hypocrite, nor even with your brother, who quite obviously is. I don't mind what they do, what becomes of us. Had I lived in former times, I should have been indifferent to war, to famine, pestilence, pogroms and torture.'

'Would you have renounced your faith?'

'Certainly, if at that price I could have kept my art. I should always have had my race, anyway. But'—he flashed an almost accusing finger at Christopher—'if I were you, if I cared as you do, I should not remain inactive, I should propagandize for anarchy among all the intelligent people I knew, since that is the only mode of living for intelligent folk. The leaders of to-day are treating the people as if they were Versuchstierchen, and the earth one great laboratory. Why the world should be transformed into an experimental theatre in the name of Mensch just because it was turned into a circus arena in the name of Jesus, I can't fathom.'

At other times he would round on Christopher, attacking his point of view from that of the established order, for he loved argument for its own sake, and argued with a gusto inspired by his fundamentally untouched cynicism.

'What can you want as an improvement on what you have to-day?' he would ask him. 'Here you live in a community of people every one of whom would have been considered a superman two hundred years ago, and a saint a little earlier than that. Superstition has been broken on the rack of sense, the family has almost disappeared in favour of the community, work and play are synonymous. Art flourishes, science rules. War and epidemics have vanished, the attitude towards sickness transforms pain into pleasure; we can remain young as long as we like, and a generation lives and dies together; we have lost universal fear and found universal friendship. Above all, quite a lot of us are becoming intelligent.'

'Do you think so? Do you think all that really amounts to so much?' retorted Christopher. 'What have we gained individually in richness and depth of personality? Do you really believe St. John exists, except as an embodiment of this state's problems, and the mental machinery necessary to cope with them? It is the same, in a lesser degree, with all of us. We are becoming so utterly gregarious that most of us already have no kind of existence apart from the herd. Mental and manual workers, entertainers, mothers, it is the same everywhere. The individual has been gradually pushed out; his will counts as nothing against the general will; all of his interests that might conflict with those of the herd are from childhood trained, twisted, sublimated, so as to render them innocuous; and when it occasionally happens that he still endeavours to assert himself, science takes him into her loathsome workshops, where she repairs him according to the way he ought to go, not the way he wants to.'

'Well, what substitute do you propose for the present state?'

'In the old days one could appeal to the ideal state as against the bad or undeveloped state; you can only appeal to God against the ideal state.'

'Such an appeal, concretely carried out, would mean anarchy. I shall be interested to see what you will do.'

'Something must be done. I haven't the slightest interest in the community. Let it take care of itself. But I will not have the individual sacrificed to it.'

'Ah, so it will be the immortal soul versus the body corporate,' said Arcous softly. 'That should provide an interesting show.'

III

Though she went to Weil's workshops every day, it was generally expected that Nicolette would within a short time decide to adopt the career of motherhood after all. The local Council of Employment had willingly agreed to the architect's application for her assistance in his model designing, which was now graded as artistic work of fourth-class importance. This done, they referred his request to the Motherhood Council for final consideration.

The administration of all matters appertaining to careers was regulated by experts who were appointed on somewhat similar lines to the officials of ancient Freemasonry. Democratic government by votes for all was an institution of the past. Whatever profession a man or woman adopted, proficiency at it and competent knowledge of its various branches was the sole passport to advancement. Those who desired posts of regulation or control were obliged to qualify for them by examination. In order, however, to avoid the creation of an 'official' type of mind, the councils were composed of acting and honorary members, the latter being the most distinguished representatives of the profession in question. In all cases it was possible to call in as many advisers as the applicant whose case came up for consideration desired.

The Motherhood Councils were composed of women who had borne at least three children, and who, in addition, had proved themselves to possess a certain knowledge of the theory as well as the practice of their craft. They had to give evidence also of a real understanding of the less personal problems of the day, social, political and economic, and of more than a slight acquaintance with the biological sciences. Each council consisted of a nucleus of women qualified to deal with the special problems of the district, but this core was continually augmented by advisory experts, according to the nature of the case to be decided. Decisions were never based on rules of precedent. The council was required to bear in mind certain general considerations, such as, for instance, the number of children it would be necessary to produce in a certain area within a given period, the relative proportions of the sexes required, and the available female material from which to breed. Each problem to be decided was discussed from at least three angles: that of the commonwealth or the general, of the division of the community or the local, and that of the individual. Whether the matter under consideration referred to a large group or to one single person, the procedure adopted for its examination was invariably the same. In order to avoid endless debate and to facilitate a prompt decision, each of the regular members of the council was expected to have gone, into the problem under discussion previously and alone from these three points of view. They then listened in assembly to the views and arguments whatever additional expert advisers it had been of found necessary to call in.

The council summoned to give a decision on Nicolette's application to be allowed to assist Weil was composed of four women only, for the matter was one of comparative unimportance, and did not require consideration by a full membership. One of these was Antonia; another, to Nicolette's satisfaction, was Leila, whose small boy

Toodles the third she had loved so dearly three years ago; was an exceptionally clever young person called Miomi Lander; and the fourth an elderly woman, Claire Tamston, the senior member, who was the only one likely to be definitely antagonistic.

Antonia considered that her personal interest in the matter precluded her from giving judgment on her daughter's case, but this did not prevent her from expressing a view for the consideration of her colleagues.

'Of course I was surprised,' she said in her usual soft tones, which seemed to insist ever so gently on her desire to be understanding and helpful, 'when I found that Nicolette did not wish to mate with Raymond. It would have been suitable. At the same time she did convince me' (with the subtle help of Christopher, but this Antonia did not mention) 'that her reluctance was simply due to the feeling that she was not yet sufficiently prepared for her career. In the circumstances I should have liked her to continue her studies. More than that I cannot say just now.'

'I thought,' said Leila then, and her kind eyes dwelt with encouragement on the girl's face, 'that she had completed her course?'

Nicolette nodded in confirmation, but said nothing.

'It would be a pity in my opinion,' continued Leila, 'if she postponed her decision long. We naturally wish to breed from the best available material, and it is essential for women of our position to set an example. I have not the least doubt, from my personal knowledge of her, that Nicolette is certain to make a brilliant success of motherhood, and at the same time to find in it the whole satisfaction of her personal ambitions. But it would surely be a mistake to begin her career while she still feels unde-cided or immature. A slight postponement would not, in my opinion, be detrimental to her future.'

Claire Tamston was a big woman with a deceptively small voice.

'It is astonishing to me,' she said, glancing at Antonia with just the slightest tinge of suspicion and dislike in her eyes, 'that your daughter should have these curious hesitancies. I fail to see how a young girl of her person-ality and education should for one moment doubt that motherhood is the career for which she is fitted or that the earlier she can embark on it the better. She is the sort of young woman we need for the production of sons and daughters who will do honour to our state and carry on its glorious tradition. I am against a postponement. The motives for it seem to me trivial, and the work she wishes to do temporarily could be done by any boy or girl who has no such important ultimate destiny.'

'I differ from you,'—Miomi Lander smiled at the older woman. She was a subtle creature, was Miomi. Her man-ners were so perfect that they invariably left the onlooker in doubt as to her intentions. She had a sense of humour and could differentiate between the relative importance of the problems before the council, an ability that Claire Tamston unfortunately did not possess.

'What we want to avoid above all things is getting unsuitable people into the profession. Naturally Antonia would like her own daughter to do as she did, and the rest of us are keen on example as well as babies. But as

Nicolette cannot give us either until she has mated, it is clear that from her point of view the important thing is to find a young man for her. The race is the ideal, ultimately, and later on one can be satisfied to do one's work as one is bidden, for its sake. But the first time there must inevitably be the appropriate stimulus. As we obviously cannot provide it, we must give her the chance to find some one who will. I propose to leave the matter entirely to her own judgment. Let her find the mate, and the children will follow as a matter of course. If they should not, it would be quite a different affair. As for Weil, his work is so important now that Reconstruction is having such admirable psychological effects, that I certainly think we should let him have the assistant he wants. He does seem to want Nicolette.'

'A dangerous precedent,' murmured Claire, who swelled with dissatisfaction as she saw the decision of her colleagues going against her.

'This phase of society is based on precedents, most of whose dangers have been proved to be chimerical.'

'How long does she intend to remain with Weil?'

'Let us give her six months,' proposed Leila, 'and then go into the matter again. In the meantime he will have an opportunity to find some one to replace her.'

'On that understanding I will accept your decision,' answered Claire. 'I would emphatically not do so in every case, but this girl is clearly a little out of the ordinary. I suppose,' she added, turning to Antonia and revealing her disapproval more openly in looks than in words, 'that you will attend to the necessary precautions?'

'By all means,' replied Antonia, and Nicolette, watching, decided that the latent hostility between them should be turned to her own profit.

'That is settled then, Nicolette,' said Leila, smiling on her sweetly. 'You shall be appointed to assist Weil for a period of six months, and we rely on you to uphold your prestige, which involves that of your whole caste. Is that satisfactory to you?'

The last question was invariably asked of every applicant who applied to a council, and also of those who came up on account of transgression of some rule. At the present moment Nicolette interpreted it in a purely formal manner. So far, so satisfactory.

She therefore answered, 'Quite, thank you,' endeavouring to return as well as she could the other woman's benevolent smile.

'And hurry up about that young man,' added Miomi, as they all rose to go.

10 ANTIBODIES

You will not easily persuade me that man's future will be less
surprising and tragic than his past.

—J. B. S. Haldane, in a criticism of the synopsis of this book

I

Antonia was in for a difficult six months, and she felt
aggrieved about it. The unadmitted cause of her annoyance was Claire Tamston, for whom she felt a daily growing
antipathy. Claire never omitted an opportunity to inquire
with affected interest after Nicolette's welfare, and Antonia interpreted each inquiry as a renewed reflection on her
own integrity. Claire was an abomination, with her self-
satisfaction, her suspicions, her public spirit. But Antonia
had been well disciplined and was no fool; she knew that
the precept 'Love thine enemies' was the basis of all government by consent. In ancient days judges had worn in
some countries special robes in which to preside in their
courts. There was now no need for such childish symbols
of auto-suggestion. Antonia as a member of the council
was at her best, for she held that concord among arbitra-
tors was the essential basis of justice towards appellants.

The self-discipline she practised in public, however, was
not proof against a certain irritation in private. Dignity had

demanded of her that she should formally agree to supervise Nicolette's activities, but this was an unexpected task which had been thrust upon her by her own loyalties. Antonia and St. John had met but twice within the past month; she was used to making her own decisions without reference to him, but in this matter she would have welcomed his advice.

She felt that Nicolette had put her into an old-fashioned and slightly ridiculous position. It was absurd that she should require supervision at her age, and at a period when maternal authority over children other than babies had long been abolished. Yet in view of the laws of the day it was obvious that a girl dedicated to motherhood, and in whose case immunization had not even been mooted (Antonia shuddered when she thought of that horrid possibility), must not run the slightest risk of contamination.

Then she remembered Miomi's wise words, and took comfort. The obvious thing to do was to find a mate for Nicolette as soon as possible, a lover whose kisses would plead more eloquently than a mother's words could do. Antonia was reserved even with herself on the subject of sex. It did not give her much pleasure to review her own girlhood and early womanhood. There are pages in such reminiscences even the bravest women, and men too, hesitate to reopen. They contain records of so many slight disloyalties, false ambitions, and mental, if not physical, seductions. Antonia had censored a few of hers many years ago; the rest she had by now managed comfortably to forget and if ever she had known qualms when she recalled her behaviour during Christopher's pre-natal days, she had long come to regard herself as the pattern of devotion to duty.

It occurred to her that Christopher might be helpful in dealing with the present problem. It had occurred to him too—although from a different angle.

The 'two children,' as she called them (though she never thought of her others as un-grown-up), had come to see her one evening.

'How splendid you look, Nicolette,' she said, observing with pleasure the change in her daughter. The second softening, into young womanhood, was beginning to round out Nicolette's long delicate outlines now. Her thick curls were tinged with a lovely nut-brown gloss, the eager eyes looked out softly and happily from between their long lashes. Her small breasts, thin arms and legs, were swelling into the first perfection of maturity. It was obvious to others besides Arcous Weil that she would soon be an exquisitely beautiful young woman.

'I'm contented,' she answered with a joyous glance at Christopher. 'I love working with old Weil. I could go on like this for ever.'

'But that won't be possible, you know,' Antonia admonished gently. 'You will dislike me if I always pull you out of your day-dreams, but you must think of your future.'

'Oh, well, I have five and a half months before I need do that,' Nicolette replied flippantly. She simply could not take Antonia seriously.

'But I have not. Don't you realize, they've made me more or less directly responsible for it? It's a most curious position to be in.'

Nicolette looked sharply at Antonia and began to have some glimmerings of her dilemma.

'I beg your pardon, you dear,' she said, suddenly sitting upright, for she had been lazing on some cushions. 'It is hardly fair of me, is it?'

'Oh, I know you never meant to give me any trouble; please don't think I am complaining,' answered Antonia, responsive to her amiability. 'But I don't want you to lose yourself entirely in those workshops. You know there is nothing I want to do less than supervise you as if you were a small child, but the position is unusual. You obviously cannot go about among a lot of Neuters and Entertainers as if you were one of them; you must have some kind of a chaperon.'

'She has, already,' put in Christopher soothingly.

'Whom?'

'Me. And if I won't do, what about Emmeline? She could replace you whenever you like, you know.'

'Oh, I trust you absolutely, both of you, you know I do,' protested Antonia, a little emotionally. 'But it would be so nice if you could form a group of suitable young people of your own age.' (Back of her consciousness she felt the disapproving eyes of Claire Tamston looking on a shade less harshly.) 'What sort of young men do you like, Nicolette?'

'I only know one at the moment who attracts me in the very least,' Nicolette answered dreamily. Antonia's face lit up with eager anticipation.

'What is he like?'

'An adorable creature. Tall, fair, thin, but thoroughly healthy, clever, quick-witted, sensitive. . . .'

'How old is he?'

'A little older than myself.'

'What does he do?'

'He's an artist.'

Antonia's face fell a little.

'Oh! Has he been mated already?'

'You might ask him. He hasn't told me so.' She smiled maliciously at Christopher, who grinned back at her from behind their mother.

'And you like him?'

'More than any one in the world. I'm already mated to him in affection.'

'What is his name?'

'The same as your own.'

Antonia's brightness faded out like a light switched off. Yet she could not help smiling plaintively as Nicolette and Christopher burst into peals of laughter.

'You little wretch!' she lamented.

'Whose fault is it?' asked Nicolette, still malicious. 'You give me a brother with whom I've been in love since childhood, and then you expect me to mate with the thoroughly unattractive youths produced by other people. You ought not to have set me such an excellent standard.'

Antonia could not scold; could not help feeling happy and proud when she looked at them sitting there before her, side by side. 'The two children.' Hers—how utterly and unmistakably hers!

'Well, then, it's up to Christopher to find a mate for you. If he approves of the young man, you will.'

'I'm not sure I want to,' said Christopher slowly, his arm around Nicolette, his eyes on Antonia.

'Oh, Christopher, don't you make a fool of me now,' she pleaded.

'But I'm in earnest. I don't want her to mate; at any rate, not yet.'

'Christopher! How can you talk like that? How perverse you are! Is it possible you have been encouraging her in this ridiculous refusal?'

'There was nothing ridiculous about it in the first place, except Raymond,' he declared frankly. 'Why should Nicolette do as every one else does? I did nothing for years, and they did not touch me, nor did you try to coerce me.'

'But that was utterly different!' she almost moaned.

'Look here, mother,' and Antonia paid attention now, for he never used the filial expression unless he was quite serious, 'how do you know that we are not both "different"?'

He paused for a moment to allow her to appreciate his point. But Antonia was too practised a skater to fall through that thin ice. 'Have you never felt a little—well—perverse, yourself? Why do you expect Nicolette to conform so completely to the mean? You may have been able to do so, perhaps, but you know very well that there is something "different" about me. Why not then about her?'

'But you are an artist, my boy. You will be a famous man one day. Nicolette shows no sign of any talent like yours.'

'Because she has never had the chance. You specialized her training so early. Supposing you had been on the false track from the beginning? Supposing she cared for music as much as I do, and wanted to do something else instead of breeding?'

'I am certain she could not do anything so successfully,' answered Antonia obstinately. 'What talent has she?'

'Her voice, for instance. I think that with training it might be an exceptional one. Have you ever thought of that?'

But Antonia had not and did not intend to do so now. His last words had suggested appalling possibilities. Immunization. . . . As usual, she refused to contemplate unpleasant prospects.

'I refuse to let you suggest such silly ideas to me,' she said, and they both saw her frightened, absolutely resolved that the subject should not be pursued; 'and I beg you not to suggest them to Nicolette. She should at least have every opportunity to find a mate who appeals to her—mentally and physically.'

'By all means,' he soothed, knowing that he had gone rather far with her. 'But you must realize that she is not to be coerced, and that if there is danger of her making a mistake, it is because of the mistakes that have already been made. Let her be as free as possible during the next few months. It is the least any one can decently accord.'

'Certainly she shall have her way for the time being,' answered Antonia, who had made up her mind to discuss the problem with St. John at the earliest opportunity, and also to talk to Emmeline, who had obviously been encouraging 'the children' in their perversity.

II

Nicolette now lived almost entirely out of doors. Although she and Christopher had always spent long hours together in the open, there was a definite reason why they did so at present. Away from buildings they were away from people, and on their walking, flying, riding, or swimming expeditions they could take the companions they chose without provoking unfavorable comment. Arcous was nearly always with them during his leisure, but he quietly attached himself more closely to the brother than to the sister. And he began to surround them, very carefully and casually, with one or two intimates of his own.

There was Bruin, whose name was Brian Keck. Arcous had early wished to make or to supervise the making of his own colours, and for this purpose he had taken a course of synthetic chemistry. During the time he had spent in the laboratories, he had come across this fellow on one or two occasions. Bruin was rather fat, he had a longish thick nose and small brown eyes set very close together. His body was covered with hair which he systematically destroyed with depilatories as soon as it grew, because he admired a smooth skin. A faint odour of sulphur seemed always to hover about him. Arcous and Bruin admired one another profoundly. Neither took the slightest interest in the technical side of the other's work; sheer force of one strong personality attracted to another pulled them together. But Arcous did know that Bruin had the same love of power as himself, and that he cherished strange dreams. Bruin was destined for Christopher.

There was Morgana Dietleffsen, who had chosen that personal name because she was a distant descendant of Morgan, the famous geneticist. Morgana was a tall fair girl whose features were not beautiful, but the blueness of her eyes and the scarlet of her lips were unforgettable. She lived with Brian, but really loved Arcous.

The five of them had climbed one afternoon to the hermitage of the old Extonian. He was Alexander Murray, the only survivor of the obliteration of that doomed community, but he had not escaped unscathed. He was a famous entomologist, and the scenes he had witnessed there had mingled disastrously with impressions of years of observation of insect life. They attached superlative importance in the state to the lessons of entomology, so that his marked idiosyncrasy was tolerated. He had established on the top of his hill a magnificently equipped laboratory, surrounded by open-air reservations wherein millions of ants and beetles could be experimented upon under ideal conditions. Christopher, Bruin and Morgana knew the place well; Nicolette and Arcous had not yet been there.

'You won't see Murray himself, of course,' Bruin told them as they set out on their tramp of twenty-five kilometres. 'No one ever does except his assistants, and they invariably ignore him. For the past thirty-six years he has completely broken off diplomatic relations with the rest of the human species. He has to lecture once a month by radio; that was the sole condition imposed on him when he came here; for the rest his only companions are his bugs.'

'What is the matter with him?' asked Nicolette.

'Megalomania. He's an authority on Parasitology. He was in Exton, all those years ago. He wrote his most important books during the last years, between the assassination of Goldring and the final obliteration. Even then he was not communicative. He travelled all over the world, and would only come back from time to time in order to put his collections in order and write his observations. He never was interested in men, and he was almost entirely ignorant of what was taking place around him. When the end came, the Patrol warned him to clear out. He was the only person there they wished to spare. He came here and has lived on the top of his ant-hill ever since.'

'What was the real story of Exton?' Arcous asked. 'I have heard about it vaguely, of course, but I have never bothered to read it up.'

'Oh, it's a marvellous story. The sort of thing that almost excites one.'

'It's the classic illustration of the power of the commonwealth,' added Christopher. 'I can't recall a single other instance of such complete efficiency.'

'There probably never will be another,' said Morgana. 'What fun if there were.'

'Do not be so certain,' said Christopher darkly, and Arcous glanced at him swiftly.

'Well, let me hear the whole story'—he turned impatiently to Bruin.

'Christopher can tell it more fully than I can,' answered the Bear, as he lumbered slowly uphill. He was already sweating and disliked exerting himself.

'It happened as Bruin told you, just thirty-six years ago,' began Christopher accordingly. 'At that time the commonwealth had cleared up most of the obvious messes, but enough remained to be done in holes and corners to keep the Patrol interested in its job. Golding was at the head of it then, and it was organized as efficiently as the Spanish Inquisition had been. People had recovered from their first shock of surprise at finding that a scientific power, armed with invincible weapons, had come to replace the old nationalist ones. A few wars were still carried on here and there under various pretexts, because they were such a useful means of getting rid of the incorrigibles. Education was going well, the female orders were already established, and the dramatic example of the Gay Company fired the imagination of the backward.

'But, as you know, there have always been certain races who were temperamentally intractable. The most troublesome of these at the time were the Celts. There were large numbers of them on this continent then, mainly descendants of the Irish and the Welsh. They tended to herd together in large communities. When they were not quarrelling among themselves, they loved to annoy those who came from outside to investigate and arbitrate among them. Exton was the biggest of these places. That was before the time when the relative sizes of the communities and the numbers of children annually produced in each had been fixed. There were several hundred thousand people in Exton.'

'Help!' exclaimed Arcous. 'However did they manage to control them?'

'That was the obstinate problem,' answered Christopher. 'They set up a strong Patrol committee at first, but that form of administration could not continue indefinitely. The whole point at the beginning, as now, was to create autonomous communities. So they decided to give them a chance. But the native Celtic slothfulness was too severe a handicap under which the new regulations had to start. Hygiene was almost impossible, and with the support of religion (or rather superstition) withdrawn, example had no force. The means were at hand, but not the morale. They had their hotels just as we had, but there was a constant battle to compel each of them to sleep in his or her own room.'

'Surely,' said Nicolette in amazement, 'they were not so dirty as that! Do you mean to say that a man and a woman actually slept in one cot?'

'Certainly,' answered Bruin.

'My dear, do you realize that in the twentieth century whole families still slept on the floor of one room?' asked Morgana, who had studied hygiene and was well up in the subject.

'No, I can't,' said Nicolette, so obviously disgusted that they all laughed at her expression of dismay.

'Well, they did worse than that. In some places the pigs and the hens cuddled up with them.'

'Spare us the more revolting details of ancient history if you can,' pleaded Arcous, who shared Nicolette's physical fastidiousness. 'They remind me of the story of my immigrant ancestor, whom they found one day dipping his fingers in a glass of hot water. "What are you doing that for?" they asked, and he answered tearfully: "The doctor has ordered me a course of baths for my rheumatism, and I'm getting used to the water."'

Morgana was annoyed at his Jewish habit of self-depreciation. 'I though your ancestors were Sephardim,' she said, 'and not Polish immigrants.'

'So they were,' replied Arcous with a smile, 'but we all claim common descent from old Adam, and the mud of the Garden still sticks to us. Let's get back to your black sheep, Christopher. They interest me.'

'I made a slight mistake when I said that they no longer had the support of religion. Superstition and sentimentality still upheld them. That marvellous system alleged to be Christianity (of course it was nothing of the kind) still had a kick in it. They had to put up with Entertainers instead of "fallen women" for their sensual indulgences, but they found plenty of objects of pity and scorn to make a fuss over. Parasites of all degrees flourished on them. The Employment Councils had a tremendous job, because if a man would not work there was always another who was willing to keep him. They were excessively humane and had a horror of elimination. The duds lived longer than the honest men. At about this time old Murray came out of his trance. He had just been studying parasitology in the ants, and he took Wheeler's fine passage for a text on which to base his parallel. Let me see if I can remember some of it . . . "Man furnishes the most striking illustration of the ease with which both the parasitic and host rôles may be assumed by a social animal!" . . .'

'And,' added Bruin, who suddenly stopped trudging uphill to turn around and declaim in loud dramatic tones, 'Biology has only one great categorical imperative to offer us, and that is: "Be neither a parasite nor a host, and try to dissuade others from being parasites or hosts."'

'Fine, fine!' exclaimed Arcous enthusiastically. 'Go on!'

But Bruin was fanning himself with a gigantic leaf.

'You can look up the rest if you want to,' he said abruptly. 'I've forgotten it.'

'Anyway, the old hermit hasn't,' said Christopher. That's what drove him up here in the end. He wrote his first volume on the subject with the passion of a Jeremiah and the patience of a Darwin. Incidentally he destroyed another ridiculous illusion of ignorance: that the ants show an example that should be copied by man. It was one of those dangerous untruths that half-educated people were so fond of quoting. However, at the time his writings had little effect. They were too intelligent for those people, and he was already looked on as a harmless eccentric. They were hostile and, as far as they dared be, unkind to him.'

'He was a Scot, you see,' put in Arcous.

'How these Celts loved one another,' said Morgana.

'Oh, not much less than the others, only they were more naïve about it,' said Christopher. 'You must remember that love was "done" or rather overdone, till it was assigned its proper place.'

'Like a beefsteak that no one could stomach although they kept on serving it up,' illustrated the irrepressible Morgana.

'Shut up, Morgana, and let Christopher get on,' said Arcous roughly. 'We shall reach the top of the hill before he comes to the end of his story.'

Unable as usual to withstand him, Morgana obeyed.

'They certainly wallowed in proteins and fat,' said Christopher, 'and it was almost impossible to get them to migrate and merge with other peoples, although that had once been such a pronounced Celtic character. But their decadence was incorrigible. At last the central executive became impatient with them and sent Patrolmen to investigate. Their reports were so serious that Goldring determined to go himself and make a clean sweep. He immediately set up a reformatory board. The psychologists were delighted, for they had never had such a complete case before them. But their joy was short lived. No sooner had they ordered a few eliminations and expelled the ring-leaders than Goldring was assassinated.'

'How?' asked Arcous.

'Strangled by a religious maniac, O'Donnell. They got him, anyway, for the experimental work on stimulation of growth of brain cells in the adult.'

'Mathias's law,' grunted Brian. 'Most important.'

'But what a job they had!' continued Christopher. 'Anyway, they managed to restore some kind of order for a couple of years. Fanniez had taken over after Goldring was moved on, and it was the sort of thing he liked. They did manage to infuse a little public spirit into a few of their more intelligent people, and they were just beginning to learn to rule themselves. Then came the climax.'

'I remember about that,' said Arcous. 'The outbreak of infectious disease.'

'Yes. A gorgeous mess. Imagine the sensation it created! First of all it began in other places, right along the trail from Chile, where the exiles had gone. It seemed to start in four places at once, and no one had the slightest clue as to its origin. All the victims were pronouncedly unstable types, so they were got rid of as soon as possible.

Naturally, after all the years of freedom from disease of that kind, its appearance caused a certain amount of panic, particularly in the more advanced places.'

'Nucleus escaped, didn't it?'

'Yes, happily our record wasn't broken. It's still intact. But that was entirely due to the fact that we didn't lie in the lines of communication.'

'Who were the carriers?' asked Nicolette.

'Four blighters who had escaped over the frontier and had managed to get smuggled back to Exton. Apparently they all had old mothers or some such Celtic witches who wanted to see them once again. The disease simply flew round the place. Nowhere in the whole commonwealth could conditions have been more favourable. To begin with, the people who had it were so annoyed at the though of being shown up, that they hid themselves and one another. That couldn't go on very long, and they were soon spotted. All the women in the place were ordered to be immunized. Every child was cleared out to isolation stations. But although they might have got rid of the physical effects, the mental damage done was a different matter. The old slogan was dragged out of hiding too. "Disease is no crime!" and so on. There was a quite a little bout of mania again. The thing came before the Supreme Council, and even Mensch had to agree in the end that there was no alternative: Exton had to be obliterated. In any case, it simply was not worth keeping. So they went.'

'How?' asked Arcous again.

'Oh, the usual way—smoked out like a rotten hive.'

'And no questions asked?'

'Hardly any; it was almost entirely a local affair, you see. Added to that there was universal indignation at the menace the Extonians had brought on the race. The collective conscience was beginning to work efficiently; the propaganda of the Company was bearing fruit, and the Patrol was trusted.'

'What about old Murray?'

'Oh, they had got him away some time before. He had gone into a slight frenzy when the disease first broke out, and imagined that he was infected with parasites, although he never got it. And that's still the bee in his bonnet. He thinks that every one and everything is after his blood, and takes insecticide baths three times daily. But he still does work that hardly any one else could, they tell me. He has a superb technique after all these years.'

'What,' said Arcous, with his usual eagerness to probe Christopher's mind, 'do you really think about that wholesale massacre?'

'I think,' answered Christopher, 'that it was a justifiable expedient, but a deplorable precedent. The so-called value of human life is always a debatable factor; its sanctity is a matter of sentiment, not reason. But if ever I think I would like to start a revolt, the lesson of Exton sobers me.'

'That's only a matter of weapons,' answered Arcous, and called after Brian, lumbering ahead: 'what do you say, Bruin?'

He turned round and glowered at them.

'You've hit it,' he grunted briefly. 'Weapons are what we need. For every one of theirs, one of ours. Well, it might be done some time. Who knows?'

They had come to the top of the hill now, and began to approach the boundaries of the entomological reservations. Before them they could see the tiny hermitage that was the home of the old Extonian, and at a slight distance from it the substantial laboratories and dwelling-places of his assistants.

'Let's sit down and rest,' suggested Morgana, 'and talk about this. I do think the first thing to discuss is our position and what is to be done about it.'

'What do you mean?' asked Nicolette, as they squatted on a shady patch at the very edge of the hill whence all their world lay spread beneath them.

'I mean that it is time we women were no longer subjected to such abominable tyranny. Here we are, pushed into their beastly rigid castes and divided off into breeders and non-breeders to serve the race. I don't care about the race. But I care for experiment. When I was sixteen I wanted to experiment with everything, including my own body. No one tried to stop me, but of course I had to be immunized. Now I have exhausted that, and I should like to have a child. But they forestalled me. The most interesting experiment of all is denied me. And the same will happen to you.'

'But I don't want a child,' answered Nicolette smilingly.

'Not now. But you will. Sooner or later we all do. If you don't sooner, they won't let you later.'

'Well, that's got to be,' asserted Arcous. 'You can't have it both ways, and you can sublimate your maternal cravings.'

'For your benefit,' retorted Morgana angrily. 'Of course the arrangement suits your sex admirably.'

'And the majority of your own,' he replied provokingly. 'You won't get much encouragement if you begin trying that kind of reform.'

Morgana turned from him and appealed to Christopher. 'Don't you think,' she said, 'we should have an opportunity? Why not have it both ways?'

'I absolutely agree with you,' he said. 'I think it's disgraceful that intelligent people should be robbed of their free will in any way. But governments never did and never will make special laws for intelligent people.'

'Then why not make our own?' demanded Morgana. 'We're too amenable, too reasonable, altogether. We're simply being flattened down.'

'You see,' Christopher told her, 'public opinion has become so much a part of each individual's own opinion that we are becoming totally absorbed in the herd, so finely welded to it that we cannot detach ourselves. Every one of our herd instincts has been comfortably satisfied—at the expense of our individual strivings. To stand alone has always been difficult; to make a gesture of defiance, painful. And for us it is almost impossible, because there's no glamour left in it. All it would lead to would be treatment or a silent elimination. Where there's no shouting there are no martyrs.'

'Well, here's an interesting situation,' said Morgana bitterly. 'Five intelligent and young people, all for various reasons dissatisfied with existing conditions, and yet not one of them prepared to have a fling at them.'

'Not prepared is the only bit of your pessimism I agree with,' replied Christopher. 'But that's not final.'

'Well'—suddenly Morgana's eyes were brighter, for an idea had developed in her mind—'let's all say what we want and how far we are prepared to go to get it. You begin, Bruin.'

'Oh, why bother,' he grumbled. 'I've told you already.'

'It's the only reason why I bother with you, as you know,' she retorted. 'As for me, I want complete, complete freedom.' She looked lovely as she threw out her hands towards the valley before her.

Arcous appreciated the picture she made, but could not, as usual, forbear to taunt her.

'And you dare call yourself a scientist,' he scoffed.

'Certainly I do. Laws are merely formulae that we adopt to suit our own uses. The more efficiently we manage to state them, the more clearly we recognize their limitations. The laws to which man is subject apply to him as man, not as men. I can't put it in English, but I can in German. Substitute "Mensch" for man and you will get my meaning. The laws they are trying to bend us to are all framed for men and women. The only law I recognize is that which governs the behaviour of human beings.'

'God's?' suggested Christopher softly.

She looked at him for a second with wide open eyes.

'If you will,' she answered. 'It is almost impossible to express what I mean except mystically.'

'I'm all for the gods,' agreed Arcous. 'I know just what I stand for in this commonwealth. I'm only the foremost artist in it. I am just a pair of eyes, a pair of hands, and an æsthetic sense. So I don't feel revolted as you do. I do my thinking vicariously. But I do it through you rather than through Adrian Richmond. Where there is neither revolt, nor mysticism, nor pain, there can be no art. . . . I am with you.'

'I don't want to be pushed nor will I be held back,' declared Nicolette. 'I seem to have known my way once, but I have lost it. I shall never find it again if I am not left alone.'

'You must be left alone,' exclaimed Morgana, and the three young men seemed, as she spoke, suddenly to edge forward round the two of them. It came like that, flashingly, a leap from vagueness to certainty. They seemed to have pooled their separate defiances, and now Morgana's words had precipitated them into crystal clear resolution.

Nicolette must be left alone to find her way. Whichever alternative she should shortly be compelled to choose must not be, for her, the irrevocable one.

'Yes,' drawled Bruin. Something in his own line was to be done, and he was all awake now to devise the means. 'Are you prepared to be immunized?'

'If I am obliged to make a decision,' answered Nicolette slowly, 'yes.'

Arcous tried to keep the gladness out of his eyes.

'Can't anything be done about it?' Morgana's impatience made no impression on Bruin. He rolled on to his back, pulled a tuft of grass, and munched it slowly.

'Possibly,' he said at last, with his eyes on the sky. 'I have heard rumours. . . . I might be able to get you some stuff to push in first. . . . I should have to make a trip abroad for it, though.'

'I'd go,' volunteered Christopher.

'No use, my boy. Too technical for you, this job. Of course,' he said, turning to Nicolette and peering at her over his own large body, 'you'll be taking risks, you know. Either way. Do you realize that?'

'Of course,' she emphasized his words. 'But let us say we're collaborators. We shall all find out something we rather desperately want to know, shan't we? For me it seems the only way, and for you there doesn't seem to be another, does there?'

Her words and her glance were for Christopher, and he answered both as was expected of him.

'There does not,' he said quietly.

Arcous smiled and murmured: '*Vive l'anarchisme.*'

III

'If you want anything really reliable,' had said Bruin's friend, 'I advise you to go to Monailoff for it. I haven't time to make the stuff, and also, though I'm with you theoretically, I had rather it were not traced to me, if anything unusual is going to be done. You can have all the references I've got, but they don't amount to much. The last man to do anything with it was Schier, in 1942. But I don't think there's ever been an experiment on a woman. Magdalens don't turn Marys as a rule.'

It was some time since Brian had seen his friend Monailoff, and he had never met Bruce Wayland, whom he found with him when he got there. Bruce was rapidly acquiring world fame; not so much because of the things he had done as those he had caused his 'young men' to do. His own work was drawing him daily further from the laboratories, but he never lost touch with them. His imaginative qualities and his daring, tempered by practical knowledge, drew these young men to seek the advice he never withheld. They took their dreams and their ambitions in all their crudity to him and laid before him their most secret aspirations. All that to the orthodox would have appeared most ludicrous and fantastic, Bruce considered with the cool imperturbability he would have applied to the most conventional of problems. You could not shock him, for he had no mental and few physical prejudices. So the young men came unafraid, and departed comforted. Occasionally one of them, acting on his suggestions, accomplished a bit of brilliant work, that would never have been tackled without his advice. Then the rule-of-thumb men made unpleasant remarks, and the number of Bruce's youthful worshippers increased tenfold.

But if Bruce was a torch-bearer, Bruin was an explosive. In the ordinary way of work he was noted for an impeccable reliability, a man to be trusted with the most delicate and complicated jobs. Not very inventive, they said of him, but unrivalled in his own line. His ability, within certain definite limits, was taken for granted. No one, except Morgana and Arcous, had probed further nor attempted to find out just where his limits lay, and being a taciturn fellow with an obsession, he volunteered no information to those who did not ask for it. 'I'm only doing the opposite,' he had said reproachfully when, as a small boy, they had found him walking on his hands with his hat on his feet. And to do the opposite, in the laboratory, was his obsession. Whenever and wherever possible he reversed every process he carried out. Gradually the obsession led to a vision, which, like all visions, had in it something sublime and something ridiculous. He himself, having no personal ambition, mocked the absurdity and affected to despise the magnificence. But Morgana egged him on, and, caring intensely as he did for her respect, he played with bits of his vision occasionally, to give her pleasure.

The scientific commonwealth was founded on force, as it had to be for self-protection. Bruin was one of those violent pacifists for ever chafing under the restraint they impose on their own brutal tendencies. And as an outlet for these he began to criticise, to disparage, and finally to condemn the social order of his day, built, as it seemed to him, on an ignoble foundation. But only a trained psychologist, a trained chemist, or a trained physicist can combat with any chance of success such trained opponents. As previous wars had become increasingly problems of scientific invention and management, fought with weapons with which perhaps half a dozen men had supplied millions, victory inclined invariably to those nations who could supply the men of finest scientific skill. It was a question of finding counter-weapons more certainly than new ones; as he had said to Arcous, 'For every one of theirs one of ours.' And so, in secret and purely for fun, he studied this matter of providing them.

In his case it was a harmless hobby, hardly likely ever to become a dangerous pursuit, for in spite of Morgana's passion for intrigue and lust for power, Brian did not take it very seriously. He knew that such a task as his could never be carried out on a scale large enough to loom menacingly before the Leaders; and apart from technical difficulties that were insurmountable, the vigilance of the Patrol was as efficient as became so proud a body.

But one could do little things. Personal liberty, within the defined limits, was considerable, and was apportioned largely according to the intellectual merits of the person concerned. There were loopholes, and particularly in regard to precedents, for the unusual will always remain the unexpected.

Brian was willing to be of assistance to Nicolette because he had a sympathy for Morgana's point of view, and what he might not have abetted in her case, he would in that of her friend. He considered Nicolette, as they all did except possibly Arcous, destined ultimately for motherhood. She appeared to him as the exception among women, in whose case the usual precautions might well be waived. And the experiment in itself appealed to him irresistibly. Hers might be a test case of considerable interest, and should, therefore, be proven. He knew that the authorities would look upon this, as on all exceptional behaviour that involved general issues, with disfavour; nevertheless, having no intention of contributing personally to any future experiment in parenthood she might make, he considered his share of providing her with a means to evade immunization justified on objective grounds. And Brian too was brave and admired courage.

The conversation with Monailoff was strictly technical.

'I can let you have the stuff in about a month,' he said, 'if that will do.'

'Excellently. She still has two at her disposal.'

'Do you think she will carry the thing through?'

'One cannot tell, but it is extremely likely. It is a matter in which the brother will have considerable influence.'

'How So?'

'He is a mystic with a strong inclination towards martyrdom. He cannot find a medium himself, so he will probably urge her towards the complete self expression that is denied him.'

'What is he likely to do if her irregularity should be discovered?'

'Take the entire responsibility on himself and fight the authorities on her behalf. It would delight him.'

'Have they any adherents?'

'Not at present. They have no programme, you see.'

'I do. Who can have, nowadays? I think for that very reason our civilization is marching rapidly towards its end. Remember the words of that earlier mystic: "Earthly excellence can come in no way but one, and the ending of passion and strife is the beginning of decay."'

Bruce entered at that moment, eruptively, in his usual way, and having heard only the quotation immediately retorted: 'If conflict really is an integral part of nature, surely we shall see conflict in man and between men develop in new directions as we rise in the anthropological scale.'

'It is to be eagerly awaited, if you are optimistic enough to think so,' answered the other.

'Certainly there seems small chance of such educating conflicts at present. That is why,' he turned to Brian, 'I will do what I can for your friend. May I tell Wayland what you want? He is always suggestive.'

'Certainly,' answered Brian, 'if you think the matter sufficiently important. It may not interest him.'

'Everything interests him,' said Monailoff with a smile. 'Particularly biology. He wants,' he explained to Bruce, 'some anti-immunizing substance, that will combine with Sp.902 before it reaches the female tissues. I think I can make it for him.'

'That *is* interesting,' boomed Bruce emphatically, 'and just the sort of thing I should have expected him to come for. I think your notion is quite sound, but I should be inclined to—incidentally,' he turned and smiled on Brian rather mischievously, 'may one ask whether you propose to carry out a practical test?'

'Decidedly,' replied Brian, pleased with Bruce's instantaneous appreciation of the situation. 'But my share in it will be confined to this mission, and to injecting the stuff when I've got it. Whether the experiment will be carried through *in toto* I cannot predict. That does not rest with me.'

'Oh, but it must be,' said Bruce, to whom the audacity of it appealed. 'I am willing to volunteer myself to oblige the admirable young woman. The point is, of course, whether one should ask permission first, or go ahead and wait for trouble afterwards.'

'Why should there be trouble?' asked Monailoff. 'It will a be a valuable experiment.'

'Scientifically, but hardly socially,' retorted Bruce.

'You do not quite understand race psychology in these matters. Especially of the woman. If you invent a biological religion, as we had to do for them, and call it vocational motherhood, heretics will be as surely attacked by the female inquisition as Protestants were by the Catholic one. Remember that women, broadly speaking, are always a century behind men in mental development. This will lead to quite an interesting situation.'

'If it leads to anything,' said Brian.

'Oh, it must. It would be a pity to be inconclusive in such an excellent test case. Lots of us think things want stirring up. This will provide us with a useful ladle. But your young woman must have considerable pluck if she is going through with it. May one know more about her?'

'I hardly think it necessary, at present,' answered Brian, as cautious as the beast whose name Arcous had bestowed on him in fun. 'Later perhaps, if anything comes of it.'

'Well, you can depend absolutely on me if you want assistance in any way. I shall be in Nucleus in three months' time, and will call on you to hear how matters have progressed. In the meantime,' he added with a grin, 'I'll look round for a suitable young man to assist in the next step, should one be required. Remember me to Morgana.'

IV

Once the decision was irrevocably taken, all the torturing doubts were, of course, Christopher's. This method of defiance was, after all, a new proposition. It was by no means entirely their own. Neither of them knew enough about biological technique to have devised it themselves. It had been evolved by the council of five. Arcous, the sly catalyst, had pushed them to a certain point, and there they had met Morgana, who had added her feminine touch to a revolt that, as it had lain in themselves, was hardly at all sexual in principle; and with her was Brian, the ready instrument to help carry out the joint purpose.

Nicolette was delighted and almost surprised at her luck. Things had at last been straightened out. She had stood so indecisively at the parting of the ways, between motherhood, for which something deep within her still craved in rebellious, crooked, yet clamorous fashion, and that other life of the mind and the senses in which Arcous would loom as large as Art, and from which she seemed to shrink almost as keenly as she was drawn to it. The picture of the wider implications of what she was about to do hardly touched her imagination. She felt that perhaps it might be symbolic, but that side of it seemed more a matter for Christopher to deal with. All she realized vividly was that she would be given a respite, that the irrevocable decision would be postponed, and she expected fervently that within a short time she would be shown clearly which path to choose. Nor would it, so, be too late to turn back. Although the word had no place in her vocabulary, Nicolette hoped (how she hoped) for some one to claim her at last.

Christopher looked further and with a greater dread. He was honest enough and brave enough to realize that once the lawless step taken, he would be tempted to make a tool of Nicolette, to use her as his weapon. Never for a moment did he doubt that her mating would be long delayed; he foresaw the consequences, and what they would mean to him as well as to her.

'Are you quite sure you want to chance it?' he asked her more than once, and always she replied: 'Wouldn't you?'

'That's just it. I feel it's up to me to do something, and not to let you do it for me.'

'But I'm not committing myself. That's just the beauty of it. I'm only taking a precaution in case I should wish to later.'

'Oh, it's an opportunity you'll never be able to resist. It's the sort of thing I should be doing myself; striking a hefty blow for individualism. And all I can do is to egg you on.'

'But the whole experiment may fail,' protested Nicolette, though she did not herself believe this. 'Even if it does not, I don't see what equivalent thing a man possibly could do. Anyway,' and suddenly she went and laid her arms about him, and pulled his head down to her own, 'whatever is done we do together, my dear. The deed might be mine, but the will to it, like all my resolutions, comes from you. There is no point in attempting to separate our thoughts and actions. They are inextricably united.'

Then Christopher almost wished she would do nothing, after all. For if she did, it would be clear evidence that she could love another as she loved him, a possibility he could hardly contemplate with equanimity.

It was not even necessary for him to advise on Nicolette's future employment. The temporary arrangement with Weil had proved very satisfactory. In addition she could make herself socially useful in a score of ways, for she had a mind for detail as well as considerable patience.

But particularly Nicolette wanted to enjoy herself. She felt conscious of a change in her mind and body during the past months. The 'growing pains' seemed to have ceased; she felt happily sensual, healthily vigorous. Her perception seemed to have become sharpened; her pleasure in all things was rich and keen, there was now a shining about her, a lustre, which even the dullest among her companions noticed, and which entranced the artist in Arcous to the point of intoxication. This was particularly remarkable when she was with Morgana, whose vitality was mainly nervous, whereas Nicolette's was a spontaneous sparkling up of youth towards beckoning experience.

Notice of her decision had been formally sent in to the council. Her secession, since she had definitely chosen her future way, was now merely a matter of routine. Whatever impression it may have created in the minds of those women who had previously endeavoured to persuade her otherwise, was not now voiced, since discussion of an accomplished fact would have been futile.

Until after her immunization, however, she would still be subject to tutelage. So it was that she remained in the little room that had housed her more or less continually since childhood. In response to Morgana's invitation, she frequently visited her and Brian in the laboratory where they worked together.

There, one afternoon, she bent over a microscope, keeping her eyes on the slides they slipped in for her to look at, while Brian spoke softly, his head close to hers.

'I have got the stuff,' he said. 'It has just reached me. Do you think you can push it in yourself?'

'Oh yes,' she answered, 'quite comfortably.'

'Well, do it intra-muscularly,' he advised. 'I think that will be the most efficient way.'

'I'll bring it along,' added Morgana, 'so that you can do it just a few hours before. It will be wise to wait as long as you can.'

'I want to warn you, though,' added Brian, 'that there's a certain risk attached. What I propose to do is to jam your immunizing mechanism pretty thoroughly. The effect may last for a few weeks, and during that time, if you get an infection of any kind, the consequences may be unpleasant.'

'I'll chance it,' Nicolette answered calmly.

'Right-o. The stuff has been used before on rabbits and guinea-pigs and a few monkeys, but never on a human being. So I'd be glad if you'd let me know whatever you feel in consequence, though there'll probably be nothing exciting. If you feel especially uncomfortable, let one of us know.'

'I will. What a pity you cannot publish a paper on it.'

'Oh, there's nothing in this part. The sequel—that remains to be seen.'

'I doubt whether I shall worry much about it yet,' Nicolette answered with a smile. 'I shall be so busy in the next few months.'

Brian glanced at Morgana, but neither of them spoke. It seemed so obvious that a sequel was inevitable. As physiologists, they disliked inconclusive experiments.

V

Morgana had packed it all up in a neat little case: alcohol and iodine for sterilization, hypodermic syringe, and a small glass-stoppered phial containing the precious fluid.

The look of the utensils pleased Nicolette. There was always something so trim, so clear-cut, about this kind of apparatus. These people who worked in labs surely must take pleasure in the mere handling of their instruments. It was not her line, but even she could respond to their stimulation. All tools were more or less the same, of course, in this way. Whatever art or craft they might serve, always they seemed honest and willing agents to carry out the purpose of the master-mind. Slowly and carefully she bared her thigh, applied the iodine, dipped the needle in alcohol, and then at the pressure of her finger watched the pale fluid jump from bottle to hypodermic. Now she tossed a curl off her forehead, bit her lower lip in the intensity of her concentration, and with a firm gesture stabbed her smooth tinted flesh. She sighed a deep sigh of relief when it was all over, but she did not notice it. She had been bent on the job.

VI

Christopher asked nothing when they met in the hall. He was waiting by the letter-rack, where a blue slip lay in her pigeon-hole. Nicolette tore it open, glanced at a date, and handed it to him.

'To-morrow morning,' she said laconically.

He raised his eyebrows; she smiled at him quite gleefully, but he did not return the smile.

She tucked her arm through his, and felt that he was trembling.

'Let's fly,' said Nicolette.

VII

Once, in the dim days of the late nineteenth century, a noble ancestress of Nicolette's had run away from home and gone on the stage. She had not previously announced her decision, but in any case, the blow to her parents would have been unmitigated. She did not gain much theatrical success, but, having met several duchesses, she could look and speak like one. A young peer, to whom this achievement seemed, from the stalls, more remarkable than it was, married her on the strength of it. Nevertheless, her family were irreconcilable. If her parents could have frustrated her desertion by shutting her up in a convent, they would at least have had the pleasures of revenge. Antonia suffered somewhat as they had suffered when at last the impossible was about to become fact in Nicolette's case.

Fidelity to custom embitters most women's lives from time to time, but never more keenly than when their daughters defy it. Customs may change, but fidelity is a clinging habit. All the unpleasant emotions which had assailed poor Lady Geynes when Marcia revealed herself were reproduced in the unfortunate Antonia when Nicolette, shortly before attending the council, proclaimed her intentions. It seemed so 'unnatural,' and the limit of the most understanding creature's sympathy is usually reached at the 'unnatural.' Antonia's disappointment was, like all of its kind, more social than personal. The caste instinct was powerful within her, and she resented far more the blow to her ambitions than the frustration of any grandmotherly yearnings. As was to be expected, she sought reasons for her daughter's behaviour in every direction but the essential one, and her resentment finally crystallized in antagonism towards Emmeline, to whose sinister neuter influence she attributed her daughter's decision. Dominated now by her repressions, it did not occur to her to hold Christopher responsible.

Antonia's mistake was fortunate for Nicolette. For incontinently she had dashed with her tale of woe to St. John, compelling him, for one whole quarter of an hour, to desist from his great problems in order to concentrate on this small one. But St. John's respect for Emmeline was firm. It was based on a just appreciation of her splendid qualities, revealed during years of reciprocal labour in the cause of humanity.

'I will certainly see Nicolette if you wish,' he told Antonia, 'if she has anything to say to me in the matter.' Rationalization of the paternal instinct was neither the fashion of his day nor of his temperament. The question of Nicolette's future lay entirely outside his province; it had no more concern for him than would have had the similar problem of any girl in her position.

She saw him one day, as she was strolling alone along a shady avenue that led from Nucleus to the hills. St. John had always been a prodigious walker, and his twenty kilometres a day had become a firm habit. He was returning now to tackle the evening's work, which would consist of several intimate conferences, a semi-public debate, and he knew not how many hours of subsequent dictation. She resolved not to approach him, for she knew that on these walks he worked out and reviewed decisions to be carried out later on. It was, moreover, a matter of etiquette not to accost any one out-of-doors without encouragement. She turned, therefore, in the same direction, leaving him to overtake her and to speak if he wished.

'Why, yes, of course it is—Nicolette.' He smiled down at her with his usual rather vague cordiality. She fell into step with him then. 'I seem to remember,' he continued, 'that we were to have had an interview. Why not now?'

'Certainly,' she answered, smiling back, 'but what about?

'Don't ask me! Was I not to have been consulted about your future career, or something?'

'Possibly, but not by me.'

'Excellent. You obviously are my daughter. Then I take it you have decided all about it?'

'Momentarily, yes.'

'That is very satisfactory. Go step by step. I am sorry we do not meet more often. But keep your sense of perspective. Nothing is more absurd than the human tool which imagines itself the master. Really fine tools are rare, we know, but most sort of instruments can be turned out pretty easily. The idea is the hand that wields them, but the force behind it is as inaccessible to our understanding as the mind of a sculptor would be to a chisel. There is no direct contact. Ideas, abstractions, are all we can know; therefore they are all we need bother about. Our job is to be instrumental in turning them into action. But don't imagine for one moment that individually you are more than an instrument. Oh, the trouble I have in persuading some of my colleagues that they are not the commanders of the universe.' He sighed comically. 'And even more, that it is not their business to ask who or what is. What does it matter, so long as there is something to be done.'

'But is there?'

'What an admirable young woman you are! You feel like that too, then, do you? Well, on the whole there probably is; at any rate, there is a certain amount of evidence of a scheme of sorts going on. But don't imagine for a moment that you can either assist it or thwart it to any considerable extent.'

'But some people are not content with that; they want to know more,' replied Nicolette, thinking as usual of Christopher.

'Well, tell them from me they won't,' he answered kindly, understanding her hidden allusion. 'Though the curiosity is an admirable thing in itself, as a basis for action later. You know the majority of people unfortunately become stabilized at an early age. They are a nuisance, and in extreme cases a danger. A certain minority, on the other side, are victims of a permanent instability that may become equally troublesome, though they are far easier to deal with. The people we want nowadays are increasingly those who will remember the word that should be the hall-mark of all government, all education, all human thought, in fact; the word Provisional. With that constantly in view, you can settle down to anything comfortably and usefully.'

'Have you been studying Publicity?'

'Yes; I've been having a look round. I'm increasingly dissatisfied. Just at present I can discern a growing hardening everywhere, and a proportionate move towards stabilization. It won't do. It is spreading; creeps right to my very door. I have to walk like mad to get away from it occasionally; to let ideas shake me up and keep me flexible. And then back again to the daily task of shaking up others. Well, here we are. I've been delighted to meet you. Whatever decision you take, be certain it's a satisfactory one. Remember me to your brother.'

As he ran up the steps of the Council Building he thought: 'Curious, one's children. Sometimes they're so nice.'

And then forgot all about them.

11 USNESS

Schau ich nicht Aug' in Auge dir,
Und drängt nicht alles
Nach Haupt und Herzen dir,
Und webt im ewigen Geheimniss
Unsichtbar sichtbar neben dir?
Erfüll' davon dein Herz, So gross es ist,
Und wenn du ganz in dem Gefühle selig bist,
Nenn' es dann, wie du willst.

—Goethe, *Faust*

I

Arcous laid down his brush and flung himself on the floor. He rolled over on to his stomach and stayed quite still, head pillowed on arms, every muscle relaxed. Without speaking, Nicolette dropped the pose and slipped on her gown, for it was cold in the big bare studio. She was slightly stiff and stamped her feet as she walked the length of the room and back, before wriggling into a comfortable position on the divan that faced the easel.

There was a silence, during which the trickling of the rain outside sounded very loud. At last Arcous spoke.

'No more use to-day.'

'Well, I think we've done about as much as you could expect.'

'Nicolette, I apologize. I should not have kept you so long. But you know how it is—one forgets until one absolutely drops with fatigue. It's so glorious working like that, in a fury of concentration.'

'I suppose it is. I wish I knew what it is like.'

'Don't you? Not a little?' He came and sat beside her then, and his eyes as they scanned her held more than artistic appreciation.

'No, not a little. I day-dream all the time I am posing,' she answered. 'I tell myself stories. I don't feel bored, but I am not participating.'

'But it's a masterpiece,' he pleaded, gazing now at the almost finished picture. 'Yours as much as mine. No one has ever inspired me to work as you do. Just look at that glorious creature there. That's you.'

'No, Arcous, it's more than me. It's a symbol. If it were a portrait it could not be so wonderful. To make a work of genius you must be in touch with something much more universal than just one single person. The goddesses in themselves represent so much. Diana, Minerva, and Venus. How real they must be to you.'

'And not to you?'

'Oh, yes, they are. She is me, in a sense, your girl, letting go of Diana's lovely cool hand, and turning her back on Minerva's wisdom. I'm not sure about Venus, though.'

'I am,' he answered promptly. 'Especially about her averted smile, and the eagerness of the girl's gesture.'

'Yes, that smile is perfect. And the indifferent way she averts her head, looking far away through the arches. What inspired you to draw her like that?'

'The same reason that made me call it "Anticipation."' She does not anticipate—she knows; but if the girl could read her expression and realize how sure she is, it might frighten her. To get that poise, that tiptoe stretching out, I had to hide Venus's face from her. She might have drawn back to Minerva after all, if she had seen it.'

'Perhaps she will, even now.'

'Ah. So you do understand her feelings a little?'

'Possibly,' Nicolette admitted reluctantly, realizing that he had again allowed her to set a trap for herself.

'Well, I assure you she won't withdraw. Look at the beautiful young man Venus is beckoning to. I don't see why the girl should be reluctant.'

'I like her reflection in the long mirror behind Venus.'

'Yes, that's a clever touch,' he admitted with his usual frank conceit. 'It reveals just that perfection of the girl's face and form of which she herself is unconscious. Over her own person innocence seems to throw a misty veil, so that it does not fully reveal its beauty until seen in the mirror of Venus.'

'I love allegory, don't you?'

'As a means, but not an end in itself. The great point about "Anticipation" is that it conforms to all the rules of true pictorial art as laid down by Lessing in his "Laokoön" essay. You have here the supreme moment before the climax. On either side of the outreaching girl, but behind her, you have Diana and Minerva, the goddesses who have guided her hitherto, but not sufficed her. Having thrown off the veils of childhood and the reins of tutelage, she turns towards the third—the most mysterious, the so far unknown, who does not even beckon her. Venus always waits.'

'Yes, she certainly seems inevitable. And the young man?'

'Do you like him?'

'He rather surprises me.'

'Why?'

'Well, he's not quite the sort of young man I should have expected you to choose.'

'What did you expect—a self-portrait?'

He looked at her very closely, and as usual, when he did that, she felt herself blush. She returned his glance, and there was a suggestion of pleading, a humbleness in Nicolette's eyes, that made her appear younger than ever. It was a different expression from the frank, confident look her friends were recently used to find there. Before she could speak, he continued:

'Do not worry. I know quite well it cannot be. You have had a curious effect on me, Nicolette. You can trust me —now.'

He rose abruptly and began to walk up and down before her as he talked, speaking more easily from a height and a distance.

'I can see quite clearly that it is impossible. Now you may know that I endeavoured by every means to make it otherwise. I wanted your body, not only for my art, but for my senses. Why should I go on, though? I detest logic. And then you would not be mine, in that way, at all. You have already given me all you ever will. In that respect no one else will have you. But there is in you such an infinite capacity for giving that the man who cannot claim all must prefer nothing. There are women like that, I know, though they are rare enough. I have never before met one, but I know. Women from whom the one they choose need ask nothing, because it would be impossible for them to withhold anything. I never ask superfluous questions. And on the whole I am glad to recognize that this cannot be. You are too adorable to be loved less than completely, and I too unyielding to make such surrender. Beware of Christopher, though.'

Nicolette had been contemplating him for the first time with real affection. She was genuinely grateful to him for his understanding, and yet now it had been said at last between them she lost completely that inexplicable interest she had always felt in him so long as she had only guessed his thoughts. The mention of Christopher, however, galvanized her attention.

'What do you mean?' she asked, and sat up amongst the cushions.

'Christopher's doomed. We all know it.'

'Who?'

'Well, Bruin and I. There's no chance for him. He's lived three or four hundred years too late. Now all his ambitions are centred on you. He thinks your lover will be his friend, will see your future relationship in his way, as a gesture. He will find him his supreme enemy.'

'If you think I shall ever desert Christopher you make a mistake,' she announced defiantly.

'This won't lie in your power,' he explained. 'But wait. It's futile to discuss it. Like trying to have a friendly chat with Iphigenia about Orestes. Let's get to work again if you're not tired.'

Nicolette rose and threw off her gown. She did not reply. 'Where there's honey look out for the sting,' she thought. But she did not succeed with her pose this time, and went away, leaving Arcous to add a little more gold to the mirror of Venus.

II

They were all pleased to see Bruce in Nucleus. Naturally enough there were plenty of people on whom his personality jarred, for his tremendous physical and mental vigor were apt to exhaust companions of minor calibre. He had allowed himself somewhat unwillingly to be roped in and harnessed to a comparatively dull service. But once there, he got unlimited fun out of the opportunities for experiment which offered themselves, and he neglected none on the ground that it might prove embarrassing to his older colleagues. The stabilization of which St. John had complained to Nicolette was symptomatic of conditions throughout the commonwealth; but where Bruce was peace did not abide very long.

He had enough to do to keep him busy all day and all evening during the weeks he planned to stay in Nucleus, but the change of environment brought with it a change in the colouring of his mind. He could, with a little method, find time for everything, even if he commenced by doing nothing; all he appeared to want to do, as soon as he arrived, was to look up his friends. He knew quite well that his chief motive for the journey was the desire to meet Nicolette again. He had thought of her more and more frequently as time went on, but had never called her up. He had been traveling about so much that for several months he had not even seen Anna, who was busily engaged in preparing for the birth of her child. When Bruce was absorbed in his occupation he had a knack of letting other intentions rest, with no thought of the possible consequences of inertia.

He was staying in the guest-house of the college of applied psychology, where he had promised to give some lectures during his visit. He had not been there more than two hours, before he managed to evade the various people who had hospitably placed themselves at his disposal, and went in search of Nicolette, whom he naturally expected to find at her old address. The head clerk at the hall desk informed him briefly that she had changed her dwelling. 'But you can find her certainly at this time at the Weil studio,' she added, and gave him instructions how to reach it.

It was not until Bruce was well on his way there that he chanced to wonder why he should be seeking Nicolette in this place. He tried to remember whether she had told him her plans for the future when she had been in Centrosome, but he could not recollect having heard them. They had been together several times, but there had been so much to do and see that they had hardly discussed personal affairs at all. If he had asked, she would certainly have told him. And then he recalled that their conversation, when not concerned with the things and people around them, had been mainly of Christopher. 'She is probably with him,' he thought, 'but—I wonder what she is doing and where she is living.' For he could guess that the change of address had more than superficial significance.

It was to Arcous's studio on the top floor that he was directed on arrival. Josef Weil was away, so the mistake of his informant was a natural one.

More and more puzzled, Bruce entered after a masculine voice had called out a curt 'Come,' in reply to his knock at the door. Arcous's back was towards him, for he was bent over "Anticipation," set on its easel in the middle of the big, bare apartment. Bruce advanced a few paces and then stopped, his glance attracted by the picture. He stood very still, with his eyes fixed on the easily recognizable central figure. Arcous turned to select another brush and saw the visitor.

'I beg your pardon,' he said immediately, as he came towards him. 'I thought it was one of my pupils. What can I do for you?'

'I must beg yours,' replied Bruce, gazing at him with frank curiosity. 'I am looking for Nicolette Richmond, but they must have directed me wrongly.'

'Oh no, she is in the building, but in my father's room; she's his assistant. They probably thought she was sitting to me, but the picture is practically finished. Let me take you down to her.'

'Thank you. I am Bruce Wayland. I've just come over from Centrosome, I had no idea she was here.'

'Oh, so that's who you are,' said Arcous with one of his rare and charming smiles. 'Come this way. She has been here for several months now.'

'And you,' asked Bruce, as they entered the elevator, 'are the famous painter, surely?'

'We both are,' replied Arcous, pleased at the tribute, 'that is, my father and I both work here. But he is away just now.'

'Is Nicolette one of your pupils, then?'

'Oh no. She has been sitting to me and she has helped my father with his plans for Reconstruction. But she can explain herself. Here we are at last.'

He opened the door of a long narrow room, crowded with shelves, books, drawings, small-scale architectural models, costumes, armour, and figures. 'A visitor for you, Nicolette,' he called out, and slammed the door behind him.

Bruce did not at first see Nicolette. 'Come along here and help me down,' she sang out, and then he spied her, perched right at the top of a librarian's ladder between the end wall and the window. He crossed the room and stood below it, and gazed up to where she clung, struggling with an armload of heavy old books.

'Why—it's Bruce!' she exclaimed. Involuntarily, surprise loosened her hold; two of the fat tomes came crashing down, missing his head by a few inches. 'Oh, I am sorry—look out, I'm coming myself.'

He caught her off the ladder when she was eight steps from the ground, and swung her in a wide arc on to her feet.

'Yes, I've found you at last,' he answered as he took the remaining volumes from her arms, 'and I'm all agog to know what mischief you're up to.'

'A perfectly respectable, if not an eminent job,' she said demurely. 'Sit down and talk. I thought it was Christopher. I'm expecting him almost at once. How lovely it is to see you again.'

'And to see you. Even here. But what are you doing?' he insisted.

'Getting the next Reconstruction plans ready for Nucleus.'

'And the young man upstairs?'

'Oh, Arcous? How did you meet him? I suppose they thought I was sitting and took you up there? How stupid of them. Did you see the picture?'

'Only long enough to recognize your portrait.'

'Ah. Well, about three months ago I decided I would not become a mother. So I had to take the usual alternative. I had been helping old Weil for some time, and liked it.'

'But what really happened?'

'Nothing did. That's the point. When I got back to Nucleus, after visiting your people, I was going to be mated. But it didn't come off.'

'What did Christopher have to do with it?'

'Cute little feller!' She smiled mischievously at him. 'Something, no doubt, but not so much as you probably think. You don't seem very pleased.'

'I don't know whether I am or not. It's such a tremendous surprise. I'll have to hear more about it.'

'All right, you shall later on. How's Anna?'

'Flourishing. Baby's due some time soon, I believe, but I haven't seen her since she went to the Garden.'

'A boy, of course?'

'Rather.'

'What fun.'

'Tell me, Nicolette, what does Antonia say to this step you've taken. Was she surprised?'

'You bet she was. So was I, at first. But Bruce, I don't think you'll mind so much when you know all about it. And'—she looked at him curiously for a moment, and then withdrew her eyes as she added, 'And why should you, anyway? I don't quite understand.'

'It's entirely due to my stupidity, Nicolette. Somehow I imagined I had made it clear when you came over. I was only waiting till you were old enough to talk about it. In the meantime I let things be. I never imagined that you would do anything unusual. You seemed so clearly destined for motherhood. I'm a short-sighted fool, I suppose, but I never think much about anything except my job. Do forgive me.'

He got up, for like St. John he could never stay long in a chair, and tried to walk about the encumbered workroom. There was not enough space for his long strides, however, and he sat down again, uncomfortably.

'I don't think either of us was unjustifiably stupid,' said Nicolette softly and slowly. 'I made a mistake too. I'm just this minute realizing it. I couldn't have had any one else after I'd met you, but it did not occur to me that it was you I wanted. Consciously, I was only occupied with Christopher. After all, it may be unusual, but it is not so surprising, when you remember that we both think more about things than people, and about other people rather than ourselves.'

'Perhaps that may be the reason. At any rate, I don't suppose I shall think much about anything but you in the next few weeks. You have grown beautiful, my dear!'

He rose from his chair brusquely, and knocked it over as he did so. But neither of them bothered about it. Nicolette's eyes met his unflinchingly, and she smiled as he put his arms around her, and between each kiss. A picture flashed into Bruce's mind as he pressed her to him—of a young man from Nucleus who wanted some stuff that would combine with Sp. 902, and he seemed to hear an echo of his own voice saying, 'You can depend on me absolutely if you want assistance in any way.'

Then Christopher came in.

III

Bruce passed a restless night. He was hot with desire for Nicolette. Mouth, eyes, arms, the whole of his body, even the skin and the hair, desired the final intimate contact and union with this one creature. Lazily and gently, at their former meetings, something of the kind had stirred in him. But the emotion at that time had been tempered by brotherly, almost fatherly restraint. The small girl whom he had comforted and jollied with and chaperoned, the little mother of the future, had been an object of playful veneration. Now the moment of her unfolding had come, and her beauty, sheathed no longer, had aroused his desire. What he now felt was no longer an emotion of half-lights and controlled temper, but the full-blooded longing of the male who has been called and has answered.

There was more to the matter, however, than this sensual response, as he realized when he lay on his bed thinking it over. He had never tolerated the least thwarting of his ambitions; his intelligence had not only force but cunning and craft at its command; the straight way to his objective had always seemed too easy. He was never fully roused unless there was undermining and overcoming and circumventing to be done. . . .

Here, all was obviously far from simple. He had come to claim a mate, and was to find, perhaps, only a temporary liaison. There was something grotesque about the whole situation, which had been apparent to him from the moment he had gone to seek her in the Weil studios. Nicolette's childish explanation, her hints at a secret in the background, more explicit in her manner than in her words, revealed quite plainly the existence of a problem still to be encountered by him. He could not, just then, achieve a conscious and definite notion of the plan of it; only one clue, but that the essential one, was at present lacking—he determined to discover it forthwith. His thoughts naturally drove straight at Christopher in this connection. Their conversation had been a brief and trivial one, but again Bruce had used his eyes, finely and expertly trained as they were, to more effect than his ears. This boy was curiously, dominantly abnormal. That the cause of his condition was a sexual abnormality was plain; its sources, however, were still obscure. One would have to know more of his history.

Bruce endeavoured to recall what Nicolette had told him of Christopher long ago. He was different from other people, she had always insisted; talented, yet showing little predilection for one form or another of activity; beautiful, yet despising personal conquests; proud and reserved, yet with her unusually intimate and communicative; antagonistic to his brother Adrian; disdainful of his mother, but almost as devoted to the determined Emmeline as to herself. What else?

Nicolette had been reserved and vague on this point, but Bruce now remembered some allusions to her brother's mysticism. This might be worth investigating. If the hypothesis Bruce was already beginning to form was appreciably correct and could be verified, the problem of Christopher would soon be solved. But he wanted more information, and decided that he would make inquiries immediately.

Admitting for the moment no more than that all was not usual with Christopher, he began to link up that obvious fact with Nicolette's behaviour towards him. It was clearly maternal in character. Her every gesture towards him was solicitous, amusingly and prettily hen-like. There seemed a constant vigilance at the back of her glances at him. Undoubtedly he had transferred to her in some way a sense of responsibility.

Now when Bruce had put it to her, Nicolette had instantly admitted her need of himself. This moved him to gasp a little with pride and joy as he remembered how willingly she had come to his arms, how readily she had confessed her inability to mate with another, how tenderly she had tried to exonerate him from self-reproach for his tardy coming for her. But even so, if this unfulfilled desire had appeared in her consciousness masked as a refusal of maternal duties, other influences had been responsible for her further behaviour, for the definite step of immunization, for her plunge into an atmosphere obviously alien to her personality, for the intimacy of Arcous Weil with both of them. Certainly Christopher was closely concerned with all this, and his intentions had for some time been gaining an ascendant influence on her actions.

Next day he went to call on Antonia, and on the way happily met Adrian Richmond, bound in the same direction. Adrian, with advancing maturity, was beginning to grow out of his hitherto humourless suspiciousness. Responsibility during many years had armed him with a sense of proportion. He would take himself a shade too seriously until the end of his days, but almost continual contact with St. John's mellow and philosophical mind had had its softening effect on his own. The lack of sufficient intellectual appreciation of his father's genius was made up for by unremitting loyalty.

'Delighted to see you,' he said cordially as Bruce overtook and hailed him. 'I was expecting you to look me up in the course of your affairs.'

'I should have done so to-morrow,' Bruce replied. 'Just now I am "functioning socially." Going to call on your mother.'

'Excellent. So am I. Have you seen—'

'Nicolette, yes,' Bruce interrupted. 'I intend to see her fairly frequently while I am here.'

'Oh, Nicolette! I was going to say, St. John. And . . . how did you find Nicolette?'

'Marvelously beautiful,' he answered simply. 'Don't you?'

'Oh!' murmured Adrian again, and glanced quickly at Bruce. 'I suppose you knew about her decision?'

'I did not. I was completely surprised. I am anxious to know all about it. Perhaps you can give me some information. I had unfortunately lost touch with her since she was over. You know I am rather a one-thing-at-a-time man. I was immensely attracted by her, but it never occurred to me that I had waited longer than I should have done. It looks as if I shall repent it.'

As Bruce had intended, Adrian was flattered by these abrupt and unexpected confidences. Bruce's intimacy with other members of the family had not extended to Adrian. But they had known each other, had been colleagues on several occasions. And so he knew that shock tactics were those to which he invariably responded most readily.

'Yes,' said Adrian. 'It is a pity. My mother was upset, as you can imagine. But, of course, steps should have been taken long ago to secure Nicolette against the influence of my younger brother, as I told St. John. He's a neurotic, and I have not the slightest doubt that he has been responsible for a lot. Filled her head with some sorry nonsense, and there you are.'

'I wonder if it is as simple as that,' suggested Bruce.

'Oh, my mother will not corroborate me. She puts it down to Emmeline. As you know, there is always a certain latent antagonism between the mothers and other women. Antonia is irrevocably biassed where Christopher is concerned. I'm not denying that he may become, as she believes, an effective artist. But neither am I convinced that his temperament, to use the colloquialism, is artistic. I would rather suggest a slight perversity. He is so extraordinarily hostile to our community and its laws. That is not usual with our artists, who are among the most contented types. Nearly all of them are influenced by the spirit of Reconstruction, but they are not drawn to reactionary ideas for sheer—well, cussedness.'

'But then——'

'Oh, I know what you are going to say. Only, as yet Christopher has not given us sufficient indications to warrant an examination. I think myself, though, that he soon will, and I may have some inquires made. In any case, whatever you can do to withdraw my sister's interest from him a little, will be beneficial to her.' And then Adrian, looking straight into Bruce's eyes, gave one of the secret signs current among those who had at one time or another been connected with the Patrol.

The matter would go no further for the present. The next move was up to Christopher.

IV

It was difficult for Nicolette to refrain from 'showing off' Bruce to her friends. It was not so much the fact that he was already well known, and likely to be famous in due course, that prompted her. Partly her pride was the usual pride of the healthy young female in her mate, but chiefly it was actuated by a deep and powerful respect for the superiority of his mind. For he was not the sort of person one ever had to make allowances for, or who needed sympathy, tolerance, understanding. His intelligence was a perfected instrument, as integral a part of him as his physical vitality; he was almost incapable of imagining the difficulties that faced those less well endowed than himself.

Since Nicolette had moved to the artists' dwellings, she had a large room for her own needs. On the evening of the second day of Bruce's visit, Christopher, Brian, and Morgana came there to meet him, and one or two others came for a short time as well. The conversation, as Nicolette told him later, reminded her of a chess tournament, at which a champion takes on all the other players simultaneously. 'Now let me see,' she teased him, 'if I can remember the subjects you tackled them on. You began with Christopher on music. Then Ewen, your young physicist friend, got on to sound. We all joined in a bit, to his annoyance, and there were some jokes about Farnell's talking machines. After that we had more on communication, and before we could stop you, you were on to the use of crystalline liquids in television. Then—I don't remember how, you started something about the racial boundaries controversy—oh yes, that was Morley's fault, that red-haired patrolman; and after that you told us those thrilling stories of the experiments on the adrenal cortex of negroes. And there was a lot more I can't remember, because Morgana got bored and prevented me from listening.'

'I must apologize, darling,' said Bruce contritely; 'I didn't mean to bore you, but I wanted to find out what they are doing here. After all, it's what I was sent for!'

'I wasn't bored a bit, only Morgana got impatient. She won't like you. I think she had expected more personal talk.'

'But it isn't interesting. After all, who cares what we think, or are? It's what people are doing that is worth hearing.'

'Of course it is. We do talk about ourselves to a ridiculous extent.'

'Quite natural at your age. Anyway, I want to talk about you now. Come and sit down.'

He lifted her on to his knees and ran his hand through her thick curls with a sigh of satisfaction.

'What are we going to do about ourselves, you and I?' he asked, and pressed her closer to him.

'In what way?'

'Well, I want to know just what I mean to you. Once before I was a fool, and didn't talk things over with you. If it is not too late, I want to now. You see, I shall always be a bit of a bore, like I was to-night. Doing things and getting to know what other people are doing is all I care about. How do we stand towards one another?'

'Tell me first what you feel about me,' she answered softly.

'Oh, I adore you. When I first met you I thought, as far as I ever do, that when you grew up I would offer myself to you "for keeps." There is not much to be got out of sexual experience unless there is that feeling of permanency about it. It's not easy to explain, but as a man grows older he does want the knowledge of an established and lasting affection, colouring everything for him. To most men that kind of desire does not come until they are about forty, but with me it is different. I'm an instinctive monogamist. That was why I did not hurry with you. I thought I would wait until you were old enough to mate, and see if I could give you that same feeling about myself. Then we could begin having children. But when I arrive I find you have been doing all sorts of things on your own. Tell me what you really have been doing, and why.'

'What is easier than why. When I went away I was worried about Christopher. I came back and found he had a lover, and that apparently he did not seem to need me at all. I had felt that you understood about him and me—and then, there was no one. They wanted me to mate with Raymond—I just couldn't. Suddenly Christopher came back to me. I was restless . . . oh, I can see now that I wanted you, I was ready for you . . . but I had looked on you as so much older and wiser than me. When I was with you I stopped *thinking* or trying to think—we always talked about things, not people. Well, then, I wanted something to *do*. It is such fun doing things—so I joined Weil for a time. And as time went on, I got less and less interested in motherhood, and somehow I did not want to be immunized. But I had to decide. Christopher did not want me to become a mother either. You know how critical he is of everything, how he believes in anarchism and free-will. He has always been like that, ever since he was a child. He has no community sense at all. One day we were talking about things in general with Morgana and her young man——'

'Is that Brian?'

'Yes. We had been discussing Exton, and we all felt revolted. We agreed that we would try to do something for individual liberty, but we did not know what. Then it turned out that, supposing I wanted to retain my chance of motherhood, it might be possible to forestall immunization. They asked me if I would risk it. It was just the kind of thing Christopher was keen on, of course. You know he has always had a grudge against the rules. . . .'

'Something to do with his dislike of Adrian, I gather.'

'How did you know?'

'Well, it's fairly obvious. Adrian is rather trying.'

'Yes, but I think there's more to it than that. Christopher is revolted that men should be able to impose their will so completely on their fellows. He feels there ought to be another power, something more spiritual, to which one can appeal. He is mystical . . . religious . . . he wants to believe and yearns for something beautiful, something that isn't ephemeral and futile like all this. He wants it to be manifest in some way—provable. People won't listen to that sort of thing. But he—we—thought, that if we did something to startle them, something unusual, they would be roused. They would have to inquire our motive. And we could justify our belief by risking the consequences, and giving them a lesson.'

'H'm. A doubtful sort of logic, it seems to me.'

'But Christopher *isn't* logical—that's just the point!' Nicolette sat up and looked at him imploringly. Her eyes were eager and bright, her cheeks flushed. 'Don't say what any one else would,' she begged him. 'I love him!'

'Of course you do,' he soothed her, 'you dear child.' He pulled her to him, gently, and beneath her head she could feel his wide soft breast under the thin shirt, and the steady beat of his heart. That was a new sensation, new and exquisitely beautiful. As she lay there, all the nervous tension seemed to go out of her, oozing, ebbing away at her finger-tips and toes. She did not recognize it, did not know love could be like this, a bathing in alien strength that soothed like a cool wind and warmed like a gentle sun. Something new happened to her at that moment: it was as if a part of herself, the puzzled, fretful, immature part that had always been imprisoned deep in her consciousness, arose and left her, flying from this magic communion, leaving behind a strengthened being.

They were silent for a moment, lying thus so closely, so harmoniously, that it seemed as if they were being inseparably fused together.

Then Bruce said: 'Tell me the rest.'

'I decided,' she continued after a second's pause, 'that I would let myself be immunized, but that I would do something first to prevent it having effect. Brian thought it possible, and promised to get me some stuff. He was interested in the experiment for its own sake. He went abroad for it.'

'Who gave it to you?'

'I did, myself, with a hypodermic. It was quite easy.'

'And what do you intend to do now?'

'Well—what do you suggest?' She sat up, shook back her curls, and looked at him expectantly. 'I won't let Christopher down!' she declared.

Bruce gazed back at her solemnly for a moment.

'And what about the child?' he asked.

'If you're willing I'll have it, and risk the consequences.'

'I think your pluck is magnificent, my dear,' he answered, 'but what about the child? Have you considered it from his or her point of view?'

'That does not matter, surely. The child has nothing to do with the point at issue. It's only got to be born.'

'Oh! And supposing it is not allowed to live? I am not so sure that it will even be allowed to be born.'

'I could go away and hide, and only let them know afterwards.'

'And if you did—what then? They could still eliminate it.'

'But that would be outrageous!'

'Not a bit, according to the rules. No more than your conduct would appear to most people. You would have lied, cheated, committed the gravest possible infringement of the biological law; it's a serious thing, you know, what you're contemplating.'

'We mean it to be!'

'All right, then. If you are prepared for the consequences you must decide. But mothers have a way of becoming fond of their offspring and of wanting their children to live. Especially the first child.'

'Then you will not agree?'

'On my own terms, perhaps, but not on Christopher's. As an experiment, although it's unusual and a bit risky, it can be done. I can justify it, though of course they will object vigorously at first to our not having asked permission. And to that picture Arcous has done of you. But that could probably be arranged. The rest is out of the question.'

'Then you want me to betray Christopher? To take away his last chance of vindicating himself? It would be the end of him!'

'I want you to convince him the scheme is impossible. It's fantastic. And I think it quite unjustifiable to expose you to the risk.'

'But we should all be in it, not merely me. It's a collective scheme. After all, the rule is detestable. It should be abolished. If we take a stand, and let it be known, we can make it into a strong agitation for personal liberty. We should gain sympathy. The movement would grow.'

'Little darling, you would not gain an atom. To begin with, nothing would ever be known. Even now, the Patrol may have an inkling of what you are planning, and be just waiting for you. I know about these things. Do you think that people who, in the common interest, can eliminate whole cities and keep enormous tracts of land clear of a single human being, who command the intelligence and the weapons they command, would consider five silly little people like Christopher and you and me and Brian and Morgana? Does any one else know?'

'Arcous.'

'Your artist friend?'

'Yes. He's one of us.'

'How can you be certain? He's a Jew, and they're much too sensible to take life seriously. He probably thinks it's a great joke, and that's the only thing they can never keep to themselves. No, dear. It won't do. But we won't discuss it any more now. Think over what I have told you. I shall be in Nucleus for another six weeks. After that we might even travel a little together, as you are technically free to live with me if you want to. You must get to know me, to find out if you really do love me. Then we shall see. I am not sure, you know,' he said with a smile, as he lifted her on to her feet, 'if you really have room for me in your mind, or whether you're in love with that charming brother of yours.'

'He is charming, Bruce, isn't he?' Like the child she still was, she wound her arms around his neck pleadingly. 'And you must learn to love him, too.'

'I will, my dear,' he answered as he kissed her good-night, 'if we can help him to think like a man.'

V

Nicolette decided that the time had come to take an inventory, to find out to whom, for example, Bruce had delivered his ultimatum. For it was clear that in this crisis the matter of supreme importance was to discover, more or less exactly, what it was 'she' wanted.

Nicolette was not intellectual, nor even clever. But she possessed, like her father, that fundamental honesty of mind and character that must recognize fearlessly the impermanence and instability of the human 'self.' It was precisely on account of this vague, hitherto not even defined doubt of her 'real' self that she had been so adaptable, so excellent a convert. She had never been sure of anything whatever, least of all her own thoughts, so that it had been easiest hitherto to follow a lead and to pretend to herself and others that she took certain things seriously—more seriously, at any rate, than most people.

So-called absolute standards of thought and conduct were, of course, generally condemned in her day, save by such violent reactionaries as Christopher. He was one of those people who only managed to find some escape from the conflict of their emotions by sub-editing them. Two or three generations ago most men lived, or at any rate had managed to get through existence, by such methods. Clichés, headlines, symbols of all sorts were like the rungs of a fire-escape ladder, on which they had managed to climb out of reach of the torments of thought.

Nicolette determined that she would try to think things out. And then there jumped into the range of her mental vision a picture of a carpet of blue scillas, a vivid tag of memory, connected in some obscure way with other tags that represented a flight with Christopher and one of their many talks together a few years ago. This flower-picture appeared to be mingled with a feeling of acute satisfaction, and it started a train of others. They seemed, all of them, to be little things like children or bits of scenery or flowers (many of them flowers) or small masterpieces in porcelain or sculpture. . . . They were many, yet all small, and all harbingers of the purest pleasure she could know, apparently, a pleasure to be obtained in no other way and that, certainly, had never come to her through any grown-up person whatever.

Then, the other night, she had laid her head on Bruce's breast, and there, for the first time in contact with a human being, she had known that emotion in its perfect form. What did it mean?

When she had attempted to describe to Bruce this sensation he had given her, he had appeared to understand exactly what it meant and had said that he had felt it himself, with her, and only when with her. 'The absence,' he had said, 'of all sense of tension, and a feeling that the bonds of our personalities had loosened, so that in some way a fusion, a melting into one another, seemed to be taking place between us.' If you said 'Us,'—called it 'Usness,'—the thing, the formless emotion or sensation or whatever it might be, seemed to respond to that name, to take on form.

And that alone, of all sensations possible, seemed to correspond and be in harmony with her feelings about those absurd small things, feelings difficult to describe, even to translate into thought, because they were dependent on such tiny stimuli, but which, nevertheless, now she attempted to discover herself, did seem to provide the nucleus of the real Nicolette. Trying to imagine the absence from her world of perception of all the things that could arouse this emotion in her, she concluded that it would be an intolerable world, one in which she would suffer, be—it was difficult again to find a word for something so alien to her imagination—yes, be unhappy. . . .

Because of this and no more, she knew herself indissolubly bound to Bruce. There was Christopher, whom she had loved consciously all her life, with whom she had formed an intimacy which neither of them had thought possible to establish in relationship with any one else—yet all this passionate affection, which had declared itself in speech and deed and finally in an almost despairing appeal to Bruce to understand it, counted for nothing as against the sensation of 'Usness.'

It was mysterious, appalling; it was an insoluble riddle, apparently—but there it was. She would soon begin to know the meaning of the word 'unhappy,' she would be disloyal, she would betray Christopher's utter trust in her, she would refuse at the crucial moment to back him up—but however this might affect her self-respect, however keenly she might criticize herself, there was nothing to be done but see it through.

It was amazing to discover that Christopher had no part in 'Usness.' If she had not known it with Bruce she would never have been certain, and even now she doubted. Possibly she was thinking on erroneous lines—she was no expert thinker—but she could only go on, or rather let the thoughts run through her mind in their own way. It was an unpleasant process, self-analysis, but it would have been less difficult if she had practised it earlier, if she had developed her self-education.

All this thinking took place at various times, and came to her in jerks, as it were, in disconnected images that arose spontaneously and imaginatively. It was the result of the mental disturbance caused by Bruce's refusal to collaborate in the plan, and nothing could be done, one way or the other, until she had arranged her self-knowledge in some sequence and learned as much as was necessary to act upon.

Most of the process appeared to occur when she was alone, when she was doing her job, or resting after a swim, or just before she went to sleep, but it was going on all the time, consciously or unconsciously. Bruce watched, and let her be, till in due course she should make her decision known to him. Whenever she asked a question, whether apparently connected with this one problem or not, he answered her as impersonally as possible. She could have been influenced easily enough—but success so attained would have been of no use, either to him or to her. For the rest, they talked mostly of the 'things' they both cared for, leaving 'people' alone as much as possible.

Why had Christopher no share in 'Usness'? Because, so it came to Nicolette one night, he was eternally looking for Meaning. These intimate sensual satisfactions were either the only expressions of meaning or they were nothing. Nicolette found it hard to define this. But she tried to put it in terms of her very elementary knowledge of physics. All these small things that through the senses and nerves and memory conveyed these big emotions were each one of them just a complicated arrangement of quantized electrons and protons. When one thought of small things so, it was quite pleasant, but certain people, like Christopher, could not bear to apply their minds to the conception of these whirling and dancing charges in large groupings. Size, after all, was just a quantitative conception, but one which very few people could face with equanimity. Nicolette was one of these people, and so was Bruce. They were not troubled to find out mystical meanings, to wrench a god concept from the stars, to insist on the hypothetical existence of a plan or pattern that could be apprehended by human intelligence. Such a conception seemed to them to matter hardly at all; as little as they themselves 'mattered.' But to Christopher and to many men who had preceded him, nothing else had ever really mattered.

Why then had she joined him in his gestures of antagonism to the community, and been willing to be his tool in his attempt at revolt? Whatever explanation she might be able to advance for this would, she guessed, appear illogical and unintelligible.

Well, she had loved him and she knew him unloving, yet dependent to an indescribable degree on this loving atmosphere, no matter whence it emanated. People, women especially, always loved Christopher. There were Antonia and Emmeline and Morgana besides herself to love him, and even, probably, Lois. But whatever quality of love they had been prepared to give, only her own appeared to be what he had needed, the affection of which he could avail himself in order to thrive. . . .

Then there was fun in defiance, and there was particularly the need to get, without even knowing just what it was, the kind of love she wanted. Others should perhaps have been able to provide it for her; perhaps not; in any case, she had had to seek for it in her own way, no matter how crooked and curled and apparently abortive a way that might prove. Nicolette knew now that what she had found was not what she had thought herself to be seeking; but she had no doubt at all that 'it' was Bruce, and their future life together, and the continuance therein of 'Us-ness.' She decided that it was futile to endeavour to think about it in rational terms, since she had neither the means nor the method, and since—she was honest enough to be candid with herself about this—the whole matter was one over which she had no voluntary control. Life might have 'Meaning,' but since, senseless or sensible, its imperatives appeared to be unescapable, she would leave it at that.

12 UNREALITY

As the cloud is consumed and vanisheth away: so he that goeth down to the grave shall come up no more.

—Job 7:9

I

The day after the party in honour of Bruce had taken place, Christopher had abruptly left Nucleus. As soon as he had stepped into Weil's room and seen them together, he had known that Nicolette had found the instrument to enable her to fulfil her bargain. But he found the emotional strain of the situation unbearable. He would come back, later, when she had told Bruce, when, no doubt, she would call him to her side. Then his moment would come, then the crisis of his engineering would unfold itself. Until then he must avoid Bruce.

II

At the end of Bruce's six weeks in Nucleus, Nicolette was quite ready to go away with him. They journeyed for three months to many places by different ways, flying, motoring, and walking. They met men and women of various communities, chiefly members of the Company, with whom Bruce conferred and discussed mutual problems;

they enjoyed the generous communal hospitality of their day. Before the end of the journey the expected had happened: Nicolette found that her experiment had been successful, and that she was with child.

The knowledge left her in no doubt that motherhood was after all her vocation. For the joy this knowledge brought her was surprising in its intensity and its vastness. During two days she gave herself over entirely to the purely sensual delight with which it filled her. While Bruce, pursuing his programme, kept appointments and attended conferences, she remained in her room or wandered about in the open, happily dreaming. Already the embryo in her womb was to her Someone, was her son, and the sun that caressed her eyes, the perfumes which delighted her nose, the food she ate, the sleep which refreshed her, were His; passing to Him by the marvellous processes of which she knew a little and of which more could be learnt. Now she recognized thankfully how the training of her girlhood had prepared her adequately for what was to come, had paved the way for the learning of those further lessons for which she was greedy. All the time she was anxious to know in detail about the physiological changes taking place within her, and towards the end of the third month she began to fret to return to Nucleus, in order that she might devote herself entirely to His comfort.

And in the joy of these hours of complete abandonment to the dictates of His needs, Nicolette realized for the first time the genius of those who had perceived the necessity of developing motherhood on vocational lines.

Thanks to their foresight she would be able to give him health, strength, and a suitable environment from the beginning.

Bruce postponed his engagements in order that they might talk over thoroughly their future programme. It was a day of springtime, bright and gentle, but sharpened by an invigorating breeze, so they decided to walk.

'So Sp. 902 seems to have been successfully neutralized,' said Bruce with a smile. 'That's jolly interesting.'

'What will they say, do you think?'

'I don't know definitely. The thing to do will be to get your friend Brian to publish a paper on the subject. I can't quite foresee what the consequences will be. As soon as we get to Nucleus I'll see one or two people and put the matter to them. Of course, it is so important that the biological people will want to go into it pretty thoroughly. They will probably want to have the experiment repeated before they pass on the results from the theoretical to the practical side.' They both laughed.

'I suppose it will all have to be done very carefully?'

'Of course. There is no doubt that if I had not taken your funny scheme in hand, it might have led to some complications. I haven't the least doubt that the Patrol would have done something pretty drastic to all of you. As it is, they need hardly know. But I will admit this to you now: there are always discontented people about. I think, myself, that if that stuff of Monailoff's had become generally available, there might have been some bother. I shall have to talk to him when I get back.'

'I shall have to see Morgana and try to explain to her.'

'No. Morgana must not know for the time being. She's inclined to be hysterical and unbalanced; and she knows what Brian did. She's the person who will have to be watched most carefully. I don't want you to see her at all. You must arrange to stay quite quietly somewhere until you go to your Garden.'

'But I must tell Christopher everything, Bruce; I insist on that. No one else, not even you, shall break it to him. Between him and me this is a . . . a tremendously serious matter. I must at least tell him myself. I don't know a bit what he will do; it will be terrible for him.'

'Where is he now?'

'He went away without explaining very clearly why, but I think I understood. He went to that hut by the lake where he stays to compose. I expect he is there, now, probably preparing his plans for when we come back. I thought it wisest not to tell him that you would not agree until I knew for certain what would happen.'

'Why?' Bruce knew fairly well, of course, but he wanted to hear her explanation.

'Because I knew from the beginning I would do just as you and not as Christopher suggested.' Nicolette stopped walking and turned on the path, facing him with confident frankness. 'It did not take me long to realize, Bruce,' she said proudly, though her voice dropped a little, 'that I had been playing a game with myself, and unfortunately with Christopher. Oh, Bruce, if only I had known what I wanted when I came back from Centrosome! Christopher will suffer so hard now, simply because I had no sense. Surely I should have known all the time!'

Bruce drew her to him, and with his arm around her waist they continued to walk on slowly.

'It was I who should have had more sense, my little love,' he said. 'It was I who misled you. You can tell Christopher so'—Nicolette shook her head—'or I will, if you like. As for him, he misled himself, and it does not stop at that, either.'

'What do you mean?' Nicolette was unable to follow him.

'Some day I will tell you exactly, but not now. The point is that Christopher must learn to face matters squarely as you have done. He is growing up, and even he must try to put aside childish things. Otherwise . . .' Bruce left the sentence unfinished.

'Would you like to sit down and rest a little?' he asked presently, but Nicolette shook her head.

'Not yet. Oh, Bruce, you will never understand Christopher!'

'I do not consider him as enigmatic as you, my love. There is not very much the matter with him that cannot be put straight, if he will only give me his confidence.'

'He won't,' answered Nicolette decisively. 'Not to you nor to any one else.'

Bruce was silent.

'The trouble I anticipate I can't quite define. But I know his emotions are very violent. I remember——' She hesitated.

'Yes?'

'Oh, just something he confessed to me once when we were children. But he does need protecting.'

'That is what you have always imagined, I know. But you must allow me to disagree with you. Now that you have your job for the future,'—they looked at one another as only parents of a longed-for child can look—'you must give up this maternal craving to encourage Christopher's babyishness. You have done him no service that way, truly. All you little mother-pots need is babies. A little mothering of the rest of the world before you have them is very nice, for you and every one else. But it must not go too far, as it has done in your case and Christopher's. And at the present moment, until I can settle you down where you belong, I must be responsible for you, and help you out of the various entanglements I got you into. We will go to see Christopher together on our way to Nucleus.'

'But I will see him alone first!' Nicolette insisted on that.

III

'I wish Christopher would come back,' Morgana repeated obstinately.

'He won't,' answered Arcous, 'so try again. "One wish is as fair as another."'

'Don't quote things at me,' she said crossly. Ignoring him, she turned to Brian. 'What is this all leading up to?' she demanded. Brian lay on his back inhaling through a glass tube a stimulating gaseous mixture of his own concoction. Without waiting for an unlikely reply, Morgana continued: 'Christopher goes off into the wilds. Nicolette and her young man depart on a semi-public tour. Neither of you show the slightest attention. What is going to happen?'

'What always happens when young people grow up,' Arcous stated tritely. 'Christopher has found his job and is satisfied; Nicolette has found a lover and is ditto. Bruin and I being sensible, are not surprised; you being perverse, are.'

'I don't think Christopher knows,' said Morgana with heavy emphasis.

'Knows what?'

'That Nicolette has failed him, and does not intend to carry out her part of the bargain.'

Arcous raised his fine black eyebrows in that ironic gesture which never failed to annoy her excessively. 'Don't pretend,' she went on with growing indignation, 'that you don't know either. Or you,' she turned angrily to Brian, who seemed to be settling down to pleasant visions.

'Do you mean—that experiment?' he murmured lazily, egging her on in the expectation that she would continue her monologue while he meditated in peace.

'Of course I do. You both know what I mean. I mean the pact we all made and that Nicolette agreed to: that she was to have a child, and so signalize our revolt against these stifling rules.'

'Perhaps Brian's dope was no use,' suggested Arcous mischievously.

'Well, why does she not tell us? It's four months since Bruce came over; they have been together almost constantly; the matter ought to be decided by now one way or the other. And why, if she has nothing to hide, does she stay away so consistently?'

'You forget he is on a special tour; they may be away another two. There's nothing in that.'

'Then why doesn't she call us up or communicate in some way?'

'Why should she? Her brother probably knows. After all, it's their affair.'

'Oh, is that how you look at it? I thought we were all rather keen about it.'

'My dear, don't be absurd. You surely never expected any one over twenty to take that intended revolt of yours seriously? There we were, on a hot day, arguing for want of something else to while away a long walk, and now you talk as if anything ever came of heated argument.'

'Only cold feet, apparently, in your case,' she retorted rudely. 'Christopher meant it, and I meant it, and Nicolette meant it—then. And if Bruin didn't mean it, why did he go all that way for the stuff?'

Bruin was asleep, after having carefully disconnected his glass stem and rubber piping from the complicated parent apparatus, so the conversation continued as a duet.

'A, because you badgered him into it; B, because the journey was an excuse to get away from your badgering; and C, because there might have been a chance of making some biological wheels go round the other way,' explained Arcous with deliberate patience.

'You neither of you care one jot about me or any one else in the world,' complained Morgana bitterly.

'Except about our jobs, no,' he answered brutally. 'Neither would you, if you were sensible. What has this to do with you, anyway? You refuse to understand that Nicolette is in love with that chap Bruce. In love, my girl. It happened ages ago, when they first met. She didn't especially mind what she said or did until he came back. She was just waiting, entranced, like a sleeping beauty. She's woken up now—and *voilà!*'

'Fairy-tales and nonsense,' she retorted. 'Love! What is love? A degree of preference between copulating with one person or another.'

'To you and me and Brian, and people like us—to nearly every one, probably, except parents. In them, it's the dynamic urge towards completion; a throwing together of complementary personalities for the purpose of third parties. It's what keeps the race going.'

'A ridiculous argument! If it were true, we should have monogamy instead of polyandry.'

'Not a bit of it. The effects of these urges are not necessarily permanent. And in every profession there are degrees of natural talent.'

'Oh, you Jews . . .' She was unable to complete the sentence.

'Exactly. We know about these matters. We've specialized in them for centuries, you see. But they're rather outside your province.'

'And yours is utterly narrow and clodbound. There are other forms of love of which you know nothing, which cannot matter to you. Love of freedom, of independence. Your kind may make a race, but mine is what keeps its banner flying. It's the love worth dying for, though yours may give life—as the beasts do. I tell you, Christopher knows nothing of all this. If what you suggest of Nicolette is true, and it may be, or she would have given a sign by now, then she has betrayed an ideal for an idol. Do you think that if Christopher knew, he would not come back, would not try to recall her to her pledge? What is he going to do if she lets him down?'

'Live on his emotions, as he has always done, and write some marvellous music, by and by. Why do you think so little has been done to check his wildness? Simply because every one knows that in youth the artist has to be a little mad. Sanity comes with the experience of power, with the command of form, that enables the genius, the true artist, to compose masterpieces in cold blood. He may occasionally resort to a little self stimulation, attain a fine frenzy by getting him self into an emotional state; take drugs or women or religion. If he is not a genius he will often temporarily lose his self-consciousness, but whatever emotions dominate him, he will never express them in any other way than through the only means he really understands. That symphony of Christopher's was a fine thing. He's established now and will go on.'

'That symphony was his religion, I tell you, his declaration of love of God, of liberty and independence. It was simply a prelude to what he means, or meant, to do, with Nicolette's help. It was defiance of them all. If you think that Christopher and I are like you and Bruin and her and Bruce, you are mistaken. We are survivors from the age of freedom.' She rose from the floor whereon he sat in Oriental fashion and Brian lay sprawling on his back. She pointed a trembling hand at him. I despise you,' she said, and her voice rang with passion; 'I despise you both; all of you. I've finished with you. I leave you to your selfishness and your feebleness and your love and your dope. I'm going. I'm going to Christopher!' And superbly, furiously, she went.

'E finità la comedia,' Arcous murmured; smiled all alone, and gave Brian's limp body a prod with his foot.

'Our sweetie's gone away,' he announced gently; 'wake up!'

IV

Christopher was not certain when the symphony of the Voices would begin, but he knew it must be quite soon. The receiving set in the hall was all in order. He gave it a last glance, then went out on the wide balcony and lay down in a chair there. It was dark—he had come all this long way on purpose to hear it in the dark. There was garden land below him and there were woods, which trailed across the valley to the rising hills that framed the view. The sky above appeared to him, coming from the lighted room, blue-black and enormous. But there were many stars, and after a time it seemed lighter. Christopher was glad the night was still, and hoped it would remain so. His ears, which had by this time become at tuned to a multitude of faint sounds, noted now one, now another of the ceaseless interweaving of little night rustlings, but he was hardly aware of them, intent as he was on the music he was awaiting.

It too began at first as a whisper of little noises, faint moaning of wind and water, humming of insects, chirping of birds, punctuated from time to time by the conversation of beasts. These things soon made a pattern, blending in the theme of the VOICE. It was a murmurous, gentle, but vigilant song, and from the beginning one understood that all these small sounds were just the instruments created for the conveying of its import. It was both the composer and conductor of the hidden orchestra, was this VOICE.

Now while it spoke, always sustaining that message, the instrumentation varied. Soon the little sounds dwindled away, slowly, one by one; hardly noticeably they vanished as others, louder and more impressive, superseded them. Whereas at first the VOICE had spoken through the simple messengers of the country, it now sang through means devised by men. It was in the whirring of aeroplane engines and the purring of motor cars, in the rhythmic pushing and pulling of machinery. And soon the VOICE, though never for an instant wavering or ceasing, sang so softly, became so much a part of those instruments which interpreted it, that the listener's attention was lulled by familiarity. There were other voices to listen to now which combined to form a recognizable medley of sound. These were the voices of men, of leaders and led, of children, women, youths, the middle-aged and the old. Occasionally one alone spoke and the rest answered in chorus; sometimes there were several soloists contending against one another, and as they split through and cut, or struggled to drown rival sounds, the responses of the mob also became complex, dividing as if drawn magnetically towards this, that, or the other one of those who led them. There were discords in plenty here, sharp divisions, sudden pregnant silences, but although during these the VOICE still sounded its sweet song, they were never long enough for it to become dominant. There was invariably a crescendo of contentious shouting after these intervals, there was strife, dissension, war; mobilization, engines in motion, contending parties divided clearly into three or four major groups, each of which in turn gave way rhythmically, frenziedly, to its own particular cries. But now another Voice, a solitary Voice, began to be heard. This was clearly one man, and one only, who sang. At first his notes halted often, he would hesitate after a few bars, as if courage failed him to go on. Others would interrupt, and for a little while he seemed to join their chorus; then he would cease abruptly and in a moment or two endeavour to recapture his original theme. As he went on, he appeared to be succeeding. His tones became clearer as the others faded; he was apparently leaving his fellows, leaving the world, for as his power increased the musical background changed also in texture. He had long since left the machines behind: accompanied occasionally by a solitary aeroplane, he continued until that too was silent. For some little time while he rested, apparently, in a garden, for the VOICE was incarnated by the drip, drip of petals, the chirping of a lark, the humming of insects. But he went further, until the great rustling trees of the forest were about him, skirting a waterfall in an upward climb, and always as he walked the sound of the VOICE became clearer and his Voice lost its defiance, its anger, its sorrow, falling finally to a monotonous prayer-like murmur.

It was plain to the listener, contrasting the Voice of the prayer with the VOICE which accompanied and encouraged it, that whereas the first was simple, emanating from a man's throat alone, the second was composed of many united complexities of sound. Just how many instruments produced it, just how many were human beings and how many manipulated or mechanical contrivances used by them, it was impossible to determine. The blend was too intimate, too subtle, to permit of discrimination by an ear even so well trained as Christopher's. In any case, the message of the VOICE was now so urgent, so passionately uttered, that the hearer's attention was completely riveted by it. Gradually it appeared also to have imposed its will on the other singer; slowly, as he had begun to sing, he ended, his tones finally trailing off while those others swelled ever louder and louder. . . .

At last, after he had not been heard for several minutes, he began, haltingly, fearfully he began to endeavour to sing in unison with the VOICE. The effect of his stammering effort was peculiar; one wanted to laugh and to weep simultaneously as this plaintive human bubble of sound attempted the impossible, to express something of those magnificent, mysterious harmonies that played all about it, and yet never, curiously enough, overwhelmed it completely. It was always there, reaching up and out, valiantly aspiring to become enrolled in that marvellous orchestra that yet was One . . . and after a time, as if in compassion, the VOICE sank, so that the feebler Voice became audible, articulate almost, and having at last found its note affirmed with growing passion.

What followed was apparently a dialogue. The VOICE adapted itself to the dimensions of its interlocutor, while the other with growing confidence took on a new richness of tone. Many times the man faltered, his questions falling often into a mere whisper, trailing away unformulated. Then gaining courage anew, as it seemed, he dared assert, demand, whilst the reply never varied in gentleness and beauty. Once he even shouted, and the crystal clarity of the answer which followed after a second's pause caused his Voice to shake and tremble, to struggle on through sobs.

Then he did achieve a moment of union with that VOICE, and thereupon, clinging to it as well as he could, he went away and down from the mountain, his footsteps beating gentle time as he marched. The VOICE was with him, always, as he returned the way he had come; it was strong yet caressing, with now male, now female intonations, while his own, indubitably, had gained a new hardihood. So they came back to the world of men.

He went in among the mumbling crowd, and as he proclaimed his message to them the VOICE retreated a little into the background that he might be more audible. They certainly did not appear to hear it, but to him they harkened as, endeavouring to imitate its accents as he had learned to do on that mountain, he proclaimed his discovery and addressed them with exhortation. After a time a few others, chiefly women, joined him, and slowly their numbers grew. And as his partisans increased, there advanced with pomp and circumstance those leaders whose altercations had previously divided the people and egged them on to war. They challenged him and he replied heartily, and then, miraculously, his voice was indeed for a few short moments the VOICE. When it ceased, dying away to its usual murmur, which, apparently, was inaudible to them, they produced voices of their own, whose songs were astonishingly feeble or disgustingly distorted versions of THE SONG. He would have none of them; he defied them to the limit of his power, singing now exultantly with all his strength. Then they appeared to hurl themselves on him with cries of execration, with howls of derision, inciting one another to wilder and wilder excesses. Once, agonizedly, he called on the VOICE, but it, sunken to a mere whispering thread, did not reply. Then he was silenced.

Yet when all the tumult and the beastliness of sound had died away, the VOICE was raised again, and clearly that human Voice was to be recognized as part of it. Something of himself had gone out of it, something of the passion of self-assertiveness that had prevented it from blending previously with the song of infinity. Quite unmistakably it retained its own quality, but this was sublimated, refined, harmonized, so that the one song of the VOICE was also his song. No recognizably earthly nor human sounds were in this melody at first, but after a prelude which gave the impression of having lasted untold ages, the music appeared again to approach the places of men. This time it was not dimmed, nor was there the faintest trace of an antagonistic cacophonous chorus. As he had endeavoured to do so long ago, now other and many individual voices tried to attain the note of the VOICE and join its splendid theme. In due time, though not without trembling nor anguish, they appeared to succeed. Each one of them, without losing its identity, but transformed and purified as that first Voice had been, soared upward until it found and clung to the VOICE of the universe. It was not a crescendo, but an accumulation of music: while in full spate almost unendurably beautiful, in retreat slowly fading into silence, seeming to leave an echo. on the air, so that long after it had ended the listener had no consciousness of his personal identity.

'For ever and ever, world without end, Amen,' murmured Christopher.

That was how he heard the first performance of his Symphony of God and Man.

V

Christopher more or less stumbled into the room whence Nicolette had called, obeying her call subconsciously. There were sounds still ringing in his ears which left no room there for the perception of alien tones, or he might have been aware of a strange quality in hers. The room was brilliantly lit, and entering from the darkness, he saw her face, in the first seconds, only as a familiar blur. . . . And minutes passed, minutes of greetings, smiles, before his eyes focussed on her properly. His eyes informed his ears; he became aware, now, of a profound change in her appearance, yet his imagination was still so far away that he asked, stupidly: 'Nicolette? Is it really you?'

And Nicolette was about to answer automatically 'Yes,' before her own new knowledge slipped in a pause between the opening and closing of her lips. Was not that just the question she had come to answer? But not so.

Christopher had already met her eyes. He frowned and peered a little, still blinking. Then, passing his hand rapidly over his hair, said: 'Don't speak. I can see.'

'Can you, Christopher? Already?'

'Yes. And what I can see in your face—what you have come to tell me, dates from before your pregnancy, doesn't it? So you could still have chosen; it is obvious *how* you chose; all you want to tell me is why, isn't it?'

'If I can. It is difficult.'

'Perhaps for you. Not for me. At least not yet. It's so easy to see. Something of you, and so of mine, has passed out of your own into Bruce's keeping. Bruce isn't one of us, as I might have suspected. He's too old. Did you realize that he is too old, or were you beyond knowing even that? Are you no more young, Nicolette?'

It became easier for both of them when he had pronounced those rather fantastic words. It confirmed the nightmarish quality of this scene. It was easier at once to act stiffly, clumsily, as they were doing, the moment the *unreality* of this encounter was driven home. And as always during such periods of emotional tension, when time conceptions become absurdly distorted, thought comets flashed across the empty darkness that just now appeared to them to 'stand for' their ordinarily clear, well-stocked minds. Some part of Nicolette's consciousness was now following such a zigzag trail, that flashed out:

'Lucky we understand one another so well; we can suffer together, equally.' Whereas Christopher was aware of a ghostly, ghastly laughter, flitting about there ceaselessly.

He was trembling, and his voice was low as he went on. 'Oh yes, I think I understand the present position perfectly. But the past? That, in the light of it, seems so absurd. That you had better explain a little.' Then there was another flash in the background of his consciousness, but this he took hold of and brought out in words, as a flash of inspiration.

'I say, Nicolette, let's fly! Shall we?'

'I . . . I can't,' she answered piteously. 'It makes me sick.'

Then Christopher felt the sting of tears in his eyes, and heard himself laughing, and he continued to laugh, but he pressed her gently into a chair. He knelt beside her, took one of her hands in his, kissed and fondled it a little. Nicolette stroked his hair with the other. They were silent for a moment or two, both suffering about equally. Christopher after this small pause spoke gently: 'Never mind. I am just beginning to think . . . I don't quite know yet . . . but probably I have behaved absurdly all the time. I was your shadow baby, wasn't I? And now those games you played to make me happy are finished, because you're going to have a real one. Yes?'

Nicolette nodded. 'But couldn't you grow up too? *Please*, my dear?'

It was all getting more unreal and more easy from minute to minute.

'We'll see. But on the whole I doubt it. What should I grow up *for*? Anyway, it was nice of you to come to ask me.'

'Isn't there anything, Christopher, anything at all?'
'I shall be angry if you try to take my dreams away from me, little mother-pot. I am going to keep those till the end—right to the end. You have come to show me that they were and are only dreams, but you can't banish them. You have lived with them long enough to know that *they are* Christopher. What you call my dreams, and I my realities. You were part of them once, or rather, there was a Nicolette in them. But now—you—here——' He had begun to walk up and down, and he flung out his hand to her 'Oh, you could never persuade me that you are real, that this Nicolette-Bruce entity of which half is before me now, that it and its background, with people and rules and all the rest of it, are real. Try if you like, tell me something. Talk to me.'

'Bruce could talk to you more convincingly than I, if you would care to see him. He's waiting for me with the car. Would you?'

'Yes. I want to see you together. I haven't ever yet, really, you know. I couldn't.'

'Didn't want to wake up, you mean, don't you?'

'That's putting it your way. I might say, "Or go to sleep—forever." Opposites mean much the same thing, anyway. Call Bruce.'

As usual when Bruce entered, he filled the room with comfort for Nicolette. The dark mental background immediately lightened. Seeing these two together, now, whom she loved, she felt her self loving Christopher more for Bruce's presence. Almost she fell a-brooding on this masterpiece of sensation—Love. But they began to talk, and she to listen.

'Why didn't you come up?' asked Christopher. 'I didn't know you were waiting out there all this time.'

'Nicolette preferred it; it doesn't matter. I've been watching Mensch and Descartes. But I could not see much out there. You haven't a spy-hole here, have you?'

'No. There ought to be one, but it's rather an old hut. Have they decided about Jesus yet?'

'In principle, but not in practice. The difficulty seems to be to find an appropriate constellation. But you know how long the popular mind takes to make itself up.'

They all three of them went to the balcony and stood there a moment, looking out and up. Christopher laughed quietly.

'We're pulling down the stars for them to play with, now,' he said. 'What next, I wonder?'

'That's not quite fair to us, surely,' answered Bruce gravely. 'Do you realize that since astrology went out, great multitudes of people never glanced this way once throughout their lives? Comparatively few years ago, Mensch had a struggle to get elementary astronomy into the school curricula. Yet without it, no human being can begin to have an adequate sense of proportion. This game we've started them on now is just a beginning. In another twenty years we shall be getting them somewhere up to the mark.'

Christopher turned his back on the balcony and re-entered the room.

'Your enthusiasm spoils the stars for me, like every-thing else, Bruce,' he said calmly.

'I'm sorry, but why should poets and astrophysicists have a monopoly of them? People like you and me . . .'

'Oh, people *are* you and me; or were once, before your accursed medicine men got hold of the world and started tinkering about with them. Where's it going to end? Isn't any one going to pull them up? I marvel, when I look back to the beginning of the scientific era, that no one, not one single man, foresaw what it would all lead to—'

'Butler,' interjected Bruce.

'Oh, possibly, yes. But not in its monstrous fullness. Not in its personal implications. Not in its power over the mind and body of each one of us. I mustn't even mention the word "soul"; if I might it would not convey anything to you. Tell me what there is in this world of yours for a per-son like me! You, with your hundred per cent. man and your hundred per cent. woman, with your normality and your dreary talk of intelligence. I'm glad I'm not one of you! As long as I live, I shall feel an undying loathing of it all. You draw a map of a man's consciousness as you do of the "genes" of a rabbit. You tinker about and fiddle about with every living thing; you babble about "lethal factors" and "survival value," and all your other nonsense. Do you mean to tell me seriously that you attach the slightest ultimate significance to it all? Even as I speak to you, I can see what you are thinking. Neurosis, due to whatever you like to call it—and if we gave him so and so, and mucked about so, and with a few hefty doses of hypnosis, we could make quite a nice, normal little man of him.'

'You know why I'm talking to you like this. I know Nicolette's put you up to try to "reform" me. Something ought to be done about me soon before I make any mischief. All these years I thought she loved me—she may still think so—to-night I know she was only mothering me, trying to protect me. One finds people out so suddenly! The moment I saw you two together I knew. I fled. You come after me. I don't mind seeing you both to-night. But we'll have it out finally. You must leave me alone. There's nothing, absolutely nothing, you can do for me.'

'I'm sorry you're so antagonistic to me, Christopher. After all, I have fallen in with your scheme as far as it was practicable. When Nicolette has had her baby you will have to recognize that. But it would be folly to go to the lengths you suggested. You would defeat your own object.'

'How do you know?' Christopher asked hotly. 'Did any of the people of old who felt as I did reckon like you do? Were they prudent? Were they careful? Have none of you ever known moments of complete consciousness, of mystical union with God—yes, with God and His Saints, when a Voice has called to you "Go thou and do likewise!" There isn't any object but that, to go straight on to the bitter end, the end that is just a beginning . . .'

'I can't argue with you about mysticism, Christopher. But if you talk about consciousness, there is something to be said. There doesn't seem to be much doubt that to all of us, occasionally, come those longer or shorter periods of a realization that seems complete. In the old days this process of intensive thought was symbolized as an act of going up to a great height and holding communion with a god. When Moses went away to think, he came back with a law he had worked out, prepared to give it to his people as a divine revelation. Now whenever one "comes back" in this way the rest of the world does appear to be worshipping a golden calf. But we're trying to do away with the symbolism of mountains in connection with thought, and we manage to govern without revelations, and we study stupidity instead of punishing it. Moses was a father of science, not merely of a church, and we use precisely the same methods to-day as he did, only without the trimmings. They're superfluous already. That seems to me an encouraging sign. The more familiar we become with the processes of thought, the more easily we shall be able to maintain a high level of thinking over an increasing period. But for the next few thousand years the thinking of the human race will have to be done for it by a few men at a time. And they will make occasional mistakes, which I expect will decrease in number and importance. That those men must be "inhuman," as you mean it, is inevitable. To be human in your sense is simply to be emotional. Feeling is not thinking and one has the utmost difficulty in convincing most people of that simple fact. To admit it is to admit something requiring the utmost courage and fortitude to endure, and those who have not enough must invent a god to salve their feelings.'

'Stop, Bruce!' Christopher's cry was imperative. 'It's no use going on. I'm not listening to you. I've hardly been hearing you. My ears are full of other sounds. Bruce——' He pointed to Nicolette. Her eyes were closed. There were tears on her lashes. She was asleep.

'Bruce,' said Christopher softly, 'long ago, when we were quite small children, I used to see her asleep like that. And I have never loved her so much as in those moments. But as a lover you can do more for her than I. I am glad you have taken her, happy about that, Bruce. Now stay here with her. I am going out for a while. I prefer to be alone.'

'Won't you—' Bruce did not complete the sentence, but he laid his hand on the boy's arm. He knew he could do no more, but he was filled with pity. There was, of course, just one thing. . . .

Christopher stepped back. His eyes met Bruce's fully; his glance was keen with honest hatred, unyielding and clear.

'No, I will not.'

'Then—be careful.'

'I will. They'll have to come a long way for me.'

He went quite softly, but he did not look back.

VI

Christopher did not attempt to think at all until he had climbed a few hundred feet westward. Already the little shack in the velvet woods lay a long way below him. But now time and space, which had so often provided the theme for delightful speculations on previous flights, were nothing to him. He had passed through the belt of light mist which had been gathering earthwards when they had come in from the balcony, and the stars, more than ever like spots on a one-coloured map, lay before him. But they did not tempt him to-night to draw imaginary roads from the Sickle to Orion, through Castor and Pollux to Aldebaran, roads of discovery through infinity.

They did, however, recall him after a time to self-consciousness. They reminded him of Bruce, who had spoiled the stars for him. Still he did not notice how his hands trembled, although through familiarity his grip on the stick was firm.

'Everything seems about finished.' No, those words had no meaning. He might repeat them with his lips, he might bring them forward to stand out brightly against the sombre background of his mind, as those stars stood out against the sky it was futile, they had no meaning. 'Everything . . .' who can define that? 'Seems' . . . that's a little better is,' or 'may be,'—he rejected 'may be' violently and repeated 'is' with determination. 'Finished'—what nonsense! I mean, of course, 'Begun.'

That was clearer—much clearer. Christopher had not the least doubt that this was definitely a beginning—perhaps of something important. Beginnings—of days, of litanies, of the unfolding of flowers, of symphonies—beginnings were invariably beautiful. He couldn't think of an ugly beginning, and as he searched a score of quotations tittered through his mind. 'Our Father, which art in Heaven, hallowed be Thy name,'—what a beginning! He repeated the invocation several times, and mercifully had no need to reject the memory of the following request: 'Die Sonne tönt nach alter Weise?'; came next, 'In Brudersphären Wettgesang, und ire vorge schriebene Reise vollendet sie mit Donnersang.' And then, 'In the grey beginning of years, in the twilight of things that began.

The word of the earth in the ears of the world, was it God, was it man?'

Christopher was weeping, and when he noticed it, was a little surprised. Surely all that was far beyond tears—what had brought them down? That last unimportant word lingering in his mind, of course. Although he was sorry to find he still cared sufficiently to weep, Christopher could not shake off its influence. Words were having a curious effect on him just now, apparently. Apparently, then, one had to say good-bye. These small ceremonies seemed inevitable. He turned his head half to one side and downwards, but the clouds were all below him, and he was relieved to find that he could not, even if he wanted to, see through them.

Still, he was sorry. He let his tears run, let himself be filled with the sorrow that prompted them, the enormous, heavy sorrow that, if indulged in too long, leads to sleep. He was sorrowing for those little creatures, that curious race down there, sorrowing as the gods, as the Great God Himself might sorrow, a long way further up, every now and then. Even here, far away and free as he was, he took with him the ancient sense of kinship. He suddenly realized that it was this, precisely, he had come up here to lose.

Nothing new about this desire. He felt an invading sense of kinship with his forerunners, those who had also sorrowed for man and withdrawn from his contacts, and he felt a regret that they were not all with him here, that the *Makara* was not a vast mythological ship on which all those who had been compelled to fly from earth could have embarked with him. What comfort had common man not devised for his superiors when he had built them aeroplanes! He had abolished the necessity of dwelling precariously on hilltops or in caverns in order to await the purging of the soul and the complete filling by the divine spirit. Where they had perforce crouched, he could spring, soaring to meet revelation half-way. It was movement they had most lacked, he thought, not having known how to unleash the potential energy that should enable them to soar physically also.

Already the edges of his sorrow were fading into indifference. The higher he climbed, the more easily could he forbear to look downward and backward. The whole earth now seemed unreal to him; as clearly unreal as the last hour he had spent on it, when the message of his symphony had been succeeded by the pleading of Nicolette and the warning of Bruce. He had heard neither, for his head was filled with other voices, but he had seen them, looked upon them both as one looks with lazy curiosity at strange shapes on waking up in a half-light, after having fallen asleep in the sunshine.

Nicolette . . . had he really seen her for the first time to-night, or had some new individual slipped into the personal form of the small sister he had loved so many years? Whose were those sad, doubting eyes that had looked from him to Bruce? Eyes—oh, yes, he had *seen* clearly enough—that lightened and cleared as their glance travelled Bruceward. He was not a bit sorry to have left that Nicolette behind; it was quite certainly not the same creature, and, dwelling on the other, he exclaimed with a sudden sense of revelation: 'I invented that girl!'

Ah, yes! he had invented her, because, until now, he had felt so heavily the need of a companion on that pilgrimage he must make alone. And yet he seemed to remember having told her, long ago, when he could formulate his thoughts more easily by speaking them at her—he seemed to remember having warned her that he must go alone. He had had need of company, nevertheless, and until this real Nicolette had unfolded herself, the dear little invention had been loyal. For naturally his invention had been a sexless companion, the personification of no other emotion but loyalty. When the generative passion had turned that child-friend into womanhood the invention had crept away, slowly and timidly at first, and then at the last vanishing swiftly in a glitter of tears.

That word sex (words were like stepping stones in the pools of thought to-night)—that had to be thrown overboard too, before Christopher could soar freely towards his destination. It was another feeble monosyllable, a euphemism, masking emotions which had been institutionalized by man. You might turn away from it, withdraw, deny, deny, deny—it was useless, down there. Neutrality was not negation. On that ground you were either one of the army of propagatives, or an enemy whom they would ultimately extirpate. Moses and Luther between them had seen to that. Their modern successors did not preach; practice was more efficient. It was not the homosexual body they dreaded, but the homosexual soul; the soul in which the seeds of 'love' were doomed to infertility, the soul that was sufficient unto itself. From that high self-satisfaction one was tempted indeed, tempted to stoop down and preach to those other poor souls, seeking in their desperate want the unattainable mate; if only to help or to comfort, one offered a part of one's own secret wisdom. And at last, exasperated by their stupidity, their coarse unintelligence, one wanted to teach, not gently nor with words, but by deed or gesture, meeting violence with defiance.

Till at last, wearied of them and all they did or were, one recoiled once more into the worthier preoccupation with the quintessential problem.

Not a last thought for Emmeline, for Antonia, for St. John? No. Christopher had flown a long way by now. The *Makara* was groping her way more cautiously, travelling further and further forward, in order to get a little and a little higher. Christopher put her into climbing gear, and turned on the raiser. She would be all right now for a bit—let her have her head.

It was later that he felt the dropping of the temperature and switched on the radiator. The molecules—no, one could quite easily think of atoms now—were separating, moving about more happily, for there was more room up here. One could expand, could stretch mentally and physically, for there was room—so much room!

Later. The *Makara* was sailing along steadily enough still, on her own sweet road—Christopher's only in so far as it led further and further forward and a little higher and higher. He had ceased to think vocally for the past fifteen minutes; marvellous thoughts came in increasing numbers, but it was unnecessary up here, where there was so much room, to group them in sequence. There did seem, though, at the back of his mind, dimly apprehended, a thought that wanted to come forward, yet could not get through. It translated itself into an unpleasant sensation in order to find an easier path, a sensation as of something forgotten that made one want to click the fingers and press the tongue against the teeth—*tk, tk,* like that. Christopher could hear the click of his fingers, but was un aware that as he repeated the motion his thumb and index finger were fully two inches apart. *Tk, tk*—what was this that had been forgotten and that could not get through?

Here was God—indubitably: it was like going to the top of the mountain. He had known all along that when once those grimacing voices had been left behind he would hear THE VOICE, just so, like this, its music getting ever louder and clearer as one climbed forward and upward. His own music came back to him, but it could not compare with this, though it was the same—but this. . . . The thoughts fell away abruptly, nothing now remained but the mighty music. *Tk . . . tk . . . Oxy. . . . tk . . . tk . . . Oxyg . . .*

There was something intruding on the music. Something very small but significant, annoying, something that must be eliminated. *Tk . . . tk . . .* He could hear it now in spite of that glorious thundering. It was a mere word. Just listen for a second more and then it will fade away. *Tk . . . tk . . . Oxygen.*

Oh, was that all? 'Oxygen,' Christopher shouted, but the shout emerged from his throat a whisper. There was so much room up here. And suddenly he understood with extraordinary clearness, not that he had forgotten the oxygen and was going to die, for surely that was exactly what he had intended and there was no need for the intrusion of that ignoble clicking, none at all; he understood that he was about to enter into the kingdom and the power and the glory, and they into him—that, borne upward on the wings of those unceasing harmonies rapidly becoming visible, taking shape as their anticipated forms, he was going to . . .

For he had now cast off *all* superfluities, he was now transcendental, soaring quite free and yet fused with all eternity. . . .

He was now lying crumpled up over the stick. Purple blood was trickling from the nostril he had declined to cover with the protective mask—purple swiftly crimsoning on the glass edge of the clock face he had smashed in his fall.

The *Makara* continued faithfully to bear her passenger further and further, but ever so slowly a little upward, towards the forbidden heights whence soon she would wrench him, swooping through space, downward and backward, downward and backward—where he belonged.

13 BACK TO THE FUTURE

All science properly so-called, by which I understand systematic
knowledge under the guidance of the principle of sufficient
reason, can never reach its final goal; for it is not concerned
with the inmost nature of the world; it cannot get beyond
the idea.

—Schopenhauer, *The World as Will and Idea*

I

Nicolette still slept. Bruce walked across to where she
lay, looked for a moment, then paced up and down the
room once or twice. He went to the window and on to
the balcony. There was no sound but a faint rustling. As
he gazed out, the gathering clouds parted for a moment,
and through their frayed pearly edges he imagined he saw,
outlined against the moonlit blue above them, a moving,
dwindling spot. Then they closed again.

Mutely, he wished the boy well on his last voyage of discovery. He had always been so unhappy. Yet he had no
more sought to investigate the cause of his misery than
he would avail himself of the facile cure. Sad and proud
individualist, he had been as self-opinionated as if he had
been self-created. Never had he turned to inquire of the
woman who had made him—inadequately—nor of those

who stood beside and behind her, the ancestry and the blood whence they had both sprung. It was difficult for Bruce, who had long trained himself to view everything sculpturally, architecturally, to enter mentally into Christopher's flat, pictorial, one-sided point of view. He was penetrated too deeply by his own theories of interdependence and linkage; he was a biologist.

It was fine—the way the boy had gone. Bruce could respond emotionally to an act like that; a clean gesture of cleavage, possible only to one who saw life as Christopher did—canvas through which the knife of will could slash sharply.

Bruce never doubted that he would not come back, but as the slow moments passed his regret became keener. There was a deal to be said for self-ending, from all points of view. And he had enough sympathy to understand the appalling terror with which certain minds viewed the in soluble riddle of existence, the necessity they felt to invent an Ultimate, a resolving harmonious end. He himself was secretly sustained by complete confidence in the continued expansion of the human intellect; he accepted gladly all scraps of evidence which seemed to point to the fact that its power of discovery was kinetic. Quite clearly, if one assumed just a little, thought moved. It soared and fell, like the oceans. What, in the end, might be left of the ground it was ceaselessly attacking—whether the new tracts it uncovered would balance or even outmeasure those that constantly sank and foundered, reveal mighty cities and precious civilizations, or dying, rotting vestiges; whether this new land would itself be gloriously fertile or utterly barren, no man could tell. But at every moment during which one contemplated such problems one seemed to stand at a definite point on a line stretching from infinity to infinity. From the past to the future—from the future to the past—it was enough. Bruce was content.

He went back. He would take Nicolette away, to Nucleus, to the Garden. At once. The sooner it was settled, the easier would the settlement be. As he was about to pick her up, to carry her to the car, he paused. He turned and went to the machine-room. The little one-seater car attached to the hut stood there still, with that curious air of waiting which belongs to machines in repose. The airplane, of course, was gone. Bruce knew what he wanted. He went to the door of a small wall cupboard and opened it. Yes, as he thought, the oxygen was in its place. None had been moved. Intentional or accidental? Bruce knew it was not the latter, since automatically one never went up without the stuff. He shut the cupboard and went back. Brave boy!

He picked Nicolette up in his arms and prepared to carry her out. Sleepily she slid an arm around his neck. He pressed her to him. There was a sound of wheels outside. He stood and waited. Some one was rapidly walking up, trotting now, running. They were short, agitated footsteps. He turned to the doorway. Morgana stood there.

She glanced at them for an instant, bewildered, with dazed eyes. Then an expression of hostility, mingled with alarm, crossed them.

'Where's Christopher?' she asked.

'Gone,' Bruce replied quietly.

'Where?' she demanded, her hands pressed against her breast.

'I don't know.'

'When?'

'Five minutes ago. You've just missed him.'

Her hands dropped to her sides. She looked at Nicolette and involuntarily lowered her voice.

'Did you tell him?' she demanded softly, yet brutally.

'Yes.' Bruce's glance, though quite calm, was too strong for hers, despite its fury. She moved past him, into the room, and sat down with her back to him, wearily.

'We are just going too,' he said gently. 'Back to Nucleus. Will you come with us?'

'No.'

'Then, good-bye.'

She did not reply. He supported Nicolette's weight on one arm. With his disengaged hand he carefully closed the door behind him. Morgana was left alone.

II

As usual, she was too late. She sat staring stupidly, bestially, in front of her. Her whole consciousness was concentrated, thrown in on itself.

As usual, she was too late. Brian wouldn't do anything, Christopher couldn't do anything, she couldn't. Nicolette—mentally she clenched her fist in the girl's face and spat. Yes, she should at least have done that. Now it was too late. She had been born too late. She had loved too late, she had never understood until understanding availed nothing. For Christopher would not come back.

They had driven him away while she had been rushing to him. She would have made up to him for it all. Together they would yet have done something. She had been cheated, as usual.

Suddenly she saw themselves vividly, pictorially, on that walk to the old Extonian's laboratory.

'The only law I recognize . . .' she had declared. 'The only law I recognize. . . .' What was it she had been trying to say?

'God's?' suggested Christopher softly. They had looked into one another's eyes.

If only then she had gone to him! Now it was too late.

If he had planned to go away—and for months she had suspected that it would, it must, end like this—why could he not, at least, have waited for her? Together they would have gone so gloriously. But he had gone alone. Alone. She did not speak the word aloud, but she savoured it all the same. Now she would always be alone. Unless? She stood up suddenly, violently. What a fool she had been! It was not too late. Rapidly she felt in her pockets. No, they were not there. As usual, she had forgotten, until it was . . . She checked herself. For this, at least, it never was too late. There were a dozen ways of following Christopher, and she need not fear that she would not catch him up—this time. Rapidly she thought. She remembered this place. She had been here before. The lake—she remembered perfectly. Up the path and through the wood, and the hill sloped sharply down on the other side.

As she had come, so she went. She ran. She had to hurry. Although she would not miss him, this time. Up the path, there was a stone, she stumbled; through the wood—a night-jar was sawing the air on a dead branch somewhere—down the hill, first clay, then grass, then moss. She ran, and the wind clawed at her hair as if to pull her back. The bank—ten feet, that was enough. She threw up her hands and jumped.

'Christopher!' she shouted.

III

Bruce had adjusted the hammock bed carefully, placed Nicolette in it, settled down at the wheel, and driven off. The indicator hand on the speedometer travelled round rapidly. Forty . . . fifty . . . sixty . . . seventy . . . He kept it at ninety. They would reach Nucleus by seven o'clock. It was necessary to get there as soon as possible. Knowing Morgana a little, he imagined she would have come prepared. In the alternative case she would make a fuss, which would be just as awkward. It was necessary to avoid publicity now. And as soon as they reached Nucleus he would see certain people. She would have to be silenced. She was a nuisance. He wished she would have the sense to do the obvious thing. That would be satisfactory, from every one's point of view. Women like that were useless. Women. Well, there would only be Emmeline and Antonia to deal with in this case. He was not alarmed. That would be relatively simple. He began to think of several jobs he had to do. He would resume his tour as soon as Nicolette was comfortably settled. He was anxious to see Maxwell and find out what Svengaard had been doing.

The eminently pleasurable contemplation of his future business reasserted its hold on his mind. He plunged into calculations, details, figures; the fascination of the map-maker, of the man who has will, power, knowledge, gripped him again. He drove on.

'He' was kicking hard. She held him in her arms. His eyes, as yet vague, unfocussed, endeavoured to fasten on her face. It was an effort. He made it. It was difficult at first. But he persevered. At last they held her image. He smiled, gurgled at her, kicked lustily with joy and pride.

His kicking woke Nicolette. She found that her arms held him, but her flesh was still between them and his. He had not yet freed himself. He must wait a few months longer. But he was keen to see and to be seen. He went on kicking.

'He wants to get out,' she murmured. 'He's trying ever so hard. Impatient little creature. Bruce,' she called, 'where are we?'

'Halfway to Nucleus. Are you comfy?'

'Yes, but I've woken up. I want to come and sit beside you. We both do.'

'All right. Wait a minute. I'll stop.'

He slowed down and drew in a little to the side of the road. He lifted her over to him and set her beside him. He kissed her on the lips—'One for you,' he said with a smile—and then over the navel, 'and one for him. Slept well?'

'Beautifully.' She took Bruce's hand and pressed it to her. 'Feel him?' she asked.

'Rather.' Bruce started again, but did not accelerate beyond fifty. They could go slow for a bit. Nicolette might want to talk.

After a while she said: 'What has Christopher decided?'

He answered: 'I don't know, but I think I can guess.'

'I didn't hear the end of your talk. I wanted to listen, but he,' she patted her round belly, 'made me go to sleep. I can't concentrate for long on anyone but him. Did you help Christopher?'

'In one sense, possibly. In another, no.' He turned to watch her expression. 'I think he's dead by now.'

Nicolette stayed quite still for a second or two. 'Oh, Christopher!' but she remembered him whom she could not for an instant forget. She was a well-trained little mother-pot.

'Oh!' Then, 'How did he die?'

'I am not certain he did,' answered Bruce. 'He refused to consider the suggestions I made to him.' Nicolette nodded. 'He flew off and left the oxygen behind. It looks as if he had not intended to return.'

'What a splendid end!' said Nicolette gravely.

'I agree. I admire him.'

'He won't suffer any more. He might have suffered more deeply in the future, if he had stayed. Do you think his ideas were queer, Bruce?'

'Not in the circumstances. Tell me, Nicolette, do you know anything about his birth and the time before? About Antonia's condition and behaviour, I mean.'

'No,' she answered reflectively. I don't think I do. All I know for certain is that before I was born she had a daughter who owing to some mischance was born abnormal. Antonia never saw her, but she grieved. She wanted a girl, you know.'

'Much?'

'Oh, very much. Yet she never made a special fuss about me. Christopher was her favourite. She will grieve for him.'

'Yes. She should have done that long ago. Do you know if they talked a great deal together, if she ever told Christopher or he ever asked her anything?'

'I doubt it. Christopher was so tremendously reserved, you know. With every one except me. And Antonia is reserved in a way, too. Although she pretends to herself and every one else that she is completely candid. But why are you asking all these questions?'

'Because I thought you might like to know what was Christopher's trouble. You see he tended to be intermediate sexually. I very much doubt whether your father was concerned with that. But I imagine that your mother's ardent longing for a daughter, although she bore a son, affected him. She must have neglected her exercises— cheated somehow. Physically, at any rate outwardly, he appeared normal enough. But you know what slight modifications you get at either end of the intermediate scale. Christopher's submasculinity did not cause more than a slight mental perverseness. It could have easily been corrected. But it developed and grew into this sterile mysticism, which led to his self-ending. The excessively mystical impulse always has its root in some slight sexual perversity, both in men and women. You will hear more about it at the Garden. It is tremendously important.'

'You mean that normal men and women have not got that impulse?'

'Not as a rule. You can divide the religious into various classes, according to a scale. The extremists who advocate and practise asceticism of the body and contemplation by what they used to term the "soul," lean towards sterility both of mind and body. The religious desire for and belief in an after-life are the complements of underdeveloped physical or mental vigour in this. You nearly always find those sort of people terrified of the infinite, incapable of thinking, for instance, in terms of physics or geology or mathematics. You heard how appalled Christopher was by my attempt to make him think rationally about the stars.'

'How do you explain the so-called religion of the people in the old days, then?'

'The white race has never been fundamentally mystical. It is far too virile for that. But the alleged belief in an ulterior world was an excuse to overthrow and to establish institutions or customs in this, to go to war, or to reformations.'

'"Think not that I am come to send peace on earth,"' answered Nicolette; '"I came not to send peace, but a sword."'

'Precisely. What could be more clearly a declaration of policy than that? It served the activities of our race well. And it only endured so long as the Christian Church, like its predecessor, the Roman Empire, had a policy of action, and was run by vigorous men of action—Paul, Ignatius Loyola, Luther. When it ceased to govern and to act, to be political, Christendom in the West was doomed. Science provides our basis of policy, but the same type of human intelligence, the active type, still leads and governs.'

'You see how essential for us it is,' he went on after a pause, 'that the men and women of the governing class shall be as normal as possible. If they were not, our power would wilt away in a few centuries. We have no use for sterility, for above all things we aim to keep the race going until each individual shall have achieved complete self-consciousness. A self-conscious race: it seems to me worth while, that.'

'And to me,' answered Nicolette. But it won't be for a long time yet.'

'Not for a long time. That is our privilege, to go on building towards the completion of an edifice we shall never see crowned. And it is a test of our value that we should be able to face that realization and yet not flinch. That we should continue the experiment begun by this race thousands of years ago. In the meantime there will always be Christophers, and they will always suffer. But it's the experiment that counts for us, not the result.'

As he spoke, Nicolette was compelled by his fervour to turn and look at him. His steady hands gripped the wheel. He looked with dark, clear-visioned eyes through narrow lids straight ahead at the shining road before them, that led up and down, over hills and through valleys, to Nucleus, back to the future.

And as she looked at Bruce, Nicolette began weeping gently (so that 'He' might not be disturbed) for Christopher.

THE END

Charlotte Haldane (1894–1969) was a journalist who advocated for divorce reform and married women's employment . . . while also idealizing motherhood. In 1926, the year that *Man's World* was published, she married the eminent biologist J. B. S. Haldane. Her 1927 book, *Motherhood and Its Enemies*, made a progressive argument for easier access to contraceptives for women . . . while enraging feminists by arguing that only after having borne children could a woman be regarded as "normal." She went on to found the Science News Service, and reported on WWII from the Russian front.

Philippa Levine is Walter Prescott Webb Chair in History and Ideas, and Director of British, Irish and Empire Studies at the University of Texas at Austin. She is the author of, among other books, *Eugenics: A Very Short Introduction* (2017), *The British Empire: Sunrise to Sunset* (3rd edition, 2019), and the forthcoming *The Tree of Knowledge: Science, Art and the Naked Form*. With Alison Bashford, she is coeditor of *The Oxford Handbook of the History of Eugenics* (2010).